MURDER IN NOVEMBER

Lucy felt the warmth of the dog's shoulder against her thigh, and savored it. She closed her eyes, just for a moment, feeling the delicious heat. Then she opened them and saw something in the patch of reeds that shouldn't be there. Something pink.

Maybe it was just a bit of clothing, something that had gotten caught in the reeds. She studied the ice, which looked thick enough to support a single person, but she knew these early freezes could be deceptive and she didn't dare trust it. She needed to get closer to investigate that blob of bright pink.

She began making her way along the peninsula, pushing branches out of her way and scrambling over rocks until she was blocked by a thick curtain of leafless hanging vines that she suspected was poison ivy. She couldn't go any farther but was close enough to get a good look.

A bit of hot pink fleece, she realized, and more. Pink fleece and long blond hair. She gasped, her hand flew to her mouth. *Oh, no.* She reached for her cell phone, fumbling with the zipper on the pocket, and dialed 911 . . .

Books by Leslie Meier

MISTLETOE MURDER
TIPPY TOE MURDER
TRICK OR TREAT MURDER
BACK TO SCHOOL MURDER
VALENTINE MURDER
CHRISTMAS COOKIE MURDER
TURKEY DAY MURDER
WEDDING DAY MURDER
BIRTHDAY PARTY MURDER
FATHER'S DAY MURDER
STAR SPANGLED MURDER
NEW YEAR'S EVE MURDER
BAKE SALE MURDER
CANDY CANE MURDER
ST. PATRICK'S DAY MURDER
MOTHER'S DAY MURDER
WICKED WITCH MURDER
GINGERBREAD COOKIE MURDER
ENGLISH TEA MURDER
CHOCOLATE COVERED MURDER
EASTER BUNNY MURDER
CHRISTMAS CAROL MURDER
FRENCH PASTRY MURDER
CANDY CORN MURDER
BRITISH MANOR MURDER
EGGNOG MURDER
TURKEY TROT MURDER
SILVER ANNIVERSARY MURDER
YULE LOG MURDER

Published by Kensington Publishing Corporation

A Lucy Stone Mystery

TURKEY TROT MURDER

LESLIE MEIER

KENSINGTON BOOKS
www.kensingtonbooks.com

KENSINGTON BOOKS are published by

Kensington Publishing Corp.
119 West 40th Street
New York, NY 10018

All Kensington titles, imprints, and distributed lines are available at special quantity discounts for bulk purchases for sales promotion, premiums, fund-raising, educational, or institutional use. Special book excerpts or customized printings can also be created to fit specific needs. For details, write or phone the office of the Kensington Special Sales Manager: Attn. Special Sales Department. Kensington Publishing Corp., 119 West 40th Street, New York, NY 10018. Phone: 1-800-221-2647.

Kensington and the K logo Reg. U.S. Pat. & TM Off.

ISBN-13: 978-1-4967-1031-4
ISBN-10: 1-4967-1031-2
First Kensington Hardcover Edition: October 2017
First Kensington Mass Market Edition: November 2018

eISBN-13: 978-1-4967-1032-1
eISBN-10: 1-4967-1032-0
First Kensington Electronic Edition: October 2017

10 9 8 7 6 5 4 3 2 1

Printed in the United States of America

For all the Turkey Trotters,
Especially
Greg, Ben and Abby, Matt and Sam,
Andy and Mandy,
Em and Ari, Leon and Debi

Prologue

It was all over the morning TV news—the season's first killing frost. It came later than usual, probably due to global warming. That was the theory, anyway. But come it did, finally, coating each blade of grass with sparkly white rime, sealing automobile windows with a thick layer of frost, reducing late green tomatoes to black mush, and changing chrysanthemum plants, whose color had faded weeks before, into shriveled black stumps.

Alison Franklin didn't notice these changes, but she did sense the sharp nip in the air as she stepped out onto the flagstone patio of her father's house in Maine. She zipped up her fleece jacket and jogged down the long drive to begin her morning run. She usually went one of two ways. One route took her along scenic Shore Road with its ocean views and the other wound through the woods on old logging roads and circled around Blueberry

Pond. A cold northeast breeze was blowing off the water so Alison chose the more sheltered woodland path.

She was rounding the loop that led to Blueberry Pond when she heard the cries. It was nothing more than a yelp at first, a cry that could be the call of a crow or perhaps the yip of a fox. The calls came louder and grew clearer as she drew nearer to the pond.

Realizing someone was calling for help she quickened her pace and soon spotted a familiar figure standing on the shore of the frozen pond. She'd been spotted so it was too late to turn around. Nothing for it except to make the best of the situation.

"Alison! Thank God you're here!"

"What's the matter?" she asked somewhat reluctantly.

"It's Scruffy! He ran out onto the pond and I think he's fallen through."

Alison studied the pond, which had a coat of new ice. "Are you sure? There are no tracks in the ice and I don't hear him crying."

"Of course I'm sure! Why would you doubt me? Listen, listen! Can't you hear him? Oh, the poor thing. He's growing weaker . . ."

Once again Alison turned to the pond, casting her eyes along the irregular shore which was littered with large boulders, glacial erratics, most now covered with a thin layer of soil that supported bushy balsam pines and gnarled blueberry bushes, all hanging on for dear life. This growth made it impossible for her to get a clear view of the entire shore or to see exactly where Scruffy had gone through. She concentrated on listening for the poodle, hoping his cries might direct her, but all she heard was the sighing of the wind in the trees and the groaning protest of bare branches thrown against each other.

"Stop dithering! Poor Scruffy. He can't hang on much longer!"

There was no way out, decided Alison with a sigh of resignation. The undergrowth along the shore was too dense for her to make her way around the pond without a machete, which she didn't happen to bring along on her morning run. The only way she could find Scruffy was by going out onto the freshly frozen surface of the pond.

The ice cracked ominously as she ventured forth, staying as close to the shore as possible, but it held and she gained confidence as she proceeded. A small spit of land covered with brushy growth extended into the pond and she made her way along it, grabbing onto overhanging branches for safety. Once she got to the end of the spit she figured she would have a better vantage point from which to spot Scruffy.

She was almost there when a patch of reeds forced her farther from the shoreline. There was a sudden loud crack and the ice beneath her gave way, plunging her into the frigid black water. Her cries for help were loud and strong, shattering the early morning calm, but no one answered.

Chapter One

So the deep frost had finally come, thought Lucy Stone, stepping onto the back porch of her antique farm house on Red Top Road and surveying the withered mums that had been so bright and colorful only a few days ago. This recent long, extended spell of warm weather had been strange, even unsettling, she thought as she stretched her hamstrings. But today was more like it, she decided, grasping one ankle and pulling her foot to her bottom. This crisp weather was great for a run, a sentiment also shared by Libby, the family Lab. Libby was ready to go, and even though her black muzzle was now fading to white, she didn't need any warm-up exercises. She was circling eagerly, throwing expectant glances to Lucy as if to say "Enough of this nonsense. Let's go!"

"Okay," agreed Lucy, skipping down the porch steps and crossing the frosty lawn in an easy jog.

She picked up speed once she reached the old logging road that wound through the woods behind the house, pushing herself to improve her speed. This year she was training for the Tinker's Cove annual Turkey Trot 5K race, and she thought she might actually have a chance of winning in her age division.

There were not many runners signed up in the women over-forty category, and those who were running were mostly casual runners interested in burning calories before they sat down to a big Thanksgiving dinner. That had been Lucy's attitude in the past, but this year was different. This year she wasn't going to be cooking a big turkey dinner for the whole family. This year, well to be honest, she wasn't sure what she and Bill were going to do. Since it would be just the two of them perhaps they'd eat out in a restaurant, or maybe one of their friends would include them in their celebration.

Her feet pounded along the pine needle strewn path in a regular rhythm as she reviewed the various plans her children had made without consulting her. Of course she hadn't expected Elizabeth to come home for Thanksgiving; her eldest daughter was busy with her job as an assistant concierge at the upscale Cavendish Hotel in Paris. It also wasn't practical for her only son Toby to sit down at the usual groaning board. Toby, his wife Molly, and son Patrick had returned to Alaska where Toby had a government job working to increase and improve salmon stocks. It had been wonderful having the young family living in the old homestead while he took graduate courses at nearby Winchester College, and Lucy had really enjoyed spending time with her grandson, but that was a temporary arrangement. Now she stayed in touch with Patrick via Skype, setting aside a half-hour every Sunday afternoon.

But, she thought as she allowed a certain sense of resentment to carry her over a rather steep patch of trail, it had been rather inconsiderate of the two daughters who remained home to make separate plans for the holiday. Sara, who was studying earth science at Winchester College, had signed up for a field trip in Greenland led by one of her professors, arguing it was a once-in-a-lifetime opportunity and would strengthen her graduate school applications. Okay, muttered Lucy, huffing a bit from exertion, she understood. It wasn't her preference, but she could live with it. No, it was Zoe, her youngest, who had really driven in the knife with a nasty twist. Zoe had announced only days before that her friend and neighbor Renée La Chance had invited her to spend the Thanksgiving break with her at Concordia University in Montreal. Montreal, in Canada, where Renee was a freshman.

"Oh, well," said Lucy, speaking to the dog running beside her with her tongue hanging out of her mouth. "We can't always get what we want, can we?"

Libby didn't answer, but she was clearly enjoying herself, letting her drooping, silky ears flap behind and holding her tail aloft in an exclamation of doggy joy.

Realizing they were drawing close to the Blueberry Pond where Libby might expect a drink of water but would find ice instead, Lucy decided to use the leash she had wrapped around her waist. She'd heard of too many dogs that had gone out on thin ice and fallen through. It was a story replayed every year when lakes and ponds began to freeze. Sometimes the owners were able to call for help from the fire department. Sometimes they were foolish enough to venture out on the ice themselves, which was usually a tragic mistake.

"C'mere, girl," she said, and Libby obediently approached, allowing her to snap the leash onto her red leather collar. Then they were off again, running side by side at a rather more sedate pace. The newly frozen pond would be pretty in the morning light and Lucy wanted to take time to appreciate it. This was something new, suggested by her friend Pam, who was a yoga instructor.

"Live mindfully," Pam had advised. "Be in the moment."

This was the perfect opportunity, thought Lucy as the pond came into view. It had frozen overnight, and the ice was smooth and glistening. The pointed firs on the opposite shore were a dark green, piercing a clear blue sky. She paused on the shore, holding Libby firmly by the leash, and took in the scene. *This could be on a calendar*, she thought. *Maine in late fall, preparing for winter.* Soon the pond would be covered with snow, the familiar woods would be transformed into a dreamlike fairyland, the little waterfall at the pond's outlet would become still, frozen into a freeform sculpture.

Lucy took a few deep breaths and banished all negative thoughts from her mind. There was nothing but her breath, the pond, and the panting dog leaning against her leg. She felt the warmth of the dog's shoulder against her thigh, and savored it. She closed her eyes, just for a moment, feeling the delicious heat. Then she opened them and saw something in the patch of reeds that shouldn't be there. Something pink.

Maybe it was just a bit of clothing, something that had gotten caught in the reeds. She studied the ice, which looked thick enough to support a single person, but she knew these early freezes could be deceptive and she didn't dare trust it. She needed to get closer to investigate that blob of bright pink, and she knew there was a narrow, hidden path occasionally used by trout fishermen in the spring. Now, however, after a summer's worth of growth it was going to be tough going and she didn't want to struggle with the dog as she battled her way through the thick underbrush, so she tied Libby to a tree. "Stay!" she added for good measure then began making her way along the peninsula, pushing branches out of her way and scrambling over rocks until she was blocked by a thick curtain of leafless hanging vines that she suspected was poison ivy. She couldn't go any farther but was close enough to get a good look.

A bit of hot pink fleece, she realized, and more. Pink fleece and long blond hair. She gasped, her hand flew to her mouth. *Oh, no.* She reached for her cell phone, fumbling with the zipper on the pocket, and dialed 9-1-1.

As soon as the dispatcher assured her that help was on the way, Lucy made a second call to her boss at the *Pennysaver*, Ted Stillings. She was a part-time reporter, feature writer, and copyeditor at the weekly paper, and knew she'd stumbled onto a big story. And it was deadline day, too, which made it breaking news.

"A woman in the pond?" asked Ted. "Who is she?"

"I don't know," replied Lucy.

"And you're sure she's dead?"

"Not sure, but I think it's pretty likely," said Lucy, her voice tight with dread. "I couldn't get close enough for a good look. She's too far out from the shore and I sure wasn't going out there. The ice is too thin and the same thing would happen to me—I'd fall right through. I can't imagine why anyone would do such a risky thing."

"Well, stick with it, Lucy. Deadline's not until noon and I may be able to get more time from the printer. I'll get right on that." He paused, then added, "Get as many pictures as you can, okay?"

"Okay," promised Lucy, ending the call and making her way back through the brush to the logging road.

She'd no sooner got there when Libby announced the arrival of the first responders. Her loud yips and enthusiastic jumps threatened to snap the leash that kept her fastened to the tree. Lucy untied her but held tight to the leash, watching as the town's special brush-breaking truck lumbered into view. The regular fire trucks were much too big to negotiate the old, uneven dirt logging road so the rescuers had taken the smaller truck that was equipped to fight forest fires. The truck was towing a trailer carrying an inflatable boat used for water and ice rescues, and an ambulance followed close behind, lurching from side to side as the driver attempted to avoid boulders and potholes.

"Where's the victim?" asked Jim Carstairs as he leaped out of the truck.

"Out there," said Lucy, pointing to the reedy patch.

"We'll need to use the inflatable," he said, spotting the bit of hot pink fleece in the distance.

Lucy watched as two firefighters, apparently the youngest and fittest members of the crew, suited up in bright orange protective suits while the others unloaded the inflatable from the trailer and carried it to the shore. The guys in the orange suits fastened toggle straps that connected their suits to the inflatable, then began pushing the inflatable out onto the ice. They didn't get too far before the ice gave way and one man plunged into waist deep water. Then they both got into the inflatable and began using oars to propel the craft through the mix of ice and water.

"I've never seen one of these ice rescues," said Lucy, speaking to Jim, who as captain was supervising the operation. "It looks really difficult . . . and risky, too."

"We train for them every year," he replied. "The guys know what they're doing."

"Any chance that the victim is alive?" she asked, watching as the two firemen struggled to lift the woman's body into the inflatable.

"Doubtful," said Carstairs, striding toward the crew members who had remained on the shore and blowing a whistle—the signal for them to begin pulling on the rope connected to the inflatable, bringing the victim and crew safely to shore.

Lucy snapped photos of the operation with her smartphone, noting that the victim remained motionless, showing no signs of life, and the crew members were subdued. The rescue operation had become a recovery.

When the inflatable reached the shore, an EMT examined the victim, then stepped away, shaking her head. Lucy found herself drawing closer for a better look and was shocked to see the victim was a beautiful young woman, dressed for a run in a pink fleece and black tights. Her long blond hair, which blew gently in the breeze, was held by a jaunty pink knitted headband and an earbud dangled from its thin white wire. Her running shoes were top of the line, her sodden gray gloves were cashmere.

"Any idea who she is?" asked Lucy.

"It's Alison, Alison Franklin," said one of the crew members, a young guy with longish hair. "I've seen her around."

"Is she related to Ed Franklin?" asked Carstairs.

Lucy knew Ed Franklin was an extremely wealthy new arrival in town, a retired CEO who had quickly become a force to be reckoned with. She'd covered numerous meetings and hearings where he'd tussled with local officials to gain approval for the oversized mansion he built on Shore Road. Once settled into the mansion, he quickly offered himself as a candidate for the board of health, promising to cut red tape and bureaucratic obstruction. Much to the surprise of the entrenched office holders, who took his candidacy to be a joke, he won by a landslide.

"Yeah," said the long-haired guy. "She's his daughter."

Somehow the realization that this young woman was not only beautiful, but also a child of privilege, made her death seem even worse.

"Wow," said Carstairs with a big sigh. "What a shame."

"Senseless," said another. "So much to live for."

"I see it all the time," said the EMT, shaking her head. "I'll bet she was high as a kite on heroin or oxy."

"It looks to me like she was out for a run," said Lucy.

"That's probably what her folks thought, too. But there's a shack not far from here that's a popular spot for drug users." The EMT gave a wry smile. "I'd be willing to bet on it. This girl was using. Why else would she go out on thin ice? Nobody in their right mind would do such a stupid thing."

A tug on the leash from Libby reminded Lucy that she had other responsibilities and it was time to be on her way. Ted was waiting for her story, but that wasn't her first priority, not according to Libby. Libby wanted her breakfast.

Chapter Two

"A monstrosity."
"Absolutely appalling lack of taste."
"Ridiculously ostentatious."

As a freshly showered and dressed Lucy drove along Shore Road, passing the Franklin house on her way to work, she recalled the reactions of some planning board members when they were presented with the plans. Ed Franklin hadn't gone before the board himself. He'd sent his architect and lawyer to seek the necessary approvals. And they'd succeeded because the plans had been cleverly designed to take maximum advantage of the town's zoning laws.

The structure was enormous, much larger than the other mansions on Shore Road, but at 14, 999 square feet, it was actually one square foot less than the town's maximum of 15,000 square feet. It's true that the roof was topped with an inordinately large widow's walk, but those were allowed, and the house itself was only three stories high and just shy (by an inch) of the maximum height restriction. And while the roomy flagstone terrace seemed to extend forever, it actually stopped ten feet and one inch from the property line, more than meeting the required ten-foot setback.

Lucy had covered the meeting and had quoted the architect, who had announced in a rather challenging tone, "We have not exceeded any of the local restrictions and have been mindful of traditional New England architecture."

She also remembered quite well the various reactions of the board members, who had no choice but to grant approval to the plans. Maisie Wilkinson had looked as if she had bitten into a lemon when she cast her vote, Horace Atkins had huffed and puffed for all the world like an outraged walrus, and Linc Curtis had glared at the applicants as if he could make them disappear by staring angrily at them. Committee chairman Susan Brooks had abstained, claiming a conflict of interest that Lucy suspected was little more than an excuse to avoid going on record as supporting the project. Only realtor Wilt Chambers had spoken in favor of the plan, saying it would increase the tax base and raise property values.

As she drove by the house, Lucy thought it could have been worse. It could have been a modernistic glass box, for instance, or a faux Tuscan villa with a red tile roof, rather than the overblown Federalist-style mansion that now dominated the neighborhood. And even though it was huge, everything was in proportion, with oversized windows and chimneys, and a dramatic carved pediment calling attention to the massive front door which was made from some rare Brazilian hardwood. Lucy had heard that when seen from a distance— it could quite easily be observed from a boat bobbing on the sea it overlooked—the house seemed quite in scale with its surroundings.

But no house, no matter how grand, could protect its inhabitants from the vagaries of fortune or shelter them from tragedy and grief. In fact, it seemed to her that wealth and success could almost tempt fate. She thought of John Kennedy, Jr., becoming disoriented and crashing his plane into the Atlantic, and Gloria Vanderbilt, who saw her son hurl himself from a fourteenth floor terrace, and now Ed Franklin, who had certainly not awakened this morning expecting to learn that he'd lost his beautiful daughter forever.

Lucy was uncharacteristically somber when she got to the office, prompting Ted to comment on her glum expression.

"Pretty rough morning?" he asked in a sympathetic tone. Ted was the owner, publisher, editor, and chief reporter for the weekly paper.

"Who was it?" asked Phyllis, chewing on the earpiece of the jazzy reading glasses that either hung from a chain to rest on her ample bosom or perched on her nose. Phyllis's official title was receptionist, but she also handled ads, classifieds, and event listings.

"Alison Franklin," said Lucy, hanging up her barn coat on the coat rack.

"Ed Franklin's daughter?" asked Ted.

"That's what they say. I don't know much about

Ed Franklin apart from the permitting process for his big house."

"That was quite a show, wasn't it?" said Ted, who had relished the controversy that prompted so many heated letters to the editor.

"She hasn't been officially identified," said Lucy, "but one of the EMTs recognized her."

"Well, write up what you've got," ordered Ted. "We'll say 'tentatively identified as'."

"Okay," said Lucy with a sigh, sitting down at her desk and booting up her PC.

It was an old machine and slow to wake up in the morning, so while she waited she mulled over possible leads for the story. Her eyes roamed around the familiar office, where an old Regulator clock hung on the wall above Ted's rolltop desk, which he'd inherited from his grandfather, a legendary small town journalist. Wooden blinds rattled at the window and a little bell on the door jingled whenever anyone came in. Entering the office was like taking a step back in time, she thought, wishing for a moment that such a thing was really possible. If only the clocks and calendars could roll backwards to yesterday, then Alison would still be alive.

Lucy's computer announced with a whirr that it was up and running and she got to work.

When the paper came out on Thursday the story was front page news, but of course everyone in Tinker's Cove had already heard about Alison Franklin's fatal mishap. News, especially bad news, traveled fast in town, and the tragedy was the main topic of conversation in Jake's Donut Shack when Lucy arrived for her weekly breakfast date with her friends.

"Such a shame, a young girl like that with her whole life before her," declared Norine, the waitress, greeting Lucy when she entered the busy little café. "Your friends are already here," she added with a nod toward the table in the back where the group regularly gathered.

The four women had begun the weekly breakfast meetings as a way of keeping in touch when their children had grown and they no longer ran into each other at Little League games, bake sales, and PTA meetings.

"So young and so very rich, too," offered Sue Finch. With a perfectly manicured hand, she tucked a glossy lock of hair behind one ear. "Her father is enormously wealthy. Fortune Five hundred wealthy."

"Money doesn't guarantee happiness," said Lucy, slipping into the vacant seat and greeting her friends with a smile.

"That's so true," said Pam Stillings, speaking from experience. She was married to Lucy's boss Ted, and had wholeheartedly supported her husband's struggle to continue publishing the *Pennysaver* despite competition from the Internet, dwindling advertising revenues, and ever-increasing production costs. "Good health, family, friends—those are the things that really matter."

"Pam's right," said Rachel Goodman, who was married to Bob Goodman, a lawyer with a busy practice in town. "Simply possessing money doesn't guarantee happiness. In fact, it can cause lots of problems—guilt, lack of responsibility, family disruption." She had majored in psychology and had never gotten over it.

"I certainly wouldn't want to swap places with Alison's parents, not even if they had all the money in the world," said Lucy, glancing up as Norine approached with her order pad in hand. "But there's a big difference between having enough money and not having it." Her tongue went to the new crown she'd recently had to get when a tooth broke, spending the money she'd been saving to buy a new family room sofa.

"Okay, ladies. The usual for everyone?" asked Norine with a raised eyebrow. "Sunshine muffin for Rachel, granola yogurt for Pam, hash and eggs for Lucy and"—she paused for a disapproving little snort—"black coffee for Sue."

Receiving nods all round, she retreated to place the order and returned moments later with a fresh pot of coffee. "You know," she said, filling Lucy's mug, "I've heard people saying that girl committed suicide. She must've wanted to die to go out on that thin ice."

Lucy shook her head, unwilling to entertain such an idea. "I don't think so. I hope not," she said, wrapping her hands around the warm mug. "That would be too sad."

"Depression is an insidious disease," said Rachel, adding a dab of cream to her freshly filled mug. "And so often it goes unrecognized and untreated."

"It was most likely an accident," said Pam, stirring some sugar into her coffee. "The ice might've looked much stronger than it actually was. People get fooled. We have an accident like this every winter. Remember last year, when Lydia Volpe had a close call? Her dog fell through and she tried to save the beast. Luckily for her, Eddie Culpepper saw them struggling and managed to get them out."

"That was the first thing I thought of, but there was no sign of a dog or anything like that," said Lucy as Norine arrived again and began distributing their orders.

"That's why folks are saying it must've been suicide," insisted Norine, putting down Lucy's plate with a thump that made the toast jump. "Or maybe she was high on something and thought she could walk on water."

"It looked to me like she was out for a run. She was dressed for a run," said Lucy, who was staring at the pair of sunny-side-up eggs sitting on top of a mound of hash and thinking she really didn't want eggs this morning. Truth was, she hadn't really had much appetite at all since she'd discovered Alison's body.

"I guess we'll never know," said Norine, tenting the little bill and setting it on the table.

"It comes at a bad time for Ed Franklin," said Sue. "His new wife is expecting a baby. Due any day from the looks of her."

"His wife's pregnant?" asked Lucy, doing some quick math. "If Alison was twenty, isn't it rather late to be adding to the family?"

"How old is this latest wife?" asked Pam.

"About Alison's age, I'd say," said Sue. "I saw her at the salon when I was getting these highlights."

She tossed her head. "Expensive highlights, I might add, not that any of you have noticed."

"I noticed," said Pam, dipping her spoon into her yogurt. "I thought your stylist missed a few bits."

"Monsieur Paul does not miss any bits," said Sue, not the least bit amused. "And he was making an enormous fuss over the newest Mrs. Franklin. Mireille's her name. She's very young, very beautiful, and very pregnant."

"Exactly how many Mrs. Franklins are there?" asked Lucy.

"At least two, according to Monsieur Paul. There's Alison's mother, who must be at least fifty or so, and Mireille, who I doubt is old enough to buy a bottle of wine. Not that she would have any business buying wine, not in her condition."

"That does muddy the waters, doesn't it?" mused Rachel. "Imagine what it would have been like for Alison to have a stepmother who is her own age."

"And pregnant," said Pam.

"A constant reminder of this young stepmother's allure," said Rachel. "Not to mention her father's sexual potency."

"Yuck," said Pam.

Yuck indeed, thought Lucy, pushing her plate away. She thought of the Franklin home, the mansion perched high above the roiling sea below, and wondered what emotions were in play behind those massive walls, and if some primal forces drove Alison to her watery grave.

* * *

When Lucy got to work later that morning she discovered Ted had a completely different take on Alison Franklin's death.

"You know, Lucy," he said as she shrugged out of her jacket and hung it on the coat rack, "I've been getting a lot of calls about this Alison. People are upset and most of them blame drugs. That's what they're saying—that we have to stop this heroin epidemic that's claiming our young people."

"It's true," said Phyllis. "We've had at least three calls this morning."

"I've had some e-mails, too," said Ted.

"I've heard that theory, too, but I don't think it was drugs, Ted," said Lucy, remembering the hot pink fleece jacket and the running shoes. "I think she was out for a run."

"Lucy, people don't run on thin ice."

"Maybe she didn't know about the way ponds freeze. Not everybody grows up knowing these things. Maybe she's a city kid. Maybe she made a very bad mistake. It happens—like when that trucker tried to take his semi under the old railroad overpass last month and got stuck."

"That was quite a hoot," said Phyllis. "'Course, nobody dies of embarrassment."

"Well, all I know is that a lot of people are blaming this opioid epidemic and want some answers. It's about time we put Jim Kirwan on the spot and ask what he's doing to stop these senseless deaths.

"You want me to call the police chief?" asked Lucy, sitting down at her desk.

"Good idea, Lucy," said Ted as if it hadn't been his idea all along.

"Okay," said Lucy, anticipating the chief's reaction, "but he's not going to be happy."

As she expected, Chief Kirwan was immediately defensive when she asked what his department was doing to combat the opioid epidemic. "As you well know, Lucy, we are not the only town coping with this influx of drugs. Heck, it's a national problem. It's complex. There's high unemployment among youth, limited prospects for kids who don't go to college, folks can't get ahead, and heroin is cheap and plentiful. Truth is, it's easier for kids to get illegal drugs than to buy a six-pack. It's not like we're ignoring the problem. We've got a new program with the courts—we don't prosecute if the addicts agree to go to rehab . . . but oftentimes there's no rehab places available." He sighed. "Facts are facts. We're a small department with very limited resources and we're doing all we can."

"I know," said Lucy in a sympathetic tone. "People are upset over this latest thing. You know . . . Alison Franklin's death."

"Well, people shouldn't jump to conclusions," he said in a sharp tone. "The investigation is still ongoing and the cause of death has not been determined. We don't know if drugs were involved and we won't know until the toxicology results come in from the ME's office."

"When will that be?" asked Lucy.

He snorted. "I wish I knew. The state lab is under-budgeted and understaffed."

"I won't hold my breath then. Thanks," said Lucy, ending the call.

"Just as I expected," said Ted, who had been listening to Lucy's end of the call. "The same old, same old." He paused. "Well, we're not going to settle for lame excuses. I want to know what Alison's family has to say. I bet Ed Franklin wants some answers and he's the kind of guy who gets 'em."

"Ted, you're not going to make me call him, are you? The man just lost his daughter. . . ."

"And I bet he wants people to know what a wonderful girl she was, and how much he loved her," said Ted.

"The poor man must be beside himself with grief," protested Lucy.

"That's funny," observed Phyllis. "You called him poor, but he's not poor. He's probably the richest man in the state."

"You know what I mean," said Lucy, glaring at Phyllis.

"There's no rush," said Ted. "You've got till next Wednesday. Give him a call next week . . . when he's had some time to get over it."

People don't get over an unexpected, violent, tragic death of a loved one in a few days, thought Lucy, biting her tongue. Sometimes Ted got so involved in a story that he lost all sense of perspective or even decency. But noticing how he was hunched over his computer keyboard pursuing truth and combating evil one keystroke at a time, she admitted it was that determination that kept him going.

"Okay, I'll do it Monday," she said, booting up her computer to check her e-mails.

As it happened, she didn't have to wait until Monday to call Ed Franklin. She was just about to leave the office later that afternoon when the door flew open, setting the little bell to jangling, and the man himself walked in.

Lucy had never seen him in the flesh, but everybody had seen photos of the billionaire who was frequently in the news. He was most often featured in the business pages, announcing the construction of a new condo tower, golf course, or gambling casino. These projects were always described as fabulous, luxurious, or magnificent. Ed Franklin was a man who went in for superlatives and did everything in a big way.

The man himself, however, was shorter than she expected, although that mane of silver hair and the ruddy complexion were unmistakable. So was the expensively tailored suit that couldn't quite conceal his paunch. "Who's in charge here?" he demanded in the raspy voice she'd heard on TV.

"That would be me," said Ted, jumping to his feet. "I'm Ted Stillings. How can I help you, Mr. Franklin?"

"Look here," said Franklin, plunging right in. "I've had it with all this political correctness, this so-called tolerance. It's time we put a stop to these Mexican drug traffickers bringing heroin and marijuana here and poisoning our kids. Where is the outrage? There's supposed to be a war on drugs, but if this is how we fight a war . . . well, it's no surprise we're not winning. I'm going to get straight to the point. This is what I want you to do—I want you to run an exposé of this filthy business. Let people know where these drugs are coming from and how we can stop it. I speak from personal experience here. I just lost my daughter.

A beautiful girl. Gorgeous, and smart, too. I know what I'm talking about. It's these filthy Mexicans and we've got to get them out of the country."

"I'm very sorry for your loss," said Ted, stunned by Franklin's outburst. "We all are," he added with a wave in Lucy and Phyllis's direction.

"You have our sympathy," said Lucy.

"You're in our thoughts and prayers," added Phyllis.

"That's neither here nor there," said Franklin in a gruff tone, brushing aside their condolences. "The question is, what are you going to do about it?"

"It's not clear that your daughter died because of drugs," said Lucy. "The toxicology tests haven't been completed."

"Well, what else could it be?" demanded Franklin. "She had everything to live for. And I mean everything. Looks. Money. Connections. Everything."

"As it happens, we did call Chief Kirwan today, asking tough questions about the current opioid epidemic," said Ted.

"That's a start," said Franklin, "but you've got to take it further. We have to get to the source and cut off this vicious trade. It's these Mexicans. They're like a plague, swarming across the border, bringing death to our kids and destroying our American values. Our American way of life." He paused and looked around the office, taking in the worn and shabby atmosphere. "Look, see here. I'm a businessman and I know these are bad times for newspapers. I'm always looking for good investments and I see a lot of potential here. What you need is capital so you can expand. Maybe start a magazine, an online edition of the paper. Hell, the sky's the limit if you've got vision and the cash to make it a reality."

"We're doing just fine the way we are," said Ted, his dander rising. "Thanks for stopping by."

"Ted . . . you don't mind if I call you Ted, do you?" Franklin asked, continuing without pause. "You know, I've seen a lot of guys like you. Frankly, I think you're one of those guys who'll go down with the ship, blaming the tides and currents. But you could be the captain of your destiny, if you'd take my advice. This is an issue that could make a dinky small town paper like yours into a national player." He shrugged. "But have it your way. There's nothing wrong with being a big frog in a small pond, if that's all you want to be." With that parting shot, Ed Franklin pushed the door open, making the little bell jangle, and let it slam behind him, causing the wooden blinds on the plate glass window to slap against the glass.

"Wow, he's a noisy guy," said Phyllis, smoothing her angora sweater over her chest.

"I'm pretty sure we haven't heard the last of him," said Lucy.

"Did he actually call me a big frog?" asked Ted, looking puzzled.

Chapter Three

Several days later, Lucy found herself in the basement meeting room at the town hall, covering the weekly meeting of the board of selectmen. The town meeting voters were a thrifty lot and didn't go in for frills so the room where the town's business was conducted was a very plain affair. The concrete block walls had been painted yellow a long time ago, perhaps in a misguided effort to lighten the gloom, but instead made everyone look slightly jaundiced. Fluorescent lights, rows of beige metal chairs, and gray industrial-strength floor tile certainly didn't help.

The detail that always amused Lucy, however, was the little raised platform where the five selectmen sat behind a long table. The platform was a mere six inches high, allowing the citizens in attendance to get a clear view of these elected offi-

cials while ensuring that they didn't get above themselves. Behind the table an American flag stood in one corner and the Maine state flag in the other. There were nameplates on the table for each selectman, as well as a microphones, now that the meetings were televised on local cable TV.

Attendance at the meetings had fallen off since people could watch the antics of the board members from the comfort of their homes, but a few stalwarts still showed up each week. Town curmudgeon Stan Wysocki was in his usual seat and local fussbudget Verity Hawthorne had brought her knitting. When things got slow at the meetings, Lucy sometimes entertained herself by wondering exactly what the shapeless mass of moss green that grew larger every week was meant to be. A sweater for a yeti? An afghan for a cow? A cozy for Verity's aged Dodge?

"Hi, Lucy," said Corney Clark, slipping into the seat beside her. "I'm glad you're covering this meeting."

"I cover them all," said Lucy, stifling a yawn.

"Well, tonight's going to be worth your while," said Corney, making her eyes quite large and giving a little nod that caused her expertly cut blond hair to rise slightly and then fall back exactly into place. "Big doings, that's all I'm going to say."

"Give me a hint," prompted Lucy, who knew Corney had a tendency to overstate. She was the executive director of the town's chamber of commerce and worked tirelessly to promote area businesses.

"Nope, you'll just have to wait," she said, turn-

ing to give an encouraging wave to a very tall, very
thin, very distinguished looking man who had just
entered the room.

"Who's that?" asked Lucy, who knew everyone
in town and couldn't place him, even though he
looked familiar.

"Rey Rodriguez," said Corney.

"Not the TV chef?" inquired Lucy, who had seen
his show.

"The very same," said Corney with a smug smile.

Perhaps this meeting would provide some sur-
prises, thought Lucy, watching the board members
file in.

They were led by the chairman, Roger Wilcox,
who was a retired Army man and maintained his
military bearing despite being well over seventy.
Next in line was Joe Marzetti, another long-time
member who owned the town's IGA supermarket,
followed by bearded and plump retiree Sam Bellamy and Winchester College professor Fred Rumford. The newest member of the board, Franny
Small, brought up the rear.

Poor Franny's bottom had barely met her chair
when Roger called the meeting to order, opening
with the usual period for public comment. The
public, being largely absent, had nothing to say, although there was a bit of a stir as some latecomers
arrived. These were Police Chief Jim Kirwan, Fire
Chief Buzz Bresnahan, both in uniform, along
with Audrey Sprinkle from the board of health.
The three seated themselves together in the front
row, causing Rey Rodriguez to cast a questioning
look in Corney's direction. She responded with a
smile and an encouraging thumbs up.

This was interesting, thought Lucy, aware that the two chiefs rarely made appearances at board meetings unless there was a compelling reason, usually something involving public safety. Glancing at the agenda, she saw only routine business, which the board dealt with promptly. They voted to allow the Boy Scouts to erect a bench on the town green, approved the repair of a DPW truck, and authorized overtime for a police officer to provide traffic control at the upcoming Turkey Trot race.

When Roger moved on to new business, Corney stood up. "I'm here tonight to introduce Mr. Rey Rodriguez, who I'm sure you all know from his TV show, *Let's Go Global*, on the Food Channel. Rey is also the author of many best-selling cookbooks and is the culinary genius behind two highly regarded and successful restaurants in California, El Conquistador and Mission."

Corney paused and Rey Rodriguez rose, giving the board a polite little bow. "I am very happy to be here in Tinker's Cove," he said. "I have recently purchased a property, the Olde Irish Pub, and am looking forward to an exciting new chapter in my life in this most charming and beautiful part of the country."

"Well, on behalf of the board, I welcome you," said Roger, looking a bit puzzled. "I assume you are planning to reopen the Olde Irish Pub? In that case, you will need to request a transfer of the current liquor license."

"Mr. Rodriguez is aware of the licensing requirements," said Corney. "I just wanted to get the ball rolling as he is hoping to be open for Thanksgiving."

"That will be tight, but I think it's doable," said Roger. "We'll need to consider the transfer at our next meeting. You should make sure to get it on the agenda so it can be posted. Mr. Rodriguez will have to supply some information, and we will need time to verify it, but if everything is in order I think we will be able to vote."

"That's great news," said Corney.

"I do have a question," said Franny. "Can you tell us what you have in mind for the pub?"

"Will it be a Mexican restaurant?" asked Joe Marzetti. "Tacos and enchiladas, that sort of thing?"

"And margaritas?" asked Sam Bellamy with a twinkle in his eye.

"Not classic Mexican," said Rey. "I am going to completely reimagine and renovate the present building, which will be known as Cali Kitchen. It will feature a sophisticated fusion menu using fresh, local ingredients cooked in imaginative ways while drawing on traditional cuisines including Asian, Southwestern, and even New England Yankee."

"That does sound impressive," said Joe.

"And delicious," said Sam.

"If I may," said Police Chief Kirwan, rising to his feet. "I'd like to say a few words in support of Mr. Rodriguez."

"Of course," said the chairman. "You have the floor."

"Well," began Jim Kirwan, "Mr. Rodriguez has had discussions with me. He's aware of the lack of employment opportunities for our young people and the fact that many turn to drugs and get themselves into trouble. He's interested in setting up a program in cooperation with the department to offer employment to at-risk kids, setting them on the path to gainful employment in the restaurant industry. I have to say that this is something my department would welcome, as so often we see these youngsters getting themselves in deeper and deeper until they end up in the county jail."

Buzz Bresnahan was nodding along. He was a big, thoughtful man who never rushed into anything, but he offered his measured approval to the plan.

"It's not a secret that we have a big problem with opiate abuse here in town," he said, rising slowly to his feet. "Every week my EMTs are called out to deal with overdoses, and sad to say, they're not always successful in saving the victims. I'm in favor of absolutely anything that will help our youngsters."

"I don't want to rain on this parade," said Audrey Sprinkle. She was an attractive woman in her forties who was most often seen around town chauffcuring her three daughters to after-school sports events. "But am I the only one who sees a problem here? Where do these opiates come from? Mexico, right? And here we've got a . . . well, pardon my bluntness, but we've just had a terrible tragedy involving Ed Franklin's daughter. Well, Ed, who's chairman of the board of heath, couldn't be here himself, obviously, but he asked me to come and express his concern about the influx of drugs from Mexico and here we have an applicant who is Mexican—"

"Actually, I'm American," interjected Rey with some amusement. "My ancestors have been here in the US since the fifteen hundreds. I am proud of my Hispanic heritage. I am actually descended from the Spanish explorer Juan Rodriguez de Castillo, but I am thoroughly American and proud of my service in the US Navy."

Audrey's face reddened, but she hadn't finished speaking. "I thank you for your service," she said, "but as a mother, and speaking for a father who is going through unimaginable grief, I urge the board to be cautious about putting our kids, especially at-risk kids, under the guidance of a–um—newcomer. We need to be very careful." She paused and turned to Rey. "This is nothing personal. It's not against you. I'm just for our kids," she added before sitting down.

"Well, thank you for that," said Roger. "As I said earlier, all liquor license applicants go through the same process and must provide proof of good character, financial information, and criminal records check. It's quite a thorough vetting, I can assure you."

"If I may," said Rey, "I'd like to reassure the board that I am a father and I share this lady's concern. As it happens, my two children will be working at the restaurant. My daughter Luisa handles the business end of things, and my son Matt will run the kitchen. I will be the executive chef, creating menus and developing recipes, which I envision as a part-time position. I'm not so young anymore and I'm ready to let the youngsters take over."

"Quite understandable," said Roger with an approving nod. "I do have one question, however. Why did you decide on Tinker's Cove?"

"Ah," said Rey. "I have been a Californian all my life, but now, alas, I have had several bouts with skin cancer and my doctors tell me I must avoid the sun. Maine, it happens, is very cloudy and the sun hardly ever shines."

"Lucy," hissed Corney, grabbing Lucy's pen and stopping her note-taking, "don't put that in your story!"

The old saw about the variable New England weather, that if you didn't like it you should wait a minute, didn't hold true on Saturday for Alison's memorial service. The usually fickle sun put in a rare appearance, shining brightly in a clear blue sky as mourners gathered beneath the tall, white steeple in the simple clapboard Community Church.

Zoe accompanied Lucy to the service. Although the two girls hadn't been close, they were in the same class at Winchester College, located on the outskirts of town. Winchester was a small, liberal arts college that prided itself on fostering close relationships between students and faculty, and Lucy knew that Alison's death would be deeply felt by the entire college community. Young people weren't supposed to die, and Alison's death had been completely unexpected, so grief was compacted by shock and disbelief.

"It doesn't seem real," whispered Zoe as they stepped inside the dimly lit church. "I saw her on Tuesday. We sat together in American Lit. She had me laughing at the professor, imitating the way he said Thoreau's name. 'Not Thaw-row', he said, 'but *thorough*, rhyming with *borough*.' The way she—" Zoe broke off with a sniff, and Lucy plucked a tissue from the little packet thoughtfully provided in the rack for hymnals and gave it to her. "It was just so funny," continued Zoe, after giving her nose a good blow and wiping her eyes. "She was like that, and she was really nice, too."

"Death's never easy," said Lucy, "but it's easier to accept if a person is very old and had a good life, or if they've been sick and suffering for a long time."

"It really makes you think," said Zoe, and Lucy realized that this was probably the first time Zoe had truly confronted her own mortality.

As Lucy expected, the church was crowded and they were lucky to squeeze into one of the rear pews. Unlike the usual Sunday crowd, who greeted each other and chatted until the choir appeared, singing the opening hymn, this congregation was quiet and somber. The organist, Ruth Lawson, was playing a variation on the old hymn, "Amazing Grace," and Lucy followed the tune, letting it fill her mind and soothe her jumbled emotions.

"For the Beauty of the Earth" was the opening hymn and Lucy had a tough time singing the familiar phrases, thinking of the intense emotion with which she'd greeted each of her children, and how bereft she'd feel if she lost any one of them. She hoped Alison had been loved like that, enfolded with love from her first breath.

Lucy found her eyes straying to the bereaved family in the front pews.

She recognized Ed Franklin, with that head of carefully styled white hair. His young wife Mireille was standing beside him, but Lucy could only catch a glimpse of her back. Her long blond hair was a dramatic contrast to her black coat.

The hymn ended, but before the congregation could sing the final amen, a primal cry of pain and anguish disturbed the usual pregnant pause. All eyes were drawn to a sobbing woman in the front pew opposite the one occupied by Ed Franklin and his wife. She was supported by two men, one young and one middle-aged, as she collapsed into her seat and the sobs gradually subsided.

"Her mother, Alison's mother . . ." was the whispered message that rippled through the rather staid gathering of reserved New Englanders.

Rev. Margery Harvey, the minister known to all as Rev. Marge, was quick to move things along, calling upon those present to join in prayer. When the Lord's Prayer was completed, she thanked everyone for coming and offering their support to Alison's family—her father, Ed Franklin, her mother Eudora Clare, and her brother Tag Franklin, as well as her stepmother, Mireille Franklin, and stepfather, Jon Clare.

After a responsive reading of Psalm 23 the minister called upon Tag Franklin to deliver the eulogy. Tag was the young man who had attended Alison's mother, and he bore little resemblance to his sister. He was taller, had a more muscular build, and the shock of hair that fell across his brow was light brown. With his wide-set eyes, a straight nose, and very white teeth he looked as if he could have come straight out of a Lands End catalog.

He began with the usual fond remembrances of

a shared childhood, occasional pranks, and even a few funny stories that elicited amused chuckles. But then his tone grew sharper, even accusatory when he directed his gaze at his father and said, "I wish I could say that my sister's brief life was happy and untroubled, but instead of receiving the unconditional love and support she desperately needed she encountered only selfishness. When she needed a warm embrace she got a cold shoulder, when she needed encouragement she got criticism, and when she most needed fatherly approval to sustain her she discovered that attention had been withdrawn and directed to another. Her beauty, her shining spirit, her intelligence, all went unnoticed and unappreciated."

Shocked, Lucy glanced at her daughter and saw with some surprise that Zoe was nodding along in agreement, brushing away a tear.

Then they were on their feet, singing the final hymn, "We Will Gather at the River." Lucy finally got a clear view of Alison's mother, Eudora, who was a tiny, very thin woman. Due to a puffy bouffant hairstyle, her head seemed much too large for her emaciated body. She was leaning heavily on her son and the other man, presumably her husband Jon Clare. Unlike the hale and hearty Tag, Jon Clare was a lanky, weedy sort, with a narrow head, thinning hair, and long arms and legs.

"Do you want to go to the reception?" Lucy asked her daughter, who was stuffing a wad of damp tissues into her purse. "We could skip it. With all these people I don't think we'll be missed."

"Oh, no. I want to tell her folks how kind she was to me. You know, when I had that flu last month and missed some classes she offered to go over her notes with me." Zoe sniffed. "She didn't have to do that, you know."

"Okay," said Lucy as the usher released them from their pew, allowing them to join the stream of mourners leaving the church. She had been relieved when the pastor announced the interment of the ashes would be private, unsure of how Zoe would react to the grim business of seeing an entire human being reduced to a mere pile of dust. But, like most everyone at the funeral, she was somewhat curious and eager to see the interior of the Franklin mansion.

Shore Road was already lined with parked cars when Lucy and Zoe arrived, but it was a mild day and it was pleasant walking along the rocky bluff overlooking the ocean. Far below, the surf crashed against the rocks, sending up sprays of sparkling water.

The family was not yet present, still occupied with the burial, which loosened the usual sense of restraint felt by the gathered friends and neighbors. People were greeting each other with warm hugs, chattering vivaciously and helping themselves to the generous catered buffet. Zoe went straight to the reception line, which was already forming, while Lucy accepted a small cocktail sherry from the tray offered by a waiter in a crisply starched white shirt. She was making her way through the throng to the corner where her friends Sue and Rachel were standing, when a hush fell on the crowd and Ed and Mireille Franklin entered.

Ed held up his hand in greeting and said, "Thank

you all for coming. The support of so many friends
and neighbors means the world to me and Mireille."

Mireille, who was standing by his side, was remarkably pretty, very young, and extremely pregnant. She didn't speak but bestowed a sad little
smile on her assembled guests.

"There is something I feel I must say," continued Ed. "My son Tag is no doubt deeply grieving
the loss of his sister and that is completely understandable. However, I want to make it clear that Alison was a much loved daughter and both Mireille
and I are devastated by this tragic turn of events. It
was just this time last year when Alison had her bik-
ing accident, and unfortunately became depen-
dent upon prescription painkillers. Mireille was a
rock in those dark days and got Alison into rehab,
but as often happens, recovery wasn't a simple
process and wasn't as successful or complete as we
hoped and it seems that Alison began using illegal
opioids. These drugs are insidious, terribly hard to
beat, and the dealers are relentless." He paused
and swallowed hard. "Sometimes all the love in the
world just isn't enough. Thank you for your patience."

"Nice comeback," said Sue, who had appeared
at Lucy's side, along with Rachel. They were both
holding glasses of sherry.

"I can see why he felt he had to say something,"
said Lucy, noticing that Tag wasn't present, and
neither was his mother or stepfather.

"Do you believe him—Ed?" asked Sue, sounding somewhat skeptical. "It doesn't sound realistic
to me—the trophy wife doting on the stepdaughter."

"I guess we have to give him the benefit of the doubt," said Lucy.

"Family members often have very different memories of important family events," said Rachel. "A brother and a sister, for example, might have very different interpretations of a particular birthday party. The brother might remember eating cake while the sister was upset because there was no ice cream."

"Alison's brother wasn't talking about ice cream," said Sue. "He seemed really angry about the way his father treated Alison."

"Or maybe he's projecting his own feelings toward his father and the new, young wife who displaced his mother," said Rachel.

They watched as Mireille and Ed began greeting the people waiting in the reception line, and were about to get in line themselves when Mireille suddenly began to sway and was caught by her husband. He supported her as they left the crowded room, accompanied by a solicitous older woman who followed them.

"Mireille's mother?" asked Lucy.

"I'd bet on it," said Sue, snagging a second sherry from a passing waiter.

Lucy noticed with some relief that Zoe had joined a lively group of young people. Deciding it was time to leave and tackle her long list of weekend errands, she thought she'd see if Zoe also wanted to leave or whether she'd prefer to hang with her friends.

"I don't want to interrupt," she began, joining the group, "but I really have to be going."

"I'll see you later, then," said Zoe, who was sipping on a soft drink. "We're going to stop by the cemetery together and say good-bye to Alison."

"That's a nice idea," said Lucy, rather surprised.

"It's the right thing to do" said one, a serious looking fellow with thick, black-rimmed glasses and a head of curly red hair.

"Are you sure you'll be all right?" she asked Zoe.

"It's something I want to do, Mom."

"Alison's not the first, you know," said a chubby girl with long, black hair. "There's been two others already this year."

"Drownings?" asked Lucy, shocked.

"No. Overdoses," said Zoe.

"Two at the college?" asked Lucy.

"From our class," said the boy. "Alison's the third."

"And there's been lots of close calls," added Zoe.

"We see the town ambulance on campus almost every day," said the girl.

"I'm really shocked," said Lucy. "I guess I thought college kids would be too smart to be using."

"You'd think so," said the guy. "But if they use even once, thinking they'll try it, it's all they think about. It takes over their lives. Believe me, Alison's not the last. There'll be more."

Chapter Four

Ted didn't greet Lucy when she arrived for work on Monday morning. He didn't even look up from his computer. "Don't bother to take off your coat," he said. "I need you to go straight to District Court."

"Okay," said Lucy, casting a "what's up?" glance toward Phyllis and getting an eye roll and a shrug in reply. "Mind telling me what this is all about?"

"The Downeast Drug Task Force made a big arrest last night. Three dealers. The arraignment is today." He pulled a sheet of paper off the printer and handed it to her. "Here's the press release with the names. Try to get photos, okay?"

"Will do," said Lucy, scanning the brief announcement that Carlos Cabral, 19, Manuel Perez, 21 and Eufry Victorino, 22, all from Queens, had been arrested following a three-month investigation. The three were caught in a Route 1 motel

room with 50 grams of heroin, 40 grams of pow-
dered cocaine, $5750 in cash and several firearms.
The street value of the drugs was estimated to be
$15,000.

"I'm going to follow up on the official side,"
said Ted. "I'm sure the DA will want to get some
credit, as will the Task Force."

"I always wonder why these investigations take
so long," said Phyllis. "What were they doing for
three months? It doesn't take the buyers three
months to find a dealer, does it?"

"That's one of the questions I plan to ask Detective Lieutenant Cunningham, who heads the task
force," said Ted. "Now, go, Lucy. You've got to get
over to Gilead by nine. Time's a-wasting!"

"Trust me," said Lucy, looping her purse strap
over her shoulder. "They never start on time."

Despite the fact that trials seemed quite dramatic when presented on the TV news, Lucy knew
that was because they were skillfully highlighted
and presented for maximum effect. In truth, trials
were extremely tedious and took a very long time
to establish the most basic facts. Even arraign-
ments, which were brief, required reporters to sit
through a long list of other more minor offenders.
Nevertheless, she felt a certain sense of excitement
as she followed the familiar route to Gilead, the
county seat, to cover what was sure to be a big
story.

As she expected, the parking lot in the courthouse complex was packed and there were several
satellite trucks from various TV stations. The
Boston stations were all there, as was the regional
cable news. She had to park in an overflow lot,

which meant a long hike back to the courthouse, and by the time she made her way through the metal detector and had her purse examined by a gloved officer she was running late. Court was already in session, all the seats were taken, and she had to elbow her way into a spot in the back.

Judge Irene Thaw was clearly not pleased at the sudden intense interest in the proceedings in her courtroom, and she wasn't about to expedite matters for the benefit of the assembled members of the media. As usual on Monday morning, following the weekend, there were a number of cases to be dealt with including the usual allegations of driving while intoxicated, spousal abuse, and disorderly conduct.

The air in the courtroom had become quite stale and Lucy's back was aching when the case of the three alleged drug dealers was finally announced, causing the media crowd to snap to attention. Digital cameras and smartphones were readied, video cameras and tape recorders were switched on, notebooks were opened and pens were gripped to record the moment when the alleged offenders were brought into the courtroom.

District Attorney Phil Aucoin presented the charges himself, accusing Carlos Cabral, Manuel Perez, and Eufry Victorino of Class A aggravated trafficking in Schedule W drugs, illegal possession of firearms, engaging in interstate commerce for illegal transactions, resisting arrest, and driving a vehicle that did not have a current inspection sticker. That last caused a bit of a chuckle among the gathered crowd.

Aucoin had done his homework and went on to

present the judge with the trio's criminal records, which Lucy thought were remarkably long for such young offenders. All three had spent time in juvenile facilities, and Victorino, the oldest, had recently been released from the EMTC correctional facility on Riker's Island where he had served eighteen months for assault and battery.

When Aucoin finished his presentation, the judge asked the court appointed attorney, Linda Blackman, if she had anything to add. Her attempt to defend the three was not terribly effective since she pointed out they were unemployed, or as she put it, "unable to find employment", and that situation had resulted in this misguided effort to make money by the only means available to them. She had no doubt, she said, that after further investigation the matter would be resolved as a misunderstanding. In the meantime, she wasn't going to ask for bail because, since the three were from another state, it was unlikely to be granted.

"Don't you want to at least go on record asking for bail?" inquired the judge.

"No, your honor," said Blackman, getting evil looks from her clients. She placed the case file in her brief case, shut it with a snap, and was out of the courtroom before the three alleged drug dealers were led away by the court officers to their temporary accommodations in the county jail.

"Wow," said *Portland Press Herald* stringer Pete Withers as he and Lucy joined the throng leaving the courtroom. "Their lawyer didn't want anything to do with them. That's cold."

"Well, they do sound like trouble," said Lucy.

"And it's not as if they were local kids with families in the area."

When she stepped outside she realized there was another dimension to the case. A group of demonstrators had gathered on a grassy area in front of the courthouse and were holding signs that read BUILD A WALL! DEPORT THE DRUG DEALERS! and AMERICA FOR AMERICANS! She paused on the steps and snapped a few photos of the protesters, which prompted one of them to confront her.

"Why did you do that?" demanded a middle-aged man wearing a Carhart jacket and a red and black plaid hunting cap.

"I'm a reporter for the Tinker's Cove *Pennysaver* newspaper," said Lucy. "You're part of the story I'm covering. And besides, if you're standing out here in broad daylight demonstrating, I assume it's because you want people to know how you feel."

"I sure do want people to know how I feel," said the man, changing his tune. "These scumbags come up here from Mexico and they get welfare and food stamps and free educations and Medicaid if they stub their toes, all on the backs of hard-working real Americans. That's how I see it and it's about time it ended."

"Right!" yelled another protester. "You said it, George."

"Do you mind giving me your name, George?" asked Lucy, who had written down every word.

"George Powers. I'm from Gilead and I'm fifty-three years old."

"Thanks, George. I really appreciate your openness," said Lucy. But as she made her way back to her car, she was troubled by the demonstrators' sentiments. The three young men who had been arrested were most probably guilty, she thought, but that didn't mean that everyone who had a Hispanic name was a criminal. And this was America, where everyone was presumed to be innocent until proven guilty. Wasn't it?

She had just got settled in the car when Bill called her cell phone. "Did you forget your lunch?" she asked.

"Not my lunch," he replied. "My flip book. You know, that loose-leaf with photos of my work. I think it's in your car."

Lucy twisted around in her seat and spotted the book lying on the back seat of her CR-V. "Yup, it's here. Where are you?"

"I'm at the Olde Irish Pub. I'm meeting Rey Rodriguez to discuss some renovations."

"I didn't know you were involved with that," said Lucy.

"Me, either," said Bill. "He called this morning, asking if I'd be interested. I've got my laptop with photos, but he wants something he can keep for a few days, maybe show to his investors." Bill paused, most likely answering a question from Rey. "So how soon can you get here?"

"Twenty minutes," said Lucy. "I'm on my way."

When she arrived at the harbor, she noticed several cars parked by the Olde Irish Pub. Bill's truck was there, of course, but there was also one of the gray sedans used by town officials and a huge black Land Rover. She parked next to Bill's pickup, grabbed the book he wanted, and went inside.

When the Olde Irish Pub opened more than a decade ago it had been a big improvement over its former incarnation as the Bilge, a dive frequented by local fishermen and known for cheap beer and frequent brawls. The Olde Irish Pub was welcomed by locals, who enjoyed the friendly atmosphere, good food, and harborside location. As time passed, however, the owners seemed to lose interest and the level of service declined, as did the quality of the food, and people stopped going there. It hadn't been much of a surprise when the restaurant was closed and a FOR SALE sign appeared in the window. The property languished on the market for over a year before Rey Rodriguez expressed an interest in buying it.

"You can't beat the location," he was saying to Bill when Lucy arrived.

"I'd open up the windows to take advantage of the view," replied Bill, giving Lucy a wave. "Here's my wife with the book. Lucy, have you met Rey Rodriguez?"

"We haven't met, but I saw him at the selectmen's meeting. Welcome to Tinker's Cove."

"Lucy's a reporter for the local paper," said Bill with a smile, "so you better watch what you say or you might find yourself in print."

"Never fear. We're off the record," joked Lucy. Hearing raised voices, she turned to see the town's health agent, Jennifer Santos, and Ed Franklin emerging from the kitchen.

The two were arguing and Lucy wondered if she'd spoken too soon; this might be a situation worth a paragraph or two in the paper.

"I'm telling you, you can't do this," said Jennifer. "It's not legal."

She was an attractive woman about thirty years old, who wore her long, black hair in a pony tail and dressed for work in the same flannel shirts and jeans that the contractors she dealt with also wore. The idea may have been to blend in with the boys, but it wasn't entirely successful as Jennifer's slender body was curvy in all the right places.

"This is an environmental issue," said Ed, "due to the location here on the cove. There's no way I can approve a commercial septic system that would pour grease and detergent, including nitrates, into the harbor water. And that's before we even consider effluent from the restrooms."

"It's a perfectly legal system that's up to code and it's grandfathered," said Jennifer. "It was upgraded less than two years ago."

"What are you saying?" asked Rey, crossing the room which was filled with tables and captain's chairs tumbled every which way. "That the septic system isn't good?"

"That's exactly what I'm saying," said Ed, glaring at Rey. "The only way my board will approve a license for this property is if you agree to use paper plates. All tableware will have to be disposable."

"Like a fast-food place?" asked Rey, puzzled. "That's not the sort of business I have in mind."

"Too bad, amigo," said Ed. "I'm not, I mean, the *board* is not going to let you run dishwashers that

will fill our beautiful harbor with grease and suds.
No way, José. Got it?"

"Is this true?" asked Rey, directing his question
to Jennifer.

Jennifer looked at Ed, then sighed. "I will have
to look into it," she said, biting her lip. "I'm em-
ployed by the board of health and I answer to them."
She cast a meaningful glance toward Ed. "The board
doesn't have the last word, however. They are obligated to enforce the state sanitary code as well as
local regulations."

"How soon can I expect an answer?" asked Rey.
"Time is money and I want to get this restaurant
open as soon as possible."

"I've been in business for over twenty years in
this town. I've done lots of renovations and I've
never run into anything like this," said Bill.

"And I've covered lots of projects for the *Pennysaver*, lots of board meetings, and I've never seen
such a prejudicial attitude," said Lucy.

Just then the door flew open and a young man
entered, greeting everyone with a cheery wave.
"Hi, Pop. I'm here to take a look at the new place."

"This is my son Matt," said Rey, introducing the
newcomer. "He'll be managing the restaurant."

Matt was tall and good-looking, with longish
black hair and very white teeth, and was swinging a
pair of Ray-Ban aviator sunglasses in one hand. He
was dressed in a leather jacket, designer jeans, and
fancy driving shoes.

"What a great location, right?" said Matt, nodding his approval. "It's going to be fabulous."

"Well, we're running into some problems," said
Rey. "This is Bill Stone. He came to discuss possi-

ble renovations. And this is wife, Lucy. Ed Franklin and Jennifer Santos are from the town board of health, and they say we've got some environmental issues."

"Really?" inquired Matt, raising a dark slash of eyebrow. "I went over all the specs with an environmental engineer. He even did an inspection before we made an offer. He said everything was correct."

"Well, I'm the chairman of the board of health and I'd like to take a look at that so-called review," said Ed Franklin. "You can't just come into this town and start polluting the water with your greasy Mexican gunk. I know the sort of stuff you people eat—loads of lard and oil—"

"He says we will have to use paper plates like a fast-food place," said Rey.

"That has not been decided," cautioned Jennifer.

"What exactly is the process?" asked Matt, directing his question to Jennifer. "Do we have to get approval from him? Who is this guy? The king of sanitation?"

"Like I said, I'm the chairman of the board and they'll darn well do what I tell them to do," declared Ed. "And I can tell you that we don't want people like you—"

"Now I understand," said Matt. "It's because we're Latino, right?"

"Not now," cautioned Rey, placing his hand on his son's arm.

"Yeah, and three of your compadres were in the district court this morning. Drug pushers with guns. Not the sort of folks we want in Tinker's Cove."

"Not my compadres," said Matt. "Do you know our family came here from Spain in the fifteen hundreds? We were here long before the United States was created."

"Well bully for you," said Ed, turning to Jennifer. "I think we're done here."

"Here's my card." She handed one to Rey. "You can contact me anytime with questions." She seemed ready to add something, then glanced over her shoulder at Ed who was clearly impatient for her to leave, and decided against it. "It's been nice meeting you," she said, scurrying out after him.

"What do you think?" asked Rey, turning to Bill.

"Like I said, we take out these fake cottage windows and put in plate glass. Open up the kitchen, put in some new light fixtures, banquette seating. It's going to be beautiful."

"How long will it take?" asked Rey.

"Not long," said Bill. "A couple weeks if you go with stock items, which I recommend. Custom could take forever."

Rey was smiling and nodding along, sharing Bill's vision.

But Matt wasn't buying it. "And what about Ed Franklin?"

"In the end, the board has to follow the law, and the law's on your side," said Bill.

"Ed Franklin just lost his daughter. He's grieving." Lucy gave an apologetic smile. "People here aren't like him," she said, by way of farewell.

As she made her way to the *Pennysaver* office,

she thought of the demonstration outside the courthouse and wondered if Ed Franklin was saying things out loud that many people had been thinking to themselves for some time. Maybe his hate speech would open the flood gates, unleashing a torrent of pent-up prejudice.

"What took so long?" Ted asked when Lucy arrived at the office carrying a bag from the Quik-Stop containing a pot of yogurt and a banana.

"Court took forever, then I had to grab something for lunch . . ." she said, noticing that Phyllis was holding up her hands in a cautionary sign, casting warning eyes in Ted's direction. Taking the hint Lucy decided not to mention her stop at the Olde Irish Pub, which was a personal errand, even though it meant not reporting the encounter between Ed Franklin and the Rodriguezes.

"I heard there was quite a demonstration at the courthouse. Did you get photos?" demanded Ted.

"Photos and quotes," said Lucy.

"Okay, write it up. And before you leave, I want to go over the week's news budget."

"Right, Chief," said Lucy, giving a little salute before hanging up her coat.

"No need for sarcasm," snapped Ted, who was hunched over his computer.

Lucy settled herself at her desk, eating her yogurt while she booted up her computer and scrolled through her e-mails. She was licking the last off her spoon when the phone rang and she answered it.

"Hi, Lucy," said Pam. "Something's come up and I need help."

Interesting, thought Lucy. Maybe this was the reason for Ted's bad mood. "What's the trouble?"

"Debi Long has pneumonia. She's in the hospital."

"That's too bad."

"Bad? It's worse than bad. It's a disaster."

"Pneumonia? They give you antibiotics, then you get better . . ."

"It's the Harvest Festival at the church! Debi always makes dozens of apple cider donuts and people snap them up. Some people come just for the donuts."

Lucy knew the Harvest Festival was a big fundraiser for the church, which in turn donated to numerous local causes, including the Hat and Mitten Fund that she and her friends had started to provide warm clothes and school supplies for the town's less fortunate children. She also had an uneasy feeling where this was heading.

"I wish I could help."

"Well, you can. You can make donuts, can't you? All you need is a deep fryer. If you don't have one I bet you can borrow Debi's."

"I have done it. I *can* do it, but that doesn't mean I *want* to do it," said Lucy, who used to turn out a steady stream of baked goods when the kids were little. Back then, she was always mixing up nutritious lunchbox treats like oatmeal cookies with raisins, peanut butter bars, and molasses hermits. To be honest though, she rarely bothered with donuts, considering them too much trouble, and unhealthy to boot. "I've always been more of a customer at the Harvest Festival."

"Well, I bet you'd like making donuts if you tried. It would come back to you . . . like riding a bike."

"It's the question of time," said Lucy, glancing at the rolltop desk where Ted was buried in a pile of papers. "Your husband here keeps me pretty busy."

"Never mind him. I'll take care of Ted. You take whatever time you need to make donuts. It doesn't have to be twelve dozen. Six would be good. Angie Booth said she can make six, too."

"What about Sue? Can't she do it?" asked Lucy in a last ditch effort.

"Sue is making peanut brittle, which she tells me is absolutely wonderful, though I don't know how she knows since I doubt she's ever actually eaten any." Pam paused. "Donuts aren't very hard, you know, if you use an electric fryer. You just pop them in and wait for them to float to the top, then flip 'em over." She paused. "Just be sure to let them drain well. They're icky if they're too oily."

Lucy knew from the tone of her voice that Pam was truly desperate. "Okay," she agreed reluctantly. "I'll dig out the fryer. Six dozen apple cider donuts."

"Thanks, Lucy. I knew I could count on you. You're absolutely super."

It was after four when Lucy finished writing her story about the arraignment and the related demonstration, and uploaded her photos. She jotted down some ideas for the news budget and checked her e-mails for last-minute announcements and changes to the official town calendar. Noticing something from the board of selectmen she saw a new item was added to the agenda for the upcoming meeting—a citizen's complaint about racial bias by a member of the board of health.

"This is going to be interesting," she told Ted, finally deciding to tell him about the discussion she'd heard at the Olde Irish Pub. "Ed Franklin was using derogatory words like *amigo* and *no way José* to Rey Rodriguez. And he was making up stuff about the septic system not being up to code, saying they might not be able to run a dishwasher."

"I'm not surprised that Rey is filing a complaint," said Phyllis.

"I'm not sure it's Rey," said Lucy, thinking that Matt had seemed awfully self-assured. "It might be his son, Matt."

"The hunk I saw filling up his 'Vette at the Quik-Stop?" asked Phyllis with a mischievous smile.

"Could be," said Lucy, laughing.

Chapter Five

When she got home that evening, Lucy was surprised to see Zoe using the old electric fryer to cook up a batch of Southern Fried Chicken. Each piece had a lovely brown crust and as they sat on a wire rack, they filled the air with a delicious chickeny aroma.

That aroma was clearly getting to Libby. Mouth watering, she was sitting expectantly at Zoe's feet.

"Is that for supper?" asked Lucy as she dropped her bag on the bench and began unbuttoning her jacket.

"Yup. I just got a yen for fried chicken," declared Zoe, carefully adding the last few pieces of crusty chicken to the wire rack to cool and switching off the fryer.

"Very impressive. I'm sure it's going to taste every bit as good as it looks. But I've got to ask, whatever possessed you?" Lucy knew her youngest daughter's forays into the kitchen rarely went beyond tossing a pack of popcorn into the microwave.

"I have a big American Lit midterm exam next week," admitted Zoe. "I'm avoiding studying because every time I open my notebook I think of Alison. According to my psych book it's called displacement activity."

"Oh, dear," said Lucy, concerned. "Maybe you should check those psych books for a more positive approach—one that would get you back on track with your studying."

"I should," said Zoe with a sigh. "And I will. But every time I open my notebooks I think of Alison."

"It's tough, I know," said Lucy, giving Zoe a hug. "I think you just have to make yourself get started. Once you do, I think it will get easier."

"I hope so," said Zoe, plopping into one of the chairs at the round, golden oak kitchen table. "I'm thinking of taking next semester off. This new restaurant Dad's working at, Cali Kitchen, has got lots of help wanted signs up at the college. I'm sure I could get a job there."

Lucy had a horrible sinking feeling. She'd seen how this worked. First the kids dropped out of school, then with too much free time on their hands they began hanging around with other dropouts, and before you knew it, they started experimenting with drugs. "I don't think that's a good idea," she said, washing her hands in the kitchen sink.

"Don't panic, Mom," said Zoe in an amused tone, watching her mother pull some salad fixings out of the fridge. "It's just an idea."

"Maybe you could drop a course or two, and work part-time," said Lucy, ripping open a bag of lettuce and dropping it into a bowl.

"Yeah, maybe," said Zoe with a distinct lack of enthusiasm.

"In the meantime," began Lucy as she chopped a cucumber, "since you can't concentrate on American Literature, how about making apple cider donuts for me? I said I'd make six dozen for the Harvest Festival at the church."

"I could do that," said Zoe in a thoughtful tone. "I saw Martha Stewart make donuts on TV this morning and it didn't look hard."

Lucy wondered exactly how much time Zoe was wasting in this displacement activity as she watched her pick up the neglected notebook lying on the table and flipped through a few pages.

"Of course," said Zoe, "*Moby Dick* is a really complex book and I'm way behind. I already told Mrs. Hollis that I'm not going to be able to babysit for her this weekend and I'll need some gas money . . ."

Lucy had an idea where this was heading. "I'll pay you," she said in a small voice as she began coring a tomato.

"I'm pretty sure we can work something out," said Zoe with a satisfied smile. "When do you need the donuts?"

These days it seemed to Lucy that time was accelerating and the days flew by much too quickly before she could accomplish half the things she meant to do. The town calendar followed its usual pattern of regularly scheduled meetings and she found she had a permanent case of déjà vu, finding herself once again in the basement meeting room at the town hall covering the planning board or the finance committee, and most frequently, the board of selectmen.

At least today's meeting promised to be a little bit different, as the Rodriguezes complaint against Ed Franklin was on the agenda. When she arrived, Rey and Matt were already in attendance sitting side by side in a middle row, quietly conversing. They were dressed more formally in ties and business suits rather than the customary jeans and sweaters that was usual in Tinker's Cove.

She settled herself in her usual seat, then abruptly decided to shake things up a bit and moved to the opposite side of the room and sat beside Verity Hawthorne.

"Going rogue?" she asked, looking up from her knitting and giving Lucy a smile.

"Just thought I'd see if things look different from this side of the room."

"I think we're in for a bit of drama tonight," said Verity as Ed Franklin strode down the center aisle, planting his feet heavily with each step.

Reaching the row where Rey and Matt were sitting, he paused and glared at them, then continued on his way, taking a seat in the front row where he spread his legs wide apart and stretched his arms across the backs of the chairs on either side of him. The body language spoke loud and clear—Ed Franklin was a big, important man, much too big for one little chair.

The big hand on the clock behind the selectmen's dais clicked into place on the twelve and the board members immediately filed in. Following their usual order, they sat down at the long table, each behind his or her nameplate. Roger Wilcox called the meeting to order, they promptly dispatched the usual business, then moved on to the matter of the citizen's complaint.

Rey rose and politely addressed the board members, speaking in a somewhat regretful tone as he claimed that Ed Franklin overstepped his role as a board member when he inserted himself in the meeting with health inspector Jennifer Santos. "He had no place at that meeting, the purpose of which was simply to provide an overview of the project and discuss the relevant regulations. Mr. Franklin displayed a hostile attitude. He threatened enforcement of nonexistent regulations and interfered with Ms. Santos' professional responsibilities.

"I know a bit about the restaurant business," Rey continued in a deliberate understatement. "I have been in the business for nearly forty years. I have worked hard to earn an enviable reputation as a respected restaurateur and chef, so I can only conclude that Mr. Franklin objects to me personally because I am of Latino heritage. This, as you know, is a clear violation of national, state, and local equal rights legislation.

"I also want to add that I have come to believe that Mr. Franklin has been pressuring local suppliers and garbage haulers to refuse to do business with me. As my credit rating is excellent, that is the only possible explanation for the resistance I have encountered as I have tried to contract with local suppliers for necessary products and services. I might add that in all my years as a businessman I have never before encountered a situation like this."

Matt remained quiet in his seat while his father spoke but kept his eyes fixed on the back of Ed Franklin's head. That head remained immobile. Ed Franklin did not react in any way to Rey's accusations.

When Rey finished speaking, Roger thanked him for expressing himself so clearly and bringing the matter to the attention of the board. Then he asked Ed Franklin if he wished to respond.

"You bet I do," said Ed, remaining sprawled in his seat. His tone was conversational, as if he was merely repeating widely accepted truths. "Everybody knows Mexico has only two exports—illegal drugs and people—and both are trouble. We've all read in the newspapers about the gang wars on the border and the terrible killings. These folks have no respect for life. They kill anybody who gets in their way, including police officers. I have friends in Arizona, people who've been successful in business and were looking to enjoy a peaceful retirement, and they say they have to have dogs and fences and guns to feel safe from the illegals.

"Now maybe Mr. Rodriguez here is a law-abiding fellow. I've got nothing against him personally, and my wife says his cookbooks are great, fabulous, but when one Mexican moves in you get a lot more. They're like mice. You catch one mouse and think you've solved the problem, but believe me, it's just the tip of the iceberg. I think we've got a responsibility to keep Tinker's Cove a safe, pleasant place to live and that means keeping out undesirable elements. Mexicans should stay in Mexico. America is for Americans."

While Ed was speaking Lucy watched the expressions on the board members faces, trying to discern their reactions. At first, they seemed eager to display openness and a fair-minded willingness to hear his response to Rey's allegations, but as Ed continued, their expressions hardened and they began to fidget in their seats, growing more and more uncomfortable. By the time he finished speaking, Franny Small was biting her lip, Sam Bellamy's face was red and he seemed about to explode. Joe Marzetti was clenching his teeth and Winchester College professor Fred Rumford was shaking his head in dismay. Roger Wilcox was momentarily speechless, his head lowered as he stared at the papers on the table before him.

"Mr. Franklin," he finally said, "you have not answered Mr. Rodriguez's complaint that you personally interfered in a meeting with the health agent, overstepping your position as chairman of the board of health. What do you have to say?"

"Oh, no question, I was at the meeting. And I pointed out that there would most likely be problems complying with current septic regulations considering the location of the Olde Irish Inn."

Hearing this, Matt jumped to his feet. "He said we wouldn't be able to have a dishwasher, that we'd have to use paper plates like a fast-food place! That was a clear threat! Cali Kitchen will be a fine restaurant! Paper plates would be—"

"You're out of order," said Roger with a placatory smile. "Please let me continue questioning

Mr. Franklin. If you feel you need to add something, you may speak later." He turned to Ed, raising a small booklet with a blue cover. "I wonder, Mr. Franklin, if you are familiar with this document. It is a concise summary of responsibilities and legal obligations that is given to every town official. I assume you were given one of these booklets?"

"Probably. I can't say it looks familiar," said Ed with a shrug. "A lot of paper comes across my desk. I don't get to read it all."

"I suggest you take this copy home with you tonight and read it very carefully," said Roger. "I believe you will find it helpful if you are going to continue as a member of the board of health in future."

"You're going to let him stay on the board?" demanded Matt, who was on his feet, hands clenched.

"For the present," said Roger. "But I will say this to Mr. Franklin. As much as we appreciate your service to the town, we expect you to follow all the policies the town has adopted, including the very specific requirement that every petitioner be treated respectfully, fairly, and equally. If you find yourself unable to comply with the fundamental rights guaranteed to all citizens by the US Constitution we will ask you to remove yourself from the board. Do you understand?"

"I have no problem with that," said Ed with a shrug. "I was misunderstood. That's all it was."

"We did not misunderstand you," declared Matt.

"Well, that's the thing with misunderstandings,

right?" said Ed with an ingratiating smile. "I think one thing, you think another. But I guess it's all straightened out, right?"

"It better be," growled Matt as Roger banged down his gavel. Then turning on his heel, Matt marched out of the meeting room.

There was a rather stunned silence, then the newest member of the board, Franny Small, who rarely spoke, raised her hand.

"Ms. Small," said Roger, recognizing her.

"I have something to say." She spoke in a firm voice and unfolded some papers she'd taken from her purse. "It's a quote. I just happen to have it here. It was in the bulletin from last Sunday's service at the Community Church. I'd like to enter it into the minutes, if I may. It goes like this. "'First they came for the Socialists and I did not speak out—Because I was not a Socialist. Then they came for the Trade Unionists and I did not speak out—Because I was not a Trade Unionist. Then they came for the Jews and I did not speak out—Because I was not a Jew. Then they came for me—and there was no one left to speak for me.'" She paused. "It's from a man named Martin Niemöller. He was protesting the Nazis."

"I'd like to move that the quote Ms. Small just read be entered into the minutes," said Fred Rumford.

Sam Bellamy was quick to second the motion, which passed unanimously.

"Thank you all," said Roger, nodding his head. "I think we all need to remember that America is one country with people from many parts of the world. They came here for freedom and the guarantee of equal treatment under the law. Now, if there's no other business, the meeting is adjourned." He banged down the gavel and everybody started to leave.

Lucy went up to the front of the room to congratulate Franny. "I guess that was your maiden speech," she said, smiling. "Well done."

Franny was a very small woman well into her sixties, who'd had a remarkably successful career creating a profitable jewelry business. She'd begun by making the pins and earrings out of nuts and bolts and other hardware and selling them at craft fairs. She turned out to be a canny businesswoman and the company had grown and evolved through the years as major department stores began carrying the line. Now she was retired, and although she was probably the second richest person in Tinker's Cove, after Ed Franklin, she still lived in the modest house she'd grown up in and drove an ancient Honda Civic.

"Thanks, Lucy. I had to speak up. We simply can't tolerate this sort of intolerance in our town."

"I couldn't agree more."

Franny bent closer, whispering, "Have you seen his wife? She's young enough to be his daughter!" Her eyes widened. "And she's pregnant!"

"They've suffered a terrible tragedy," Lucy reminded her.

"The wages of sin, no doubt," said Franny with a knowing nod. "Have a nice evening," she added, making her serene way out of the meeting room.

Intolerance was a funny thing, thought Lucy as

she gathered up her things. People rarely seemed to recognize their own prejudices, even when they were quick to condemn another's failings.

When she climbed the cement steps to the parking area, she was yawning, looking forward to a hot bath and bed. Hearing raised voices, she paused at the top of the stairs where she saw Matt angrily confronting Ed Franklin. The two were clearly illuminated by a street light, and a few bystanders were watching.

"We're not Mexicans," he yelled, face-to-face with Ed. "We're Americans. My father, his father, and his father going back for hundreds of years. They were all born in California."

"Get out of my way," growled Ed, attempting to edge around him. "I don't care who you are."

"Well, you better care," snarled Matt, blocking his way, "and you better call off your racist buddies . . . Becker and ProServe and Curtis Cleaners."

"I don't know what you're talking about," insisted Ed, attempting once again to make his way to his huge Navigator SUV.

"You know, and it's gotta stop!" yelled Matt, raising his arm.

"That's enough," said Rey, stepping between them. "Go home, Matt."

Matt stayed in place for a long moment, glaring at Ed, then marched across the parking lot to his Corvette. The car roared into life and he sped across the parking lot, swerving widely at the exit and zooming off down the road.

"I must apologize for my son," said Rey. "He's young and hotheaded."

"Like all you Mexicans, I guess," said Ed. "What do they call it? Latin blood?"

Rey looked like a man who'd been slapped in the face. He stepped back, shook his head, and walked slowly to his car.

"I have a feeling this isn't over," said Joe Marzetti, who had climbed the stairs and paused beside Lucy. "And it's not going to be pretty."

"I think you're right." She had noted the names Matt had mentioned, presumably outfits that had refused to do business with the Rodriguezes, and was jotting them down in her notebook.

Next morning at the office, she put in calls to ProServe and Curtis Cleaners, but both went straight to voice mail. She dutifully left messages, but doubted very much they would bother to return her call. Walt Becker, a local trash hauler, answered the phone himself.

"Hi, Lucy." His voice came booming through the phone. "What can I do for you?"

She had recently interviewed him for a story on recycling and he'd been extremely helpful, even taking her to the regional single-stream recycling facility for a tour. She didn't want to offend him by accusing him of racism, so she proceeded carefully. "Funny thing, Walt. I was at the selectmen's meeting last night."

"I'm sorry," he joked. "Nobody should have to go through that."

"I know," laughed Lucy. "It was pretty awful. But the reason I'm calling is that, well, Matt Rodriguez accused Ed Franklin of pressuring local businesses to refuse to contract with them and your name came up."

"Look, I know full well that it's against the law to refuse service because of race, color, religion, sexual preference, age . . . you name it. You call Becker Hauling and we'll haul it, as long as it's not toxic or radioactive or something like that."

"But did Ed Franklin pressure you in any way?"

"Sure. That's what Ed Franklin does. Thinks he's king of the universe. Said he'd fire me if I contracted with Rodriguez and wouldn't use my trucks anymore."

"What are you going to do?" asked Lucy.

"Look, nobody tells me how to run my business. If Franklin's unhappy with me, well, that's too bad. I've got plenty of happy customers."

"I'm sure you do," said Lucy.

"That's not to say that I've got to like everybody. Personally, I don't get that transgender thing at all, but I don't really care what bathroom anybody uses as long as they don't leave a nasty mess. And I'm not crazy about these Latinos or whatever they are. Did you see the news? Those three guys? The drug dealers?"

"Actually, I covered the arraignment," said Lucy.

"Well, then I don't have to tell you that those guys are bad guys. They're trouble and we don't need any more trouble. We've got enough of our own. But that said, business is business and I'm in the business of hauling trash from anybody and everybody who asks, just as long as they pay their bills."

"Then why did Matt Rodriguez name you as one of Franklin's buddies?" asked Lucy, determined to keep Walt wriggling on the hook. "It sure sounded like you refused their business."

"Well," said Becker, speaking slowly. "That was my girl here, Abby. She overheard Franklin threatening me and when Rodriguez called she said she wasn't sure if we could take on more business. I'll, uh, I'll give them a call and straighten it out."

"So it was just a misunderstanding?" persisted Lucy, suspecting it was nothing of the kind. She figured Walt had done a quick calculation and concluded that the bad publicity from a mention in the *Pennysaver* would be worse for his business than Ed Franklin's threats.

"Yeah," he said, quick to agree. "That's all it was. It was a misunderstanding."

There sure seemed to be a lot of misunderstanding going on these days, thought Lucy.

Chapter Six

The next morning, Lucy was dismayed to see, was a beautiful sunshiny day. A classic New England autumn morning with clear skies, golden-leaved trees, and crisp air. A perfect day for running and resuming her training program for the Turkey Trot, which she'd been neglecting.

She knew full well that she'd been avoiding running, using every excuse she could come up with—too rainy, too windy, she got a late start and didn't want to be late for work or for meeting the girls for breakfast. The truth was that Zoe wasn't the only one who was haunted by Alison's death. Lucy hadn't wanted to go back on the old logging road. The last time she ran there she'd discovered Alison's body and didn't want to relive that experience.

But she knew that she needed to train if she was going to be a serious competitor in the Turkey Trot and today was the perfect opportunity. It was early so she had plenty of time, and the weather was absolutely perfect. She had run out of excuses. It was time to lace up and face her ghosts.

When Libby saw her come into the kitchen in her running clothes, she leaped out of her doggy bed and began prancing around, tail wagging, eager to get going. The dog's enthusiasm was contagious and Lucy was smiling as she grabbed the leash and opened the door. She paused on the back porch and took a few deep breaths, then began her stretches.

Libby didn't approve of stretches. She was halfway across the yard when she stopped, realizing she was alone. She turned and barked a few times, as if to say "What's the holdup?"

"I'm coming," yelled Lucy, smiling to herself when she realized she was making excuses to her dog.

Then they were off, Lucy moving at an easy jog and Libby running just ahead, her tail up and ears flapping, her mouth spread open in a doggy smile. Lucy felt nicely loose and warmed up by the time the trail entered the woods, and she began to run harder along a flat stretch of dirt road that extended for a mile or so. She was panting and had worked up a sweat by the time the road began its uneven descent to the pond.

Her thoughts inevitably turned to Alison. *What was she doing, going out on the ice? It was such a foolish thing to do and she must have known the danger. Was she on drugs, like everybody thought? Or had there been a reason, like a dog or other animal in trouble?*

Lucy hadn't seen any sign of a struggling animal but that didn't mean it hadn't been there and either managed to get free or succumbed and sank below the surface of the icy water.

The other possibility, which nobody said out loud but which she was sure a lot of people were thinking, was that Alison committed suicide. A lot of young people encountered emotional difficulties in their early twenties, which was also the age at which mental illnesses like depression and schizophrenia manifested themselves. Suicide, sadly, was not uncommon at that age.

Lucy ran carefully, watching her footing as the path became more challenging due to ruts and rocks, but part of her mind was back in the community church, replaying Alison's funeral. She remembered Alison's birth mother Eudora, who had been so emotional and dramatic. Lucy had never quite overcome her somewhat repressive Calvinist upbringing, and couldn't help wondering if Eudora wasn't a bit of a drama queen. Then she sternly reminded herself that you never knew what people really felt inside, and that everyone dealt with grief in their own unique way. But still, it did seem a bit odd that Alison had been living with her father and his new young wife instead of with her birth mother.

Why did Alison choose to live with her father? Ed Franklin was a difficult man, to say the least, and Lucy suspected that Alison must have found him somewhat embarrassing. A young person of her generation was unlikely to share his bigotry, and even though she benefitted from his wealth, she would probably have been uncomfortable with the way he flaunted it. And then there was the young wife Mireille, who was only a few years older than Alison and was pregnant. As Rachel had said, that must have been a difficult situation for Alison to deal with.

The fragrant balsam fir trees that lined the path, giving it a sense of enclosure, thinned as she approached the pond, opening up to reveal an open expanse of sky. Libby, who had been running ahead, suddenly stopped and began to whine; Lucy remembered her doing the same thing after they'd encountered a black snake sunning itself on a rocky part of the path last spring.

She must be remembering the dead girl, thought Lucy, bending down to grab the dog's ears and smooth her raised hackles. "It's okay, it's okay," she murmured. "Nobody here but us chickens."

She snapped on the leash and was about to resume her run. She knew a few tugs on the leash were all it would take to get Libby moving again. The old logging road circled the pond on one side, but there was a parking lot and swimming area on the other side that was accessed from a paved road. A narrow footpath also led from the old logging road to the parking area and Lucy decided to follow it and run along the paved road for another half mile or so before turning back.

She expected the parking area to be empty now that the summer swimming season was over, but noticed a small black BMW idling near the exit. She ran through the lot on the pond side, keeping well away from the car, which was exactly what she had been instructed to do at the women's personal safety workshop that Officer Barney Culpepper, Tinker's Cove Police Department's community outreach officer, offered from time to time. She was about halfway through the lot when a second car pulled in and then the two cars drove off together.

Weird, she thought, heading for the exit at the far end of the parking lot. She felt uneasy after witnessing the incident and was relieved when she reached the paved road, which was fairly well-traveled. She got friendly waves and toots of the horn from several passing drivers.

Reaching the rural mailbox that she used as a marker, she turned around and began the return route that would take her home. She considered continuing along the paved road, which met up with her own Red Top Road, but that would mean missing the uphill climb from the pond on the logging road, and she knew the Turkey Trot route had a similar incline. She really couldn't avoid it. She needed the workout the hill provided, so she headed back to the parking lot. There was no danger, she told herself, because the cars had left.

But as she drew closer to the lot Libby began barking, and sure enough, that little black BMW was back in the same spot, idling. Lucy picked up her pace, sprinting along the opposite side of the lot from the BMW and was almost through when an aged Caravan with a dented fender pulled up and stopped next to the BMW, driver's side to driver's side. She didn't stay to watch. She yanked the dog's leash and pounded across the remaining few yards of parking lot and entered the safety of the woods.

What was that all about, she wondered as she slowed her pace to allow her ragged, uneven breathing to even out and her racing heart to settle

down. What was going on? There was something
odd about the whole thing that simply didn't feel
right. Was she paranoid? Maybe they were just bird
watchers or nature lovers or something. Or maybe,
she thought with a shock as she began the tough
uphill climb, she had witnessed a couple drug
deals. The parking lot was perfect for that sort of
transaction. It was secluded from view, it was reli-
ably deserted this time of year, and it had easy access to the paved town road. It was a no-brainer,
she decided, wondering why she hadn't realized
what was going on sooner. Drug deals! At Blueberry Pond.

But if she—a middle-class, middle-aged woman
whose only experience of illegal drugs was a few
puffs of marijuana in college—could figure it out,
she figured it was hardly a secret. Everybody must
know. And if everybody knew, that meant the cops
must also know. So why were they ignoring it? Didn't
they know there was an opioid epidemic? What
was keeping them from making an easy arrest?
Maybe even a lot of arrests, she thought, remembering one of the EMTs who'd responded to Alison's drowning telling her there was a nearby
shack frequented by drug users.

Back at the house, Lucy couldn't stop thinking
about the drug deals she'd witnessed. It was shock-
ing to her that this was happening so close to
home. Blueberry Pond wasn't that far from their
house, and the logging road was passable by car.
Were they in danger from these criminals? Would
they have to start locking the doors to the house,

something they'd never done in all the years they'd lived on Red Top Road? And what about the stuff in their shed? It was chock full of Bill's expensive power tools, which a desperate user could steal and sell, probably for pennies on the dollar, but enough to buy some cheap heroin. Maybe more. She had no idea how much heroin or oxy or whatever they were buying cost.

Even worse than theft, what about the home invasions she'd heard about, she thought, as she stepped out of the shower and wrapped a towel around herself. Remembering she was alone in the house and feeling vulnerable, she turned the lock on the bathroom door. True, there'd never been a home invasion in Tinker's Cove, and her fear was probably irrational, but it was there. She didn't feel safe in her own home, and she was terrified for her girls. She couldn't erase the memory of that terrible episode in New Hampshire that had dominated the news for so long, when two crazy men broke into a home and raped a mother in front of her two preteen daughters, who they'd tied to their beds. After strangling the mother they'd torched the house, and the girls died from smoke inhalation.

The story went on for months as new details were revealed, the suspects caught, and the trial unfolded. A scratch and whine from the other side of the door, undoubtedly Libby looking for her breakfast, reminded Lucy that those particular criminals had even killed the family dog. Only the father, who'd been at work, was spared.

"Okay, okay," she said, opening the door cautiously and allowing Libby to stick her nose through the crack. Summoning her courage she opened the door and proceeded down the hall to her bedroom, accompanied by the dog, who jumped on the unmade bed and rolled around, legs in the air. Then she jumped off, ran to the door, and gave a sharp yip, reminding Lucy that Libby hadn't had her breakfast yet.

Lucy dressed quickly, throwing on her usual jeans and sweater. She combed and scrunched her damp hair, grabbed her shoes and socks, and hurried downstairs barefoot. In the kitchen, she dumped some kibble into Libby's bowl, poured some cereal into her own favorite bowl, and poured out the last of the morning coffee into a mug.

The headline in the morning paper, the *Press Herald*, wasn't encouraging. REGION TOPS IN OPIOID DEATHS. A quick read revealed that Massachusetts had the most overdoses, but Maine and the other New England states weren't far behind. And no wonder, she thought, tossing the paper aside with a snort, since the cops were letting the dealers operate in broad daylight.

When she arrived at the *Pennysaver* office, she wasted no time telling Ted what she had seen earlier that morning. "I couldn't believe it, Ted," she declared as she shrugged out of her barn coat and hung it on the coat rack. "There was a little BMW in the parking lot, idling there, and other cars came and went, stopping only for a minute. Sometimes they drove off together. It was creepy and scary. They're dealing drugs practically in my backyard."

"Right out in the open, at the pond?" asked Phyllis, furrowing her brows over the harlequin reading glasses perched on her nose. Today she was wearing a brightly colored floral print jersey topped with a magenta cardigan that closely matched the color of her dyed hair.

"Are you sure it was drug deals?" asked Ted in a doubtful tone. "Maybe they were sales reps, getting samples or price lists or something like that."

"No," said Lucy, shaking her head. "It was all very fast and furtive. They hardly spoke a word to each other, not chatty like colleagues would be."

"I guess you better give Chief Kirwan a call. Ask him if he's aware of the situation."

"And if not, why not? And if he is, why isn't he doing anything to stop it?" said Phyllis with a sharp nod that made the wattles under her chin quiver. "Especially since that poor little Alison Franklin died there. She probably got the drugs that killed her from that guy."

"I'm on it," said Lucy, seating herself at her desk and booting up her PC. While she waited for the ancient machine to rouse itself, she worked out what she would say to Jim Kirwan. This was a delicate situation and she didn't want to put him on the defensive. If she was going to get any information out of him, she needed to make it very clear that she wasn't criticizing the department or his management.

"Good morning, Chief," she began. "How are you?"

"Just fine, and you?" he replied.

"Fine. In fact, I went for a run this morning. I'm training for the Turkey Trot."

"Good for you, Lucy, but I don't think you called to ask my advice on training regimes, did you?"

"Well, actually, I sort of am," answered Lucy, quick to seize the opening. "My usual route takes me past Blueberry Pond and I saw some activity in the parking lot that made me wonder if it was a safe place to be."

"What did you see?"

"A car was kind of lurking there. A black BMW with a man inside."

"Oh, you don't have to worry about him. We know all about him."

Lucy was shocked and troubled by the chief's comment and continued questioning him, determined to get to the bottom of this strange turn of events. "I'm not sure, but I think he's a drug dealer. And maybe he sold the drugs that killed Alison Franklin."

She heard the chief sigh. "First off, Lucy, the autopsy report isn't complete and we don't know what killed Alison Franklin. And second, I'm going off the record now, understand?"

"Off the record," said Lucy, eager to hear more.

"Okay, this discovery of yours isn't news to me or anyone in the department. We patrol the Blueberry Pond area regularly and keep an eye on the situation, but we don't interfere for a number of reasons. One is that we have quite a few people here in town who are struggling with dependency and we know who this dealer is—"

Lucy was quick to interrupt. "Who is he?" she demanded.

"He's responsible and his drugs are clean," continued the chief, ignoring her question. "If we cut off this supply, they'll end up going to riskier dealers, getting tainted stuff and dying."

"But wouldn't it be better if they went into rehab and got clean?" asked Lucy, shocked at what she was hearing.

"Sure, but this is the real world we're living in. I'm not saying this is a perfect solution. Personally I don't like it, but I have limited options. And I've got meager resources. I don't have all the officers I need and I don't have the budget I need to handle other priorities like domestic violence, highway safety, alcohol abuse, even animal control. We're strapped. That's the honest truth. We have to leave narcotics enforcement to the state police drug task force. They've got the knowledge and expertise and they focus on the big dealers."

"But those drug task force investigations take months," protested Lucy.

"Exactly." He paused. "That's because it's very difficult to prosecute these cases. Every *i* has to be dotted and every *t* crossed. These task force members know what they're doing and they do it well."

"Have you passed on information about this dealer?" asked Lucy.

"Yes, we have," he replied. "And now, I have other matters on my desk."

"Right," said Lucy, taking the hint. "And thanks."

Ted was all over her as soon as she ended the call. "Off the record? Did you agree to go off the record?" he demanded.

"I had to or I wouldn't have gotten anything out of him. It's a bad business. They know about the dealer. They know who he is, but the chief said all they're doing is 'keeping an eye on the situation.' "

"Are you kidding me?" asked Ted, looking puzzled.

"No. That's what he said. They have passed on his identity to the drug task force. He said his department is stretched to the limit without attempting to go after drug dealers."

"But people are dying," said Phyllis. "I think of that poor girl, drowning like that because of drugs. I can't get her out of my mind."

"This isn't acceptable," said Ted. "If the police aren't going to do anything, I think we have to. The dealing is bad, but the police cover-up is worse."

"I agree," said Lucy. "We can investigate this ourselves. We don't have to break my promise to the chief about keeping what he said off the record, I saw the dealer myself. We can follow up on our own."

"The chief's not going to be happy, and he's got a lot of relatives in town jobs. You'll never get a word out of any Kirwans in the future," warned Phyllis.

Lucy knew Phyllis was right. Dot Kirwan, the matriarch of the clan, worked as a cashier at the IGA, where she picked up a lot of newsworthy information that she passed along. Her numerous offspring, children and even grandchildren, had jobs in the police and fire department, the highway department, and the schools. Lucy would hate to lose Dot as a source, and more important, as a friend.

Ted, however, had no such reservations. "We'll do an investigative report," he said, warming to the idea. "We'll stake out the parking lot, take photos, figure out who this guy is."

"And what if we see the police observing him and doing nothing?" asked Lucy.

"We report it," declared Ted with enthusiasm. "That's what we do. We tell the truth, the whole truth, and this will be a big, breakthrough story. It will not only show that opioid addiction is a problem that crosses ethnic and class lines, that it touches all of us, but it will also show that the police, the people we expect to fight the war on drugs, are AWOL."

"So tomorrow . . ." began Lucy.

"We stake out Blueberry Pond," said Ted. "Bright and early." He paused, thinking. "Better dress warm."

Chapter Seven

That afternoon, when Lucy returned home, she was surprised to see a snazzy Corvette parked in her usual spot. The only person she knew who had such a car was Matt Rodriguez and when she went into the house she found him in the kitchen with Zoe. The two were shoulder to shoulder, rolling out donut dough on the counter. Libby the dog was sitting on her haunches beside Zoe, watching every move in case a scrap of dough fell her way.

"Hi, Mom," Zoe sang out by way of greeting. Her face was flushed and Lucy didn't think the fryer had heated up the kitchen all that much. Zoe had an adorable smear of flour on her nose. "You know Matt, don't you? He's helping me make these apple cider donuts for the Harvest Festival."

"Hi, Matt," said Lucy with a smile as she plunked her bag on the bench by the door and hung her jacket on one of the hooks. "Thanks for helping Zoe."

"It's a pleasure," he said with a broad smile that revealed very white teeth and two deep dimples, one in each cheek.

He was remarkably good-looking, thought Lucy, seeing him up close. He had longish black hair and arched eyebrows over dark brown eyes, a hawkish nose, and wide mouth. Even his ears were small and nicely shaped. He was wearing designer jeans, fashionable ankle boots, and a tight cashmere sweater that showed off his toned muscles—not the baggy jeans and flannel shirts most young men in Tinker's Cove wore.

"I have to compliment you on your kitchen," he said, looking very serious. "It's functional, but also attractive and honest. It's a room with what my father calls *duende*. The closest English word is *soul*."

Lucy didn't quite know how to respond. In her mind, the kitchen was a mishmash of things picked up at yard sales. With its battered cabinets and golden oak table that gathered all sorts of clutter, it looked nothing like the sleek designer kitchens she saw in the magazines. The compliment made her wonder about this guy who she suspected was more interested in Zoe than in Lucy's decorating.

"Matt's a trained chef, Mom," said Zoe, who knew very well that her mother would want an explanation for Matt's presence in the house, which was a clear violation of the family rule against entertaining young men when no parents were home unless they'd been introduced and gotten the parental seal of approval. "We got talking when I interviewed for a job at Cali Kitchen and when I told him I had to make these donuts, he offered to help. He's already taught me so much about pastry. There's a lot more to it than I thought."

Lucy had reached for the jar of dog biscuits, a move which didn't escape Libby's notice, prompting her to abandon Zoe and transfer her attention to Lucy. Lucy raised a finger in the "sit" signal and Libby promptly obeyed, earning a biscuit which she promptly took to the dog bed in the corner and chomped down.

"Zoe is going to be a great addition at the restaurant . . . if we ever get it opened," he said. "She's not only beautiful but she's definitely got a flair for cooking. She really ought to consider culinary school."

Lucy didn't like the sound of that one bit. "She's already attending Winchester College," she snapped, "and she hopes to go on to veterinary school."

He turned to Zoe with an expression of surprise. "You didn't tell me that! That's great! I love animals. I had the best dog when I was growing up. A beagle named Bismarck. He went everywhere with me." He paused. "I missed him more than I missed my folks when I went to college."

"Was that culinary school?" asked Lucy, wondering how old Matt was.

"No. I went to Pomona for a year and flunked out," he answered, turning around and leaning his back casually against the counter. "My dad wasn't about to let me be a dropout and pushed me to join the Navy. That's where I really got interested in cooking. When my hitch was up I used the GI Bill and went to the Culinary Institute of America in New York state."

"And how long have you been working in the restaurant business?" she asked, busy adding up the years.

"About five, I guess," he said with a shrug and a big smile. "Time flies when you're having fun."

At least thirty, thought Lucy, which made him much too old for Zoe.

"And are you married?"

"No," laughed Matt. "Like I said, I'm having too much fun."

Not with my daughter, you're not, thought Lucy.

Libby, having finished her biscuit, rose from her doggy bed, gave a shake, and went back to her previous spot next to Zoe. Lucy, realizing she had little to no control over a situation she didn't much like, decided to go out and mulch the vegetable garden with compost for the winter.

When she returned to the house an hour later, Matt was gone and six dozen donuts were neatly lined up on paper towels and cooling on the counter. Lovely donuts, perfectly browned around the edges, with a light dusting of cinnamon sugar. Really, she ought to be grateful to the fellow, but she wasn't. She even resented the fact that she really, really wanted to eat one but knew she shouldn't. She heard the TV in the family room and went in, finding Zoe on the couch with Libby, watching a cooking show.

"Thanks for making those donuts. They're beautiful," Lucy said, plopping down beside the dog and scratching her behind her ears. On the TV, Ina Garten was adding a lot of butter to a pan of mushrooms.

"You should thank Matt," said Zoe. "I could never

have made such nice ones by myself. And they taste fantastic. He put in some spices I never would have thought of . . . like cumin and red pepper."

"Red pepper?" asked Lucy, alarmed.

Ina was cracking eggs into a bowl and whisking them.

"Just a tiny bit. He said it would 'liven' the sweet apple flavor."

"That will have to be our secret." Lucy could imagine how the usual festival customers would react to the idea of red pepper in their apple cider donuts. "What is she making?" she asked as Ina added grated cheese to the eggs.

"A mushroom quiche," said Zoe. "I have to say, I didn't think much of her pastry technique. She used a food processor and Matt says that makes a tough crust. You can always tell, he says, if the pastry was made by loving hands."

Ina was now outside her shingled house in the Hamptons, serving quiche to her husband Jeffrey, who was sitting at a patio table. He really seemed to enjoy the quiche, even if the crust was machine made.

Or maybe it was the big glass of white wine, thought Lucy. "Matt seems really nice," she said, carefully weighing her words as the commercials began to roll, "but he's quite a bit older than you."

"What's that supposed to mean?" asked Zoe. "He's not my boyfriend or anything."

"He clearly seemed attracted to you," said Lucy. "Guys don't make six dozen donuts for girls they don't like."

"That's the silliest thing I ever heard," said Zoe, laughing.

"Well," admitted Lucy, also laughing, "it was a unique situation. But you've got to admit guys are nice to girls they're attracted to, and offering help is one way to get acquainted. You're very pretty. He even said so."

"He was just being polite," said Zoe.

"Maybe a bit too polite, too charming. I think you should keep things on a professional level. He's really too old, too worldly for a girl your age." Lucy sighed. "There are lots of nice boys at Winchester. Boys like Hank," she said, naming a boy Sara had dated the previous winter. "He was so nice. I don't know why Sara dropped him."

"For your information, Hank DeVries is a big loser and a druggie," said Zoe, clicking off the TV and picking up the textbooks and notebooks lying on the coffee table. "I've got to study."

"You must be thinking of somebody else," protested Lucy. "Hank was really into diving. Sarah met him at the college dive club. He was very fit and athletic . . . and smart, too. I thought he was a really nice boy."

"Mom, you should hear yourself," said Zoe, tucking the books into the crook of her arm. "*Nice* is just a code word for white and Protestant. You say that you don't approve of Matt because he's too old for me but what you really mean is that he's Latino, he's got dark skin and black hair, and he's probably Catholic. You'd rather have me go out with Hank, who's blond and Episcopalian and wears L.L. Bean boat shoes without socks year round."

"He wears duck boots in winter, like everyone else," said Lucy, stung by Zoe's accusation. "And I don't object to Matt because of his skin or hair. It's because of his age and the way he's so slick, so polished. It's nothing but charm. He's not sincere, and I don't trust him."

"But you trust Hank? That's a laugh. He's a dropout. He hangs around the college to score drugs."

"I can't believe that," said Lucy.

"Well, it's true. His family is all screwed up. He had a brother who was killed in a skiing accident. His parents are divorced. His father is a beach bum somewhere in the Caribbean and his mother sells crystals in Sedona."

"I had no idea," admitted Lucy, picturing the SCUBA enthusiast she remembered. "He seemed so clean-cut and helpful and open. I thought I could read him like a book."

"Well, it turns out the Book of Hank has some plot twists," said Zoe, leaving the room.

"I guess so," said Lucy, following her into the kitchen.

Zoe continued up the back stairs to her room, and Lucy began the job of packing the donuts on trays and covering them with plastic wrap.

Next morning, the phone rang while Lucy was getting ready for the stakeout.

"I've got that stomach virus that's going around and I'm not leaving the house," said Ted. "Believe me, nobody would want to be anywhere in my vicinity."

"That's too bad," said Lucy sympathetically, cradling the earpiece on her shoulder and pulling on a second pair of socks. "I was kind of looking forward to going undercover."

"Go ahead without me," said Ted. "This is an important story and we need to get right on it."

"I don't think I should go by myself," said Lucy, shoving her foot into a duck boot. "It might be dangerous."

"There's plenty of cover at the pond," said Ted. "And these folks are probably pretty focused on contacting the dealer and scoring. They won't be noticing the scenery."

"From what I saw the other day it seems they do come and go pretty fast," said Lucy, remembering that Chief Kirwan had told her the dealer was known to the department and wasn't considered dangerous. "I'll give it a try, but if I don't feel comfortable I'm getting out of there."

"That's my favorite investigative reporter!" declared Ted. "Uh, gotta go," he added quickly, ending the call.

Lucy wiggled her other foot into a duck boot and checked her appearance in the full-length mirror. She looked pretty pudgy, she decided, and no wonder since she was wearing many layers of clothing. She'd started with her usual bra and panties, adding a thermal top and leggings. Then she'd slipped on a turtleneck shirt, a pair of jeans, a sweater and a fleece vest. She'd topped it all off with a pair of camo-print hunting pants she borrowed from Bill, as well as a pair of his thick socks, which were making her duck boots feel awfully tight.

Of course, she told herself, she wasn't dressing for a fashion show. She was dressing for a chilly morning in the Maine woods. Once downstairs she filled a thermos with hot coffee and put on her warmest parka, as well as a wool hat with a pompom and a pair of lined gloves. She was tempted to add Bill's big mittens over the gloves, but figured they would be too cumbersome for taking photos.

Libby had watched her every move as she prepared to leave, growing more and more excited every minute, certain that she would also be going on this outdoor excursion.

"Sorry," said Lucy, patting her on the head. "Next time."

The nippy air stung her cheeks when she stepped out onto the back porch and she congratulated herself on dressing so warmly. She was going to need every layer if she was going to stay out in the cold for several hours. She felt like the Michelin tire man as she made her way to the car, which she decided was her best option for getting to the pond, and in case she needed to make a quick escape. As Ted had reminded her, there was plenty of cover from evergreens, and she planned to leave the car on the old logging road a short distance from the parking area.

As she drove down the unpaved road, she felt a sense of mounting excitement. This was a lot better than sitting in that awful basement meeting room at the town hall and listening to the local power players argue about authentic historical paint colors or raising the price of a dump sticker. She loved getting out of the office and away from the computer, chasing down stories that really mattered. That was the best part of her job and she didn't get to do it enough.

She was really getting pretty fired up. Her sunglasses were getting foggy and she was perspiring. No wonder, she realized, glancing at the indicator on the dashboard. Somebody, probably Bill, had set the heat at seventy degrees. She switched it off and opened the windows, letting the cold air blow in for the last quarter mile or so. Finally reaching the spot she had in mind, she pulled the SUV into a small clearing, parked, and got out.

Once standing, she discovered she really needed to pee. She should have thought of this before she left the house, and before she'd pulled on all those clothes, she decided as she struggled to undress enough to relieve herself. That task done and her clothing rearranged, she made her way down the path toward the parking area beside the pond, carrying a big tote bag with her camera, notebook, coffee thermos, and energy bars. As she drew nearer, she scouted for a good observation post and was pleased to discover a bushy young fir tree growing beside a large bulletin board where various notices were posted. It was especially good for her purposes because there was a small gap between the tree and the sign which gave her a good view of the parking lot.

She set her tote bag on the ground and pulled out her camera, checking the battery level and peering through the viewfinder at the empty parking area. Reassured that she could get a clear shot, she looped the cord around her neck, letting the camera rest on her chest, and pulled out her notebook. Flipping it open she wrote down the date, time, and place. Observing there was still no action in the parking area, she tucked the notebook into her pocket and grabbed the thermos. After filling the cup, which felt pleasantly warm in her hands, she wished she'd thought to bring something to sit on. Her back was starting to ache a bit and it would be nice to be able to get off her feet.

Nevertheless, she told herself, it was a lovely morning. Chickadees were flitting around in the trees, some even perching on nearby branches and giving her a once over.

"Dee-dee-dee yourself," she whispered, taking a sip of coffee. There was nothing like hot black coffee on a chilly morning, she decided, savoring each swallow and promptly draining the plastic cup.

She was beginning to wonder if perhaps she'd arrived too early in the morning to catch any drug-dealing activity. Now that she thought about it, it seemed that drug-dependent individuals might not be early risers. Maybe they had to sleep off their high, like drinkers with hangovers. She poured herself another cup of coffee and sipped it while she peered through her peephole.

The coffee cooled rapidly in the chilly air, and her cup was soon empty again. She was reaching for the thermos to refill it when she realized she was going to have to pee again, and soon. What to do? She suspected that the moment she finally freed herself from her clothing and squatted down to relieve herself would be the very moment the drug dealer decided to make his appearance. She was simply going to have to hold it, she told herself, noticing that a chickadee had now perched on the handle of her tote bag and was cocking his black-capped head one way and another, apparently believing she kept sunflower seeds in there.

"Shoo!" she hissed, afraid that the little birds gathering around her were probably used to begging from swimmers and picnickers and would give her away. The birds were unmoved, which was probably for the best. A cloud of birds rising all at once would certainly have tipped off the drug dealer. Not that there was a drug dealer or any customers in the parking area.

Lucy checked her watch and discovered she'd been watching and waiting for over an hour and nothing had happened. Maybe drugs were only sold on Tuesdays and Thursdays but never on Fridays. Maybe the delivery had been late. Maybe the dealer had been arrested. Maybe it was time to call it a day, head home, and have a nice, long pee in the comfort of her downstairs powder room.

It was a tempting idea, especially since she was beginning to shiver in the cold. She was stamping her feet and waving her arms, trying to warm up, when she heard the purr of an engine. A car! This was it! She grabbed the camera and raised it to her eyes, clicking away as the black BMW came into view. It was followed by an aged orange pickup truck, a truck that she recognized because it had been parked in her driveway many times last winter.

Lucy watched with dismay as she recognized the familiar figure of Hank DeVries leaning down from the window of his truck to give something to the person in the BMW. The deal completed, the

BMW zoomed off, but Hank lingered, sitting in the truck.

Horrified, Lucy broke cover and marched right over to the truck. "Hank! What do you think you're doing?" He'd grown thinner, she saw, and needed a shave and a haircut. It looked as if he'd been wearing the same clothes for too long. His hooded sweatshirt was grubby and shapeless.

Startled in the act of rolling up his sleeve, Hank jumped and dropped the bit of rubber tubing he was holding. "What are you doing here?" he demanded.

"Bird watching," said Lucy. "What are you doing?"

Hank hesitated as if trying to think up a plausible excuse, then gave a big sigh. "You know what I was doing. I was going to shoot up."

"That's terrible. You have to stop. You'll end up killing yourself."

"I'd like to stop. Believe me," he said.

Lucy did. "I know it's hard . . ."

"It's more than hard. It's impossible." His eyes were dull. He'd lost the sparkle and energy that had made him so attractive last winter.

"You should go to rehab. There are places that can help you."

He snorted. "They'll help you if you've got ten thousand dollars. I don't."

"There must be a way," said Lucy. "What about your folks?"

Hank was fidgeting. Dirty fingers picked at the worn, frayed cuff of his sweatshirt. "They've got their own problems. They don't need me to add to them."

Lucy guessed that he didn't want his parents to know about his addiction and she understood why. He wanted them to be proud of him, to approve of him. "There must be programs—"

"Ten thousand dollars. That's what they want. Then they'll let you in." He was beginning to shake, and Lucy realized he needed his fix.

She wanted to help him but knew it would be cruel to prolong his agony. "Well, I gotta go. But do you really mean it? Do you really want to go to rehab? If I find something for you, will you go?"

He was wrapping the rubber tube around his fingers. "I'll do it," he said.

Her heart sinking, Lucy walked away, picturing Hank injecting himself with heroin like the actors she'd seen faking it in countless TV shows. This was real, though, and she knew that sooner or later he'd overdose.

But please, God, not today.

Fearful that he might overdose, she went back to her post behind the bush and waited until he drove off. Then she picked up her tote bag and walked slowly back to her car, determined to find a way to help him.

Chapter Eight

"Lucy Stone, you never made those donuts yourself," accused Sue Finch when Lucy proudly presented them at the festival. Sue had dressed for the Harvest Festival and was wearing a professional chef's apron over her chic buffalo plaid flannel shirt and skinny black jeans.

Transporting six dozen donuts had presented quite a challenge, and Lucy was proud of her solution. She'd borrowed the Legos she kept for her grandson Patrick to play with and had constructed a six story tower which she'd placed inside a sturdy picnic cooler. She was carefully unpacking the trays of donuts, arranging them in a neat pyramid on the baked goods table, which was already loaded with a mouth-watering assortment of homemade cakes, cookies, and pies.

"What do you mean?" she protested. "I'm a good cook."

Once her donuts were safely arranged on the table, she took a look around. The entire fellowship hall at the Community Church had been turned over for the festival and was filled with row upon row of folding tables offering gently used books and household items, homemade knitted items, baskets, and other crafts, all watched over by volunteer salesladies. The festival was very popular and even though the doors hadn't yet opened a small crowd had gathered outside. Inside, the volunteers were chatting, catching up on gossip, and admiring each other's contributions to the sale.

"You must have bought them!" exclaimed Sue, still dubious about the provenance of Lucy's donuts. "And if you did, where did you get them? They look fabulous."

"I didn't buy them," said Lucy. "Zoe made them with help from Matt Rodriguez."

"The cute kid with the 'Vette?" asked Sue.

"He's no kid," replied Lucy, "but he is a trained chef. His dad is Rey Rodriguez. You've probably seen his TV show."

"Oh, right. I have one of his cookbooks. Really creative, delicious recipes."

"Well, Rey has bought the Olde Irish Pub and plans to turn it into a fusion restaurant called Cali Kitchen, and Matt is going to manage it. Zoe interviewed for a job there and Matt took a shine to her and that's how I have these beautiful apple cider donuts."

"They sure are beautiful," said Pam, stopping by

for a quick chat before the sale opened. "You've put us all to shame."

"I can't take credit for them. Zoe made them with help from Matt Rodriguez," confessed Lucy again.

"It looks like the Stone family will be enjoying world-class cuisine if Matt continues to court Zoe," said Sue.

"Zoe has a new boyfriend?" asked Pam.

"I sincerely hope not," said Lucy. "Matt Rodriguez is much too old and sophisticated for her. The very idea makes me uncomfortable."

"You're sure you're not being prejudicial?" asked Pam.

"Oh, probably," admitted Lucy. "But it's not his Latino heritage that bothers me. It's his age. He must be at least thirty, and Zoe's only eighteen."

The sound of a teaspoon tapping on a glass silenced Lucy and the other volunteers. Festival chairman Bessie Bone thanked everyone for their efforts and announced the sale was now open. There was a smattering of applause as the doors were opened and the eager customers rushed in.

The Harvest Festival had become well-known through the years for the quality of the crafts that were offered, especially the knits and baskets, and there was a good deal of rushing about as patrons searched out their favorites. Lucy and Sue's table was at the rear of the hall and didn't attract much attention at first, but word soon spread about the donuts, which people said were better than ever this year. They were all gone when Rachel arrived with Miss Tilley; all that remained on the baked goods table was a single blueberry pie with a rather burnt crust.

Julia Ward Howe Tilley—nobody but her closest and oldest friends dared to call her by her first name—was the retired librarian of the Broadbrooks Free Library and the town's oldest resident by at least a decade. Rachel was her home health aide, a position that had evolved from her friendship with the old woman following an automobile accident.

"Well, where are the donuts?" demanded Miss Tilley. "I always buy a half-dozen."

"Sorry," said Sue, "we're all sold out. All we have is this blueberry pie."

"My mother always used to say a pie doesn't have to look good to taste good," said Lucy, attempting to close the deal. "I think we could offer a substantial discount."

"Blueberry pie is a Maine tradition," said Rachel.

"Are they Maine blueberries?" asked Miss Tilley, eyeing the pie suspiciously.

"I'm sure they are," said Sue. "Franny Small made that pie and nobody is more Maine than Franny. She wouldn't use berries from the supermarket."

"You could ask her," said Pam, waving to Franny, who was standing at a nearby table.

Franny spotted Pam's frantic waving and came over, a big smile on her face. "The sale is a big success. My table is sold out."

"Miss Tilley is thinking of buying this pie you brought, but she wants to know if it contains Maine berries," said Sue.

"Of course it does. I wouldn't use anything else. I picked them myself out by Blueberry Pond and froze them. Last summer was a good year for berries. I got tons." Franny paused, and a shadow fell over her face. "But I don't know if I've got the heart to pick next summer—not after that poor girl died at the pond. I know that's all I'll think about now, every time I see that pond."

They all fell silent, thinking about Alison's tragic death, and even though they all had something they wanted to say, nobody wanted to be the first to speak.

It fell to Miss Tilley to break the awkward silence. "So sad when a young person dies."

"And a lot are dying from this opioid epidemic," said Rachel. "They overdose or get tainted drugs."

"I'm working on a story about drugs here in town," said Lucy.

"Here in Tinker's Cove. My goodness," said Franny, her eyes wide.

"Drugs are everywhere," said Sue. "It really is an epidemic."

"I simply don't understand why they do it," said Pam. "I'm high on life. I wouldn't risk my life for some synthetic version."

"I doubt very much that Alison Franklin died of an overdose," said Miss Tilley.

They all turned to look at her.

"Why do you say that?" asked Lucy.

"Because she was so healthy and athletic. I used to see her running by my house every morning when I opened the door to get my morning paper. She was always on time and she used to give me a big smile and wave at me."

"That doesn't mean she wasn't using drugs," said Rachel. "Or maybe it was her first time."

"Nonsense," snapped Miss Tilley. "I've been around for a long time and, well, you just get a feeling for people. She gave every impression of being a happy, healthy person. She radiated optimism."

Lucy couldn't help thinking that Miss Tilley was drawing a lot of conclusions from very little evidence, but didn't want to contradict her.

Sue had no such compunctions. "That's ridiculous!" she exclaimed. "You couldn't tell all that from seeing her run past your house."

"Do you know her father is married to a woman the same age as Alison?" asked Franny. "And she's pregnant."

"Her father is Ed Franklin," said Pam. "Imagine being related to him."

"He is terrible, I admit that," said Miss Tilley. "That big gold *F* on his chimney! So tasteless. But I have observed that very often the more horrible and vulgar a man is, the nicer his relations are. It's as if they're aware of his shortcomings and attempting to make amends. Just think of that basketball coach we had a few years ago. His wife was the loveliest woman."

"Well, if you don't think she overdosed, how exactly do you think Alison died?" asked Lucy.

"Well, I've heard all sorts of theories about

drugs and even suicide or a tragic accident," said Miss Tilley. "But I think she was murdered." She didn't even pause for breath after making that astonishing comment but went on to ask, "How much for the pie?"

Lucy was still thinking about Miss Tilley's provocative comment after the festival was over and she went on to work at the *Pennysaver* office. Phyllis had taken the afternoon off to help her husband, Wilf, who was having cataract surgery, and Ted was covering a regional conference on flood insurance, so she had the place to herself. After she'd uploaded the photos she took at the sale, she googled drug rehab programs and made a few phone calls. She was surprised to learn that Hank was right and the programs did require up-front payment.

"These folks are drug addicts," said the admission counselor at a place in New Hampshire called New Beginnings. "We want them to commit to getting clean. Recovery is not easy. Our program is four weeks long and even with the big financial cost we have dropouts."

"What about health insurance?" asked Lucy, who had opened a file in her computer and was entering the counselor's comments with an eye to including them in the series on drug addiction. "Drug addiction is a disease, after all."

"It varies depending on the policy," said the counselor. "But it's an unusual patient who has coverage.

By the time they come to us, they've pretty much bottomed out. Health insurance is usually tied to employment and most of our folks don't have jobs."

"So how do they come up with the money?" asked Lucy.

"Family, friends, people who love them. Parents often patch together the money using several credit cards."

"Ten thousand dollars is a lot of love," said Lucy, "especially if you're paying twenty percent interest."

"It is indeed," said the counselor. "But it's not uncommon. We actually have a waiting list."

"Let's add my young friend to the list," said Lucy on impulse, figuring that it was worth taking a chance. Maybe, just maybe, something would come up and Hank could go to rehab. In any case, the difficulty of getting into a rehab program would definitely be part of the series on drug addiction.

She remained at her desk after completing the call, cleaning up the file which she'd typed while talking on the phone. The whole situation was depressing, she thought, thinking of the mess these young people got themselves into and the difficulty of getting out. What future did Hank have if he couldn't get clean? She hated to think of him becoming a homeless straggler, relying on the food pantry for something to eat, or even worse, dying of an overdose. What a waste of a promising young man!

The sound of a police siren penetrated her dark

mood and she brightened up, realizing it was signaling the start of the high school football team's
pregame parade and rally, which she was supposed
to cover for the paper. The team was having a successful year and would play on Saturday in the
semifinal for the state championship. She quickly
put on her warm jacket and grabbed her bag,
heading out to join the folks lining Main Street
where a police cruiser with flashing lights and wailing siren was leading the procession.

The parade was a homegrown affair, featuring
the high school marching band, civic groups, and
of course, the town's four fire trucks. The high-
light of the parade was a flatbed truck carrying the
uniformed team members, most looking rather
self-conscious at all the attention.

Lucy waved and clapped as the various marchers
went past, joining the cheerful watchers standing
on the sidewalk. She snapped photos of the high
school kids in the marching band, the team members, and Jason Marzetti (Joe Marzetti's kid) dressed
for some reason as Uncle Sam and walking on
stilts. The ladies from Fran's Famous Fudge tossed
wrapped candy to the kids, and she got a great
photo of a little blonde tyke catching a piece in
mid-air.

The kid was adorable, a fair-haired and ruddy-
cheeked angel, and Lucy found herself wondering
if she would characterize a black child with a curly
Afro as adorable and angelic, but hoped she would.
She was suddenly looking at the crowd with new
eyes, realizing that it was entirely white and mostly
adult. Of course, Maine had a very small minority
population, but somehow she had never realized

that fact. How had she lived in this town for several decades without realizing this?

She had grown up in New York City, riding the subway to her high school, sharing the train with all sorts of people—Hasidic Jews in hats and long black coats, elderly Asian women with shopping bags, mixed-race couples holding hands. She visited Boston from time to time, and there she saw Muslim women in head scarves, African-American women wearing kente cloth dresses and turbans and big gold earrings, and lots of kids of all races.

Looking at the rather thin crowd with new eyes, she was shocked to realize most of the people were senior citizens. It wasn't only Tinker's Cove, she knew, that was largely old and white. It was most of rural New England, and no wonder. Property was expensive, housing was limited, and good jobs were even scarcer than affordable houses. There had even been warnings from demographers that the trend couldn't continue, as there wouldn't be enough young workers to care for the aging population. She hadn't really paid attention, but there it was—the proof—right in front of her. Not only was she getting older, all her friends and neighbors were, too. And their children hadn't stayed in Tinker's Cove but had left following high school to attend college elsewhere and make their lives in economically vibrant places like Portland, Boston, and New York.

Yet another siren was announcing the arrival of the cheerleaders, and Lucy made sure to catch some good photos of the girls atop the hook and ladder. They were dressed in the school colors and, unlike the boys on the team, were tossing candy to the crowd and enjoying all the attention.

Putting her camera down, she gave the girls a big wave and one tossed a miniature chocolate bar her way. She caught it and tore off the wrapper, eating it as she walked along the street to the church where she'd parked her car that morning. As she walked, she thought about the circuitous path that had brought her to Tinker's Cove.

She hadn't been born and raised in the little Maine town. Her family had been New Yorkers way back, tracing their ancestry to the early Dutch settlers of what was then Nieuw Amsterdam. Through the centuries, there had been various additions from Sweden, England, and Germany, but it was a matter of pride to her father that his ancestors had fought in the American Revolution, the Civil War, and two World Wars. While in college, she'd met Bill, whose ancestors included more recent arrivals from Ireland. After working for a few years on Wall Street, he'd begun dreaming of a simpler life as a restoration carpenter and they'd moved to Maine, buying the ramshackle farmhouse on Red Top Road and fixing it up.

Their story was typical, she thought. Everybody in America, except for the Native Americans, came from someplace else. And Americans didn't tend to stay put, either. Members of both their families had gone west and south. Bill's parents now lived in Florida; she had cousins in Texas and Virginia. The country was a big jumble of people from all over, who continued to restlessly follow their dreams. That was the whole point about America, she thought, beginning with the earliest settlers.

The parade over, the crowd was breaking up and the sidewalk was filled with people heading home. The afternoon light was already fading and the sky was taking on a pinkish hue. She'd reached Sea Street when she got stuck behind a young mother pushing a stroller and dragging along a tired preschooler, and was trying to get past when she heard people shouting. Turning toward the noise she looked down Sea Street to the harbor where she saw a crowd gathered in the parking area.

She was tired and hungry, having skipped lunch, and wanted to go home, but she was a reporter and duty called. Reluctantly, she turned left and walked down Sea Street to see what the fuss was all about.

As she drew closer, she realized the group was somewhat organized, engaged in a protest in front of the former Olde Irish Pub which now had signs in the window announcing new ownership. COMING SOON! CALI KITCHEN! She knew that Bill had planned to meet Rey there this afternoon to go over the final plans for the renovation and spotted his truck in the parking lot.

Some of the people in the crowd also had signs. AMERICA FOR AMERICANS was one. Another read MEXICANS GO HOME.

She was snapping photos when the camera was snatched from her hand and she turned to protest. "Give that back!" she demanded, facing a man she recognized.

It was Jason Sprinkle, who owned a plumbing business.

"No photos," he growled in a threatening tone, giving the camera back. "And if you know what's good for you, you'll get out of here."

"What do you mean?" she demanded as a thrown rock smashed one of the restaurant windows, shattering the glass and shredding the paper sign.

Chapter Nine

Lucy instinctively ducked and moved away from the group of demonstrators. Seeking shelter, she found it in the harbormaster's shack where Harry Crawford was watching the scene from the open doorway. As soon as she stepped inside, he closed the door and locked it. The little waterfront office was about the same size as a highway tollbooth, and gave a 360-degree view of the harbor and parking lot. He quickly began closing the miniblinds, at the same time calling the police department to report the situation.

"They're throwing rocks," exclaimed Lucy, who was standing by a window and peeking through the slats of the miniblind. "My husband's in there with Rey Rodriguez." The sun was sinking fast and the sky was now a fiery red, casting a lurid glow that was reflected in the pub's remaining windows.

"I've got a situation down here at the harbor,"

Harry said, speaking into the phone. "There's a mob protest that's turning violent."

Lucy was hanging on every word, at the same time following the action outside, terribly fearful for Bill's safety.

When Harry put the phone down, his worried expression wasn't encouraging.

"I don't think we're going to get much help, at least not right away. All the officers are working the pep rally." He still bore traces of the tan he'd acquired during the summer when he was out on the water every day patrolling the harbor. Peeking through the blinds, he was also keeping an eye on the protesters, and he remained on the line, updating the dispatcher on the demonstration. Turning to Lucy he asked, "Who's out there anyway? The dispatcher wants to know."

"I recognized Jason Sprinkle and Link Peterson. He used to play Little League with my son Toby," said Lucy. "I think it's mostly those guys who hang out at the roadhouse on Route 1, like Zeke Bumpus. Not exactly up-and-comers."

Harry nodded. "I call 'em Left Behinds, guys like me, except they weren't lucky enough to get full-time jobs with benefits. Those guys have a lot of resentment. I've felt it when I've had to deal with them for going too fast in the no-wake zone or fouling the water."

"This isn't a spontaneous thing. It didn't just happen. Somebody must have organized this," said Lucy, watching nervously as a handful of bearded and leather-suited newcomers arrived on motorcycles, roaring into the harbor parking area to join the demonstration. They were greeted with a loud roar from the crowd, some of whom were holding signs that they waved enthusiastically. The lights in the parking lot had now switched on and Lucy could clearly see the crowd's enthusiastic reaction. There was a great deal of hand shaking and backslapping, and a roar of approval when one of the motorcyclists produced a heavy chain from his saddlebag and displayed it in a menacing manner.

"I don't like this at all," said Lucy, thinking of Bill and Rey, who were trapped inside the restaurant. "Where are the cops? This is more important than the parade. What about the sheriff or the state troopers?"

She was nervously shifting her weight from one foot to the other and biting her lip as she peered out the window through the slats of a miniblind.

Harry came to a decision. "It would take them a half hour to get here, minimum. It's up to me. I'm gonna go tell them to disperse," he said. "I'm responsible for security here at the harbor. It's my job. I can't just hide in here."

"You can't go out there by yourself, all alone," protested Lucy. "There's at least thirty of them and only one of you. You need reinforcements with riot gear."

"The cavalry's not coming," said Harry, ducking through the door just as a woman's scream pierced the chilly air.

All heads turned, including Lucy's. She had stepped into the open doorway and immediately spotted Ruth Lawson, the Community Church organist, standing between two parked cars, shrieking and pointing into the larger one, a black SUV parked beneath a tall streetlight.

"He's bleeding!" she yelled.

Harry immediately changed direction, abandoning the demonstrators and running toward the frantic woman. He yelled over his shoulder to Lucy, telling her to call 9-1-1 and to bring the first aid kit that hung on the wall.

Lucy grabbed the kit and began running toward the SUV, using her cell phone to call for help. She and Harry were the first to reach Ruth, a tall woman whose steel gray hair was tightly permed, but the demonstrators soon came charging across the lot from the restaurant to the line of parked cars. Lucy realized the SUV was Ed Franklin's Range Rover, and a quick glance through the shattered driver's-side window revealed he was beyond help. A good part of his skull was gone and blood was spattered everywhere, as well as globs of matter she thought must be bits of his brain. The first aid box was useless. Recoiling at the gruesome sight, she turned to Ruth, wrapping her free arm around the shaking woman's shoulders. She didn't feel all that steady herself, she realized as she led the sobbing woman away.

Harry had placed himself between the restless crowd of gawkers and the Range Rover and was warning everyone to stand back. "This is a crime scene. Police are on the way."

"I saw him in the car, like he was sitting there waiting for someone," babbled Ruth. "But the angle of his head wasn't right. I thought he might've been taken ill or something, so I went closer to check on him and then I saw the—"

"I know, I know," said Lucy, guiding her to the harbormaster's shack. "Don't think about it."

"We should help him!" protested Ruth. "Get an ambulance!"

"Help is coming," said Lucy. "Harry's there. He's got things under control."

But even as she spoke, she doubted that Harry could actually control the rowdy crowd for very long. They'd been shocked into silence at first, but who knew how long that would last. Sooner or later they'd be looking for someone to blame, and she was afraid that person would be Rey . . . or even Bill, guilty by association.

She tried not to worry, focusing on Ruth, who was badly shaken. Reaching the harbormaster's shack she set the first aid box down on the wooden step and awkwardly opened the door, still supporting Ruth who was leaning heavily on her arm. She guided Ruth inside and helped her into the office chair, then switched on the electric kettle Harry kept in the shack. He was a tea drinker and all the makings were handy, so Lucy dropped a tea bag into a cup with shaking hands, and yanked up the blind so she could watch out the window while waiting for the water to boil.

The kettle was finally starting to steam when she saw one of the town's two police cruisers coming down Sea Street with lights flashing and siren blaring, followed by the fire department's ambulance. The two vehicles drove smoothly down the steep hill and into the parking area, stopping just short of the crowd. She continued to watch, glancing away only briefly to fill the cup with steaming water and to add two packets of sugar, then saw her friend, Officer Barney Culpepper, getting out of the cruiser. The flashing lights on the ambulance and cruiser were like a visual drum beat, ramping up the tense atmosphere, as he faced the crowd.

Barney was a big man who had been a cop for most of his life and wore his uniform easily, expecting and getting respect, even if it was sometimes granted grudgingly. Only a very foolish person would attempt to tangle with him. He immediately began ordering the onlookers to step back, then after a quick look into the Range Rover got right onto his radio, reporting the death. He also cautioned the EMTs who were unloading a gurney from the ambulance, holding up his hands in a stop signal so they wouldn't touch the body. The two EMTs shoved the gurney back inside the ambulance, then climbed back inside the cab, awaiting further instructions.

Lucy held the tea bag by the string and nervously jiggled it a few times to hasten the steeping. As soon as the water turned the proper shade of amber she handed the cup to Ruth, ordering her to drink it and telling her she had to go out but promising to return as quickly as possible.

Lucy hurried, winding her way through the rows of parked cars to the Range Rover, which was now illuminated by a spotlight. The crowd was still in place, refusing to disperse. She quickly snapped some photos, then drew close enough to hear what people were saying.

"We know who did it," claimed Link, getting a loud buzz of approval from the demonstrators.

"No we don't," said Barney, planting himself firmly on his thick-soled regulation black oxfords and staring the crowd down. "You'll get your chance to talk. The state police are on the way. Nobody leave. They're going to want to question everyone."

That silenced the crowd momentarily until Jason Sprinkle spoke up. "We got nothing to fear. It wasn't any of us. It was that Mexican kid, Matteo, who shot him. I saw him standing right here in this spot," he claimed, pointing at the Range Rover. "I even heard a pop, but I didn't think nothing of it. It's noisy here at the cove. Guys are prepping their boats for the winter, you know."

"That's ridiculous. You don't know what you're talking about," declared Rey, who had left the restaurant along with Bill when the cruiser arrived. He'd heard Jason's accusation.

"You calling me a liar?" challenged Jason, practically nose to nose with Rey.

"I'm just saying that my son would never shoot anybody," said Rey, stepping back. "He doesn't even own a gun."

"Who was shot?" asked Bill, taking his place beside Lucy.

Relieved that he was in one piece, she slipped her hand into his.

"Ed Franklin." She saw Rey start as if he'd received an electric shock, then quickly recover, adopting a serious expression. "Ruth Lawson discovered the body. She's in the shack," Lucy continued, speaking to Barney. "Is it okay if I take her home? She's pretty shaken up."

"No problem," said Barney with a nod, taking down Ruth's name in the leather-covered notebook he preferred to the electronic tablets recently issued by the department. "I know where you both live" He turned back to the crowd. "As for the rest of you, let's keep it peaceful. The state police are on the way and they're going to want to interview everyone, so nobody else leaves." He surveyed the group, letting his eyes rest on each and every one there, letting them know they'd been seen and noted. "And I don't have to tell you that the DA won't hesitate to prosecute anyone interfering with the investigation or anyone taking the law into their own hands."

Lucy sensed a certain rumbling hostility among the demonstrators, but took heart from the fact that the state police were on the way. After receiving a reassuring squeeze from Bill, she reluctantly withdrew her hand from his then went back to the shack. She wasn't entirely comfortable about leaving the scene, feeling that it was her responsibility as a reporter to cover the shooting, but also aware that she had a rare opportunity to question the prime witness.

When she reached the shack she found Ruth sitting motionless in the desk chair, her mug of tea in her hands, untouched.

"We've got permission to leave," Lucy told her. "I'll take you home."

"Are you sure?"

"I'm absolutely sure," said Lucy. "I told Officer Culpepper that you discovered the body . . ."

"Body!" whispered Ruth, trembling so violently that Lucy feared she would spill the tea. "You mean he's dead?"

Lucy pried Ruth's hands from the mug and set it down on the desk before answering. "I'm afraid so."

"Oh, noooo," wailed Ruth. "That's awful!"

"I think we should get moving before the state

police arrive and the parking lot is blocked off," Lucy said, taking Ruth's hands and pulling her to her feet. "Let's get you home."

"I still don't feel right about leaving," protested Ruth. "I was the one who found the . . . the body."

"I told Barney all about it and he said they'll interview you at home where you'll be a lot more comfortable." Lucy opened the door. "My car is right over there."

Ruth stopped short in the doorway. "But what about my car?"

"You can pick it up tomorrow. I'll drive you over if you want. But right now you're in no state to drive."

"Well, I don't know—" protested Ruth.

"I do," said Lucy, giving her a hug. "You've had a traumatic experience and you're in shock."

"So much blood," said Ruth, allowing herself to be led out of the shack and across the parking lot to Lucy's SUV. "I never saw so much blood."

"It was awful," Lucy opened the passenger side door and helped Ruth climb in.

She sat passively while Lucy fastened the seatbelt.

Then Lucy went around the car, got behind the wheel, fastened her own seatbelt, and started the car. "Did you see anyone near Ed's car? Anyone at all?" she asked as she backed out of the parking space.

"No. I saw that bunch at the pub, the old pub, and wondered what it was all about. It made me think twice about parking at the harbor. I almost went back to my car to park it somewhere else. I was on my way to the church—I like to practice the hymns before Sunday, you know—and I knew I wouldn't find a parking space there because the volunteers would be cleaning up after the Harvest Festival and folks would also be parking there for the pep rally parade." Ruth was gaining strength as she spoke, finding relief in the distraction of conversation.

"The festival always attracts a big crowd and this year was no different," said Lucy, turning onto Main Street just in time to see State Police Detective Lieutenant Horowitz's unmarked car coming the other way, blue lights flashing.

"The crafts are rather expensive, in my opinion," said Ruth, eager for the distraction of chatting, "but of course it all goes to a good cause. I asked Sue Finch to save me a nice mince pie. They're not very popular these days. I guess they're rather strong tasting for a lot of people, very spicy you know, but they're my aunt's favorite and I always try to have one for her."

"My mother loved mince pie," said Lucy, thinking that at this rate she'd never get any information from Ruth. "I made, well actually it was my daughter who did the cooking. She made six dozen apple cider donuts."

"My goodness! That must have been quite a job."

"It was indeed, but she had help from a friend," said Lucy, who was struggling to reconcile Link Peterson's accusation against Matt with the agreeable guy who'd helped Zoe make the donuts. "I'm just curious. What made you look in Ed's car? Did you see something suspicious? Did you hear anything? See anyone?"

"I'm afraid I was just being nosey," admitted Ruth. In a hushed voice she defended herself. "I'm not usually like that, you know, but I'd seen that car around town and I wondered what it was. It's not like the other cars, you know, the ones like this one. You see a lot of these and I suppose they're very nice and all . . ."

"Do you mean SUVs?" asked Lucy, somewhat amused.

"If that's what they're called, I suppose so. Hondas and Toyotas and Nissans . . . they're all Japanese, aren't they?"

"Ford and Chevy make them. Jeep too. I think every car manufacturer makes SUVs. They're very popular."

"Well, my father always used to say to buy American, and I've found my Dodge to be very satisfactory."

"They have a very good reputation," said Lucy, turning into Ruth's empty driveway. "But you were curious about Ed Franklin's RangeRover?"

"I was," said Ruth, picking up her handbag and squeezing the handles. "It's taller than the other UVS cars and it's the only one that looks like that. I wondered what it was, so I walked over and saw it's called a Range Rover. I think those are English or something."

"They are."

"I suppose they're very expensive, since he is so rich," said Ruth, suddenly realizing the need to correct herself. "Since he *was* so rich and all."

"I imagine so," said Lucy.

"I noticed that the windows are all tinted, not that I would have looked into the car. That's sort of a private place. But the driver's side window was down . . ."

Actually shattered by the bullet that killed Ed, thought Lucy.

"Well, anyway, I could see right in and I wish I hadn't," concluded Ruth, reaching for the door handle.

"Do you want me to come in? Just to make sure you're all right."

Ruth looked at her with her muddy brown eyes and grabbed her hand in a surprisingly strong grip. "I don't want to be any trouble, but it would be so kind of you."

"No problem," said Lucy, hoping to get more information out of her.

"You see, I never lock my door," said Ruth as they walked up the path together toward the door, eerily illuminated by a yellow bulb that was not supposed to attract moths. "It always seems such a bother, but I suppose it's rather foolish. Anyone could walk in and steal me blind." Reaching the stoop, she paused. "Or worse."

Lucy knew that locked doors were a rarity in the little town where everybody knew everybody. "Well, I always think that if somebody wants to break in, a lock isn't going to stop them."

"I suppose you're right," said Ruth, who had stopped in front of the closed front door. "I mean, even if Ed Franklin had locked the doors of his car, it wouldn't have made any difference."

"No, it wouldn't," agreed Lucy, wondering why Ruth wasn't opening the door to her house. "Shall we go in?" she prompted.

"I know there's really nothing to fear but . . ."

"I'll go first," said Lucy, turning the knob and switching on the light.

The door opened into a small hall with a stairway; the floor had been painted gray and spattered with beige, yellow, and white in the old-fashioned style, and a braided rug served as a doormat. A prim and proper living room dominated by an upright piano was on one side of the hall, a dining room with a polished mahogany table holding a milk glass bowl of obviously fake fruit was on the other, with the kitchen behind.

"Nobody here," reported Lucy, after taking a quick look. "I'll just run upstairs."

Upstairs she found two neat and tidy bedrooms, each with white ruffled curtains and a double bed covered with a white candlewick bedspread. She considered peeking in the closets and looking under the beds but decided that would be overkill. The house was definitely empty.

Going downstairs she found Ruth in the old-fashioned kitchen where a small table with two chairs painted red sat on a linoleum floor beneath a plastic wall clock shaped like a rooster.

Ruth was filling the kettle at the porcelain sink; an ancient red plastic dish drainer sat on the large drain board.

"I think a cup of tea is called for," she said. "All things considered."

"Absolutely," said Lucy, suddenly drained of energy and sinking into one of the chairs. "And if you have any, I'd really love a cookie or two."

Ruth produced some homemade oatmeal-raisin cookies and Lucy nibbled on one while they waited for the kettle to boil. Ruth couldn't seem to sit still and kept popping up to check the kettle and adjust the burner.

"A watched pot never boils," said Lucy with a smile.

"I know. It's just, well, I can't help worrying." Ruth paused, twisting her hands nervously. "You know, I'm a real fan of mystery shows on TV, and I know from watching them that the person who finds a body is always a suspect."

Lucy's jaw dropped. "You think the police will suspect you of killing Ed Franklin?"

"I'm afraid so," admitted Ruth.

Lucy glanced around the prim and neat house, and considered Ruth's work as a church organist. "I don't think you have anything to worry about."

Just then the kettle shrieked and Ruth grabbed a pot holder and snatched it off the stove.

"That's certainly a relief, Lucy," she said, filling the teapot. "But just to be on the safe side, I think I'll take my Glock into the station. They'll be able to tell that it hasn't been fired."

"Your Glock?" asked Lucy, shocked to her core.

Chapter Ten

Lucy had enjoyed a half-dozen of Ruth's home-made oatmeal cookies, but she hadn't gotten any more information about her gruesome discovery. She had learned, however, that Ruth's father had given her the Glock many years before, and Ruth went straight to the shooting range every Sunday after church to practice. She had blushingly admitted she was quite a good shot, a fact that Lucy was mulling over when she finally left to go home. She had made numerous calls to Ted to tell him about Ed Franklin, but the messages had all gone to voice mail.

She was pouring herself a glass of chardonnay and wondering if Bill would be content with soup and sandwiches for supper when Ted finally called.

"Are you sure about this? Ed Franklin is dead? Shot in his car in broad daylight?"

"I'm sure," said Lucy in a grim tone. "I saw him. Blood everywhere."

"Wow," said Ted. "Any chance it was suicide?"

She paused, forcing herself to recall the sight of Ed Franklin's bloody body before she'd recoiled in horror and looked away. Ed was leaning away from the driver's side window, and all that remained of the window were a few shards of glass.

"I don't think so," she said. "The driver's side window was broken and Ed's body was leaning away from the window. If he'd shot himself and the bullet also broke the window, I think he'd be leaning the other way. Also, I didn't see a gun in the car with him, but I didn't look for one, either. It was pretty gruesome." She paused and gulped down some wine. "There was an anti-Mexican demonstration going on in front of the old pub. It was pretty noisy so I guess nobody heard the shot. Ruth Lawson discovered the body."

"The church lady?"

"The organist."

"My word," said Ted.

"One of the demonstrators—it was actually Jason Sprinkle—claimed he saw Matt Rodriguez standing next to Ed's car. Even claims he heard a popping sound, but Rey insists his son doesn't have a gun."

"But he would have a motive," said Ted. "Ed was giving the Rodriguezes a lot of trouble."

"I bet Ed Franklin gave a lot of people a lot of trouble," said Lucy. "He was just like that. And don't forget, this is the second death in the Franklin family in a couple weeks."

"What are you saying, Lucy? That there's some sort of vendetta against the Franklins?"

"I don't know," admitted Lucy. "But it's certainly worth looking into."

That was the question Lucy pondered all weekend, and the one she wanted to pose when she went to the District Attorney's press conference on Monday morning, but she had to wait a good long while. The conference was late getting started as the conference room in the county complex proved too small for the large number of reporters assigned to cover the sensational death. Ed Franklin was a household name, known by one and all as typifying the American Dream of achieving success and untold wealth, and his murder was attracting a lot of interest.

After everyone had relocated to a larger space, actually a vacant courtroom, Phil Aucoin began by introducing representatives from the various law enforcement agencies involved in the investigation and congratulating them at length on their spirit of cooperation. Then there was a bit of a flap until the press releases he planned to distribute were found, apparently mislaid in the switch. Once found, it took only moments for the reporters to read the few printed lines and begin loud demands for more information.

"All this says is that Franklin was killed execution style by a person or persons unknown," began Deb Hildreth, who worked for a local radio station. "Do you have a theory, a motive? Are there any suspects?"

"I am unable to provide more information at this time," said Aucoin, "as it might hinder the investigation."

"Do you think Franklin's outspoken opposition to immigration might be the reason he was killed?" demanded Pete Withers, a stringer for the *Portland Press Herald*.

"I can assure the public that we are following a number of leads," said Aucoin.

"Franklin was involved in a number of failed businesses and even filed for bankruptcy a couple times," alleged Stan Hurwitz, from the *Boston Globe*. "Could the shooter be a disappointed creditor?"

"Could be," said Aucoin. "As I said, we're following a number of leads."

"Any ties to organized crime?" asked another reporter, speaking with a thick New York accent. "There were rumors . . ."

"There are always rumors about high-profile people," said Aucoin.

"What about his family?" asked Angela Hawkins, from NECN. "He had a very bitter divorce."

"Once again, we're following a number of leads," said Aucoin. "We will certainly be taking a look at everyone who had dealings with him, including his family."

Finally Aucoin pointed his finger at Lucy and she got her chance. "It's quite a coincidence that his daughter Alison died in a suspicious manner just a few weeks ago. Do you think there may be a vendetta against the Franklin family?"

The question caused quite a hubbub. Many of the reporters were new to the story and hadn't known about Alison Franklin's drowning and they began shouting questions.

"What happened to the daughter?"

"When was this?"

"How did she die?"

"Quiet down. One at a time." Aucoin waited for the unruly crowd of reporters to settle down. When everyone was back in their seats and quiet restored, he spoke.

"We have no reason to suspect foul play in Alison Franklin's death." He paused. "And with that, I'd like to thank you all for coming," he said, ending the conference.

Aucoin and the other officials made quick exits, leaving Lucy to deal with the out-of-town reporters' demands for information about Alison's death. "You can read about it on the *Pennysaver* website," she said as mikes were thrust in her face.

"C'mon, Lucy, just give us the gist," urged the guy with the New York accent as she tossed her notebook into her bag and started to make her way through the crowd to the doorway.

"I've got it!" crowed Pete Withers, peering at his smartphone and reading from Lucy's story. "Right here. 'Alison Franklin, daughter of billionaire Ed Franklin, drowned in local pond' . . . blah blah blah . . . oh get this. 'DA Phil Aucoin cautioned that the cause of death has not been determined. In light of the recent opioid epidemic, he said he is waiting for toxicology test results from the state lab, but added that these tests are now routinely mandated for all unaccompanied deaths.' "

"So they think little Alison overdosed?" asked the New Yorker, blocking Lucy's path.

"I have no idea," said Lucy, shaking her head and trying to slide by him.

"What do most people think? This is Hicksville. People talk. What are they saying?"

"You'll have to ask them," said Lucy, finding a gap and slipping through.

"Hey!" somebody yelled. "There's Deb Hildreth. Ask her! She works for the local radio station."

Poor Deb, thought Lucy, abandoning her to the media scrum as she stepped into the airy lobby and the door closed behind her.

It was a typical November day, gray and miserable, and Lucy's spirits plunged as she made the drive from Gilead to Tinker's Cove. It was horrible to think that things like this could happen in the little town that she loved. Alison's death was bad enough—it was always awful when a young person died—but Ed's brutal murder overshadowed everything. The man was shot in broad daylight, right in the heart of town. It seemed incredible that such a thing could happen. Who would do such a thing? And why? Whoever killed Ed must have really hated him, she thought, finding it difficult to imagine how anyone could simply pull a trigger and blow off another person's head.

Of course, it happened all the time. Gun shootings were common occurrences in the US, and there were the constant reports of suicide bombings and assassinations and attacks on innocent people in Europe and the Middle East. Come to think of it, she decided with a sigh, it seemed that there were actually an awful lot of people who were not the least bit reluctant to take other people's lives.

* * *

"Wow, you look like you lost your best friend," observed Phyllis when Lucy arrived in the office later that morning. Phyllis was dressed today in a harvest-themed sweater featuring a design of apples and pumpkins, and her hair was tinted a flaming orange.

"Not yet, but you never know, the way things are going," Lucy said glumly, dropping her bag on the floor with a thunk so she could unbutton her jacket.

"How was the press conference?" asked Ted, who was staring at his computer screen.

"Crowded." Lucy hung up her jacket, then bent down and picked up her bag. From the way she moved you would have thought it was filled with bricks. "There was even an obnoxious guy from New York and lots of people from TV stations."

"Well, Ed Franklin was famous," said Ted. "Any new developments?"

Lucy sank into her desk chair and leaned her elbow on her desk, propping up her chin as if her head was much too great a load for her neck to bear. "Killed execution style. I guess we could've come up with that on our own."

"Talk about stating the obvious," muttered Ted. "No suspects?"

"Aucoin's playing his hand close to his chest," said Lucy.

"Dot Kirwan says it's all hands on deck, overtime for everybody—vacations and off-time cancelled," reported Phyllis. "She's real upset since Patsy was scheduled for maternity leave next week. Now she's going to have to work until she pops."

Patsy Kirwan was the police department dispatcher, just one of Dot's many relations who worked in the town's police and fire departments.

"Of course, you can see why they're so anxious to get the killer," continued Phyllis. "Talk about cold-blooded. It gives me the willies every time I think about it."

In spite of herself, Lucy found herself smiling. "Somehow I don't think we need to worry about getting shot in our sleep by some sort of serial killer maniac."

"Lucy's right," said Ted. "Ed Franklin was targeted. He was killed because somebody wanted him dead."

"Well, the one I feel bad for is that little wife of his," said Phyllis. "She's pregnant, you know, and even if she is a gold digger like everyone says, it must be awfully hard on her losing her husband like that. Of course, she's probably going to make out fine financially and all."

"That reminds me," said Ted. "I bet AP's got a file obit up for Ed Franklin. Want to check that for me, Lucy? Give it a local twist, get some quotes from the town's movers and shaker

"Roger Wilco," said Lucy, relieved to be given a simple, undemanding assignment. And besides, she was interested in learning more about Ed Franklin's past. The past, she knew, often held the key to understanding the present and the obit did yield some surprising information.

It began with the usual summary of Ed Franklin's achievements—graduated from Dartmouth where he played football, went on to Harvard where he earned an MBA, began climbing the corporate ladder, ending as CEO of Dynamo where his high-profile leadership style made him a household name. It was Franklin's family history that caught her interest. His grandfather was a German immigrant, Emil Franck, who ran a beer hall on the Lower East Side of New York City. The beer hall was successful and he soon ventured into real estate, buying up tenements and renting them to Jewish and Italian newcomers in the early 1900s. His son, Ed's father, was thus armed with a sizeable fortune and an ambitious wife who wanted to join the highest ranks of New York society, which necessitated obscuring his immigrant origins. He changed the family name from Franck to the more American-sounding Franklin, and his wife was soon invited to join the boards of the Metropolitan Museum of Art and the New York Historical Society.

Lucy chuckled as she read this, wondering if Rachel would say Ed Franklin's hatred of Mexican immigrants was an effort to compensate for his family's immigrant past, which he somehow found embarrassing or shameful. It struck her as ironic that the man whose family fortune was originally built by exploiting newcomers to the country would become a proponent of anti-immigration policies. But maybe, she decided with a sigh, he only wanted to prohibit immigrants from Mexico and Latin America. Perhaps he would find Europeans more acceptable.

When it came to getting quotes from locals she decided to start with the folks he worked most closely with, his fellow members of the board of health. She was only able to reach one, Audrey

Sprinkle, and had to leave messages with all the others, which she doubted would ever be returned.

Audrey was hesitant to say anything about Ed, perhaps fearing he would reach out from the grave in retaliation. "I don't really know what to say except this is the most awful thing that's ever happened here in Tinker's Cove. My heart just goes out to his whole family, and that includes his first wife, Eudora. That poor woman has lost her daughter, too, you know."

"I understand," said Lucy in her most sympathetic voice, "but what was it like to work with him on the board of health?" She was dying to ask Audrey if she agreed with Ed's anti-Mexican sentiments as her son Jason certainly did, but resisted the temptation, opting to stay in safer territory. "What was his leadership style?"

"Ah, well, I guess you could say he was a strong leader," said Audrey. "But he always had the best interest of the town in mind."

"I see," said Lucy. "Any examples?"

"Sorry, Lucy, I've got to run," said Audrey, ducking for cover. "There's someone at the door."

Moving right along to the board of selectmen, Lucy called the chairman, Roger Wilcox.

"A fine example of public-spirited service," he said. "Ed Franklin donated untold hours to the town, giving us the benefit of his unparalleled business knowledge and abilities."

"But weren't some of his actions rather controversial?" asked Lucy.

"Dear me," said Roger, "my wife wants me to walk the dog. Says it can't wait."

Joe Marzetti was always a safe bet for a quotable quote, but he didn't have much to say about Ed Franklin either when she reached him at his supermarket. "Helluva businessman, I got a lot out of that book he wrote—*Never Let 'Em See You Sweat: How to Win in Business and Life.*"

"Did he apply here in Tinker's Cove any of the concepts he wrote about in the book?" asked Lucy.

"Aw, gee. I gotta problem with one of the checkouts. Gotta go."

Lucy plugged away, working down the entire list of town officials, but nobody seemed to have much to say about Ed Franklin. She knew Ted wouldn't be pleased with the story, but she filed it just before leaving for the day, hoping to put off the inevitable rewrite.

When Lucy arrived on Tuesday morning, as she'd expected, Ted wanted more. "I know the guy's dead, but this story needs some livening up. It doesn't give the reader any idea of who Ed Franklin really was." He leaned back in his chair, chewing his lip. "What about his family? You haven't tried them."

"Oh, Ted," she protested. "They've got enough to deal with. I don't want to bother them. Phyllis was right. His wife's pregnant and her husband was shot . . ."

"She'll probably welcome the opportunity to talk about her late husband. She'll probably want everyone to know how wonderful he was." He paused, smirking. "Lord knows, nobody else seems to have liked him."

"Okay," said Lucy, hoping the phone at the Franklin mansion was unlisted. Unfortunately for her, the automated 4-1-1 operator offered her the option of placing the call.

A woman answered the phone, and Lucy assumed she was a maid or some other employee, and after identifying herself asked to speak to Mrs. Franklin.

"Oh, poor Mireille. She's taking a nap," said the woman. "I'm her mom. Everybody calls me Mimsy. Maybe I can help you?"

Whoa, calm down, Lucy told herself, feeling as if she'd hit the mother lode. "Well, first of all, let me say how very sorry I am about your son-in-law's tragic death. I'm working on an obituary for the local paper and I just wanted to give family members an opportunity to say how they'd like him to be remembered."

"Ed was a great guy," said Mimsy. "He was crazy about my Mireille, and you know, a big famous guy like him, not to mention rich. Well he didn't need to, but, you know, he actually came to our house and asked my husband, Mireille's father, you know, for her hand in marriage! Isn't that the sweetest thing you ever heard? And it was especially nice since poor Sam was on his death bed. He had cancer and didn't live to walk little Mireille down the aisle."

Personally, Lucy thought it was probably a bit of a con, even going so far as to take advantage of a dying man, but she wasn't about to say so. "That is amazing," she said, doing her best to sound sincere. "Like he was just a regular guy."

"Trust me, Ed Franklin was really a regular guy.

You'd never know he was a big shot. And good to our little girl! You shoulda seen the diamond ring he gave her. It's too bad she can't wear it now. Her fingers are awfully swollen. She's got it put away in a safe-deposit box. It's too valuable to keep around the house. That's what I told her. Better safe than sorry. After all, I told her, it may be the only thing she gets to keep, after that first wife of his gets through with her. She's already contesting the will, you know."

"Is she really? What a nerve!" replied Lucy, finding it only too easy to join this gossip fest.

"The way he left things, everything was to go to his children—poor Alison and the one Mireille's expecting. In the case of only one child surviving, that child would scoop the loot. No children, then it's a crap shoot. The executors have to distribute the estate equably, whatever that means."

"But what about the older son, Taggart?"

"Taggart wasn't actually his child. Ed adopted him when he married Eudora. Tag was from Eudora's first marriage, and Ed said in the will that he had previously made generous settlements to him."

"So Eudora doesn't think it's fair that Ed's wealth all goes to Mireille's baby?" asked Lucy. "That she and Tag don't get anything?"

"You said it! She seems all fragile and sensitive and artistic but believe me, that woman is really a crazy bitch. The things she's said to my Mireille! Vicious, nasty stuff. I'm not kidding. A mind like that, she really oughta be committed. Scary stuff."

"You don't say."

"I do say! And here she's gone and decided to

drag Mireille into court and poor Ed's hardly cold. He's only been dead for three days. The papers were delivered to her this morning."

"That's too bad," said Lucy, well aware she could never use this material in a news story without inviting a libel uit, and she already knew that Eudora wasn't averse to legal challenges. "What about the funeral? Do you know what's being planned?"

"Haven't got a clue. Poor Mireille, she got up her courage and called Eudora thinking it was only proper to include her in the planning. And you know, what? Eudora told her not to bother, that Ed's lawyer was taking care of the details. Can you imagine? That's what these folks are like. It's all about the money. They don't care if he gets a decent funeral or not." Mimsy paused. "I guess you could give Munn a call. That's Howard Munn. He's Ed's lawyer. He's got an office in Boston."

"Thanks," said Lucy, wishing every interviewee was as forthcoming as Mimsy. "Please let Mireille know how sorry I am for her loss, and if there's anything she wants to add, she can reach me here at the paper."

"Will do. It's been real nice talking to you, Lucy."

Lucy shook her head after hanging up, thinking that things just kept getting stranger and stranger as suspects kept popping out of the woodwork. Matt Rodriguez was the prime suspect, of course, named by a witness. Then there was Ruth, a self-declared and extremely unlikely suspect, but there was the troubling matter of the Glock. Who knew what other weapons she might be hiding under all those hand-crocheted afghans? And now it turned out that Mireille had a very strong motive for killing her much older husband, since her baby would inherit his entire fortune. As the mother of this tiny billionaire, she would certainly have access to the estate and might actually control it. Come to think of it, thought Lucy, Mireille might also have figured out a way to kill Alison, clearing the way for her baby to inherit every last penny. And then there was Mimsy herself. It wouldn't be the first time that a coldhearted killer used charm and an apparent willingness to help to distract investigators. It was certainly something to think about, Lucy decided as she googled Howard Munn.

Chapter Eleven

The lawyer's number was easily obtained and Lucy got right on the phone to his Boston office where, much to her surprise, the man himself answered the phone. Caught off guard, she blurted out her thoughts.

"I didn't actually expect to get through to you," she confessed before identifying herself. "Sorry, I'm Lucy Stone from the Tinker's Cove *Pennysaver* newspaper."

Munn chuckled. "Well, I've got a small office, just me and a couple associates. We find that it's best to keep things simple and direct, and our clients seem to appreciate our approach. I detest those recorded messages and why should I have a girl to answer the phone when I can do it myself?"

"Absolutely. I couldn't agree more. Believe me, I spend a lot of time trying to negotiate phone systems that I suspect are designed to make callers give up in frustration. They say every call is important to them but they sure don't act like it."

Munn seemed to appreciate that and gave a little laugh.

"I won't take up much time," said Lucy, addressing the reason for her call. "I just need the details for Ed Franklin's funeral for his obituary."

"Of course. The service is at eleven o'clock Saturday at Trinity Church in Boston, followed by a reception at the Copley Plaza Hotel. Unfortunately for your readers, it's by invitation only."

"Of course. He was a very important person and I suppose a lot of other very important people will be attending."

"Yes," said Munn. "We know there's a lot of interest, however, and I do have a limited number of press passes. Shall I reserve one for you?"

Lucy was floored. In her years as a part-time reporter for a small town weekly she knew only too well that she was at the bottom of the media food chain. "That would be great. Thank you."

"No problem. I know how much Ed loved Tinker's Cove and how active he was in local affairs. He'd want to include his neighbors, but given the situation it's not practical to invite the whole town."

Lucy found this reaction encouraging and decided to press for more information. "I've been told that Ed Franklin's first wife is challenging his will. Is that true?"

There was a pause before Munn answered. "No comment, I'm afraid."

Now it was Lucy's turn to chuckle. "Can't blame a girl for trying."

"Not at all," he said. "I respect people who work hard."

"Is there anything you want to say about Ed Franklin for the story? I expect you've known him for a good number of years."

"I have indeed," he said in a thoughtful tone, "and I'm shocked and saddened by his death, especially so because it was clearly an assassination. I knew him well, personally and as a client, and I can think of no reason why anyone would want to kill him. This is a real tragedy. Ed's death is a great loss to many, and most especially to his wife Mireille and his entire family."

"Considering the fact that his daughter also died recently in rather suspicious circumstances, do you think there's a vendetta against the Franklin family?"

"I fear poor Alison's death was simply a tragic accident and unrelated to her father's murder." He paused. "I will overnight that press pass to you. You should have it in the morning."

Lucy knew the call was over and there was no point trying to prolong it. "Thank you. I really appreciate this opportunity."

Ted, however, wasn't impressed when she told him she'd been invited to the funeral. "A funeral's a funeral, even if it's in Trinity Church," he said, swinging around in his swivel chair and facing her. "There'll be music and people will say a lot of nice things about Ed Franklin that may or may not be true and then they'll party afterwards, glad it's over."

In her corner by the door, Phyllis gave an amused snort.

Lucy couldn't believe what she was hearing. "This is a big deal, Ted. There are going to be a lot of VIPs there, and maybe even his killer."

"I'm sure the killer will wear a sign or something to identify him or herself. One of those smiley face stick-ons—Hello My Name Is Hit Man."

Phyllis thought this was hysterical and she was struggling, shoulders shaking, to keep from laughing out loud.

Lucy, however, wasn't amused. "The funeral's by invitation only and I bet they haven't invited any locals. I'd be representing the whole town." She paused, dredging for something that would convince him. "We really owe it to his wife and the people Ed knew here, all the folks who worked with him on committees."

"You mean all the folks he fought with," said Phyllis.

"Well, yeah," admitted Lucy. "He was involved with a lot of people. He affected a lot of lives here in town." She could see Ted's expression softening.

He was definitely considering letting her go.

"I'll do it on my own time, Ted," she offered, sweetening the deal. "I won't even put in for gas."

"Well, when you put it that way, I suppose we do owe it to our readers," he said, turning back to his computer. Then, giving a little start, he slapped his hand against his head. "Did I hear you say something about his first wife challenging his will?"

"Yeah, that's what Mireille's mom told me."

"I wonder, do you think she's been blabbing to everyone who calls, or do you have a scoop? A scoop you've been sitting on since yesterday?"

"Well, if she told me, she's probably told others," said Lucy, defending herself. "She sounded like quite a character. Very chatty."

"Yeah, but you know Samantha Eggers," said Ted, naming the court clerk. "You wrote a flattering story about her, didn't you, just a few months ago?"

"I don't know if I'd call it flattering," said Lucy, feeling the need to defend her journalistic integrity. "It was part of that series we did on the county court."

"You did kind of suck up to her," said Phyllis with a knowing nod.

"She was very helpful," said Lucy, still defensive. "She's nice. That's not a crime, you know."

"Well, get on over there and see if she's got anything on this so-called lawsuit, okay?"

"Okay, boss," said Lucy, only too eager to get out of the office . . . and out of town.

Ed Franklin was gone, but somehow the combative attitude he'd brought to Tinker's Cove was lingering on. Paranoia and discord seemed to be spreading like some sort of infectious disease.

Heading back to Gilead for the second time in two days, Lucy stopped at the Quik-Stop for gas and picked up a hotdog for a quick lunch she could eat while she drove. It seemed to her that she was plying the same route to Gilead, the county seat, quite a lot. Fortunately, the trip was quite scenic, taking her past lovely old homes and giving her peeks at numerous coves and inlets dotted with pine-covered islands. As she drove and ate her hot dog, she thought about how Maine was changing.

When she'd first moved to Tinker's Cove, lots of people sold homemade items like quilts and whirli-gigs, setting them out on their lawns for tourists to buy. Now, most of those displays were gone, replaced with neat signs advertising art galleries, acupuncture, and computer services. The region, indeed the whole country was experiencing a changing economy, and those who didn't have college educations were joining Harry Crawford's group of Left Behinds.

Approaching Gilead, which was nestled in a valley and dotted with tall white steeples, Lucy thought it was quite an attractive New England town, apart from the county complex that included the 1960s brick courthouse and the grim granite jail with its chain link fence topped with coiled razor wire.

In the past, she had been able to come and go freely in the courthouse, but after 9/11 everything changed and now she had to present her bag for a search and step through a metal detector. Once inside, she went straight to the clerk of court's office, where Samantha Eggers had brightened the atmosphere by stripping away the dog-eared and faded notices that used to be taped any which way on the walls and replacing the dusty old Venetian blinds with attractive striped valances and simple Roman shades. The budget hadn't stretched to cover new furniture, however, so the same old tired tables and chairs remained as well as the old-fashioned card files that stood against one wall. The computer revolution had not yet arrived in the county court, where lawsuits were still entered on index cards and filed away alphabetically in drawers.

Lucy noticed there was a line of people at the counter, which was staffed by two assistant clerks, so she went straight to the drawer marked CH-CO but found no card for Clare v. Franklin. That meant she also had to join the line filled with people filing lawsuits or inquiring about suing someone or checking on the progress of their case. Samantha Eggers was visible, busy at her desk behind the counter where she was available for consultations when necessary.

She glanced up from time to time to check on the progress at the counter and when she saw Lucy, she got right up and drew her aside to the far end of the counter. "What brings you here today, Lucy?"

Samantha wore her gray hair in a short, no-nonsense cut and wore suits and low-heeled shoes. Today she had left her jacket hanging on the back of her desk chair and was wearing a flattering light blue cashmere turtleneck and a gray skirt.

"A little birdy told me that Ed Franklin's first wife is contesting his will," said Lucy, speaking in a very low voice. "But I didn't find anything in the card file."

"It just came in and we're processing the paperwork," said Samantha.

"Any chance I could take a peek?"

Samantha looked away as if studying the effect of the new window treatments, then smiled. "I don't see why not. It's going to be public soon enough. Come on in."

She raised the counter and opened the gate beneath, allowing Lucy to step inside the office area, which caused a bit of a stir among the people wait-

ing in line. Samantha ignored them, and took
Lucy to a vacant desk in the rear where she presented her with the original petition then went
back to her own desk.

Eudora Huntington Clare and Taggart Huntington Franklin v. Estate of Edward Franklin con-
sisted of twelve typewritten pages prepared by
Eudora's lawyer who happened to be her husband,
Jon Clare. The words they contained were nothing
more than various combinations of letters from
the alphabet, but Lucy felt her face reddening as
she read them. It felt as if they were alight and
burning her skin.

The suit alleged that Mireille had alienated the
affection of Eudora's husband, Edward Franklin,
and had poisoned his mind against his lawful wife
by knowingly making false accusations against her.
The alleged accusations included claims that Eudora was mentally unbalanced and accused her of
spousal abuse, infidelity, and incest, such charges
being wholly unfounded and entirely false.

The suit also claimed that the aforesaid Mireille
Wilkins had falsely claimed to be pregnant with
Edward Franklin's child, which situation caused
him to initiate divorce proceedings against Eudora
Franklin. Furthermore, the suit continued, after
her marriage Mireille Wilkins Franklin had continued to slander Eudora Franklin and had influ-
enced Edward Franklin to disinherit her and her
son Taggart Huntington Franklin, whom he had
legally adopted upon his marriage to Eudora Huntington.

In addition to accusing Mireille of lying and

slanderous behavior, the suit alleged that she had alienated Alison Franklin, the daughter of Edward and Eudora Franklin, against her birth mother. The most terrible accusation was last and claimed that Mireille had "knowingly and with malice intentionally provided illegal opioids to Alison, causing her to become addicted to said substances and contributing to her untimely death."

When she finished reading, Lucy sighed and looked up, meeting Samantha's sardonic expression.

"Do you want me to make a copy for you?" Samantha asked. "It'll cost you."

"How much?" asked Lucy.

"Twenty-five cents a page."

"Quite the bargain," said Lucy, handing the papers to Samantha, who promptly unstapled them and fed them into the huge copy machine. The machine was old and slow and produced the copies at a stately pace, but Lucy left the office with a complete set folded in her bag.

When she was crossing the parking lot she noticed several reporters she'd seen at the press conference, making their way to the courthouse. She assumed that Mimsy had been at work and the word was out; she could only hope that Samantha wouldn't be as helpful to these others as she had been to her.

Fearing she had no time to waste before the media horde turned its attention to Jon Clare, Lucy put in a call on her cell phone to the law firm named in the letterhead which was the prestigious old-school Boston firm of Bradstreet and Coffin.

Unlike Howard Munn, Bradstreet and Coffin had an automated phone system which provided the names of associates and their extension numbers. When Jon Clare's name was not mentioned, Lucy took the option of pressing star for the operator.

"I will connect you," said the operator without providing an extension number.

That made Lucy wonder exactly what relationship Jon Clare had to the office.

He did pick up, however, and confirmed that he was representing his wife, who was contesting Ed Franklin's will. "It's a story old as time, an attractive young woman stealing the affection of an older man and destroying his family."

"I saw the suit. There are an awful lot of terrible allegations against Mireille," said Lucy. "I find it hard to believe that a hardheaded businessman like Ed Franklin could be so easily manipulated."

"Well, it will all come out in court, and more," said Jon. "I can promise you that this is just the beginning. It's going to be a sensational trial." He sounded quite gleeful at the prospect.

Lucy found it disturbing. Once again she wondered about his professional status. "In future, if I need to reach you, what number should I use? I noticed the firm hasn't given you a telephone extension."

"Um, right. I'm just here temporarily. A friend is letting me use an office that happens to be empty. I'm actually, uh, retired," he said. Something in his tone made Lucy wonder if that was the truth. Perhaps no law firm wanted to hire him, or perhaps being married to Eudora was a full-time job. "Use my cell," he added, giving her the number.

By the time Lucy got back to Tinker's Cove she discovered the media frenzy had begun. There were several vans from TV stations parked in front of the police station, and she spotted several reporters she recognized filming segments for the evening news.

At the office, she presented Ted with the copy of the lawsuit, but admitted she didn't think she had a scoop. "I saw a bunch of reporters at the courthouse, just behind me, and they're already filming reports out there on Main Street. For all I know, Samantha is handing these out to everybody."

"Somehow I doubt that," said Ted, and as it turned out, he was right.

That evening, when Lucy tuned in to a Boston channel, she noted with satisfaction that Michelle O'Rourke could only report that police investigations into Ed Franklin's death were continuing, and that a court official had confirmed that Ed Franklin's will was being contested but could provide no details as the paperwork was still being processed.

The rumor mill continued to grind during the week, however, and Wednesday morning's *Boston Herald* had front page photos of Ed's mansion in Tinker's Cove and Eudora's mansion in nearby

Elna, superimposed with head shots of Mireille and Eudora under the headline CURSED HOUSES. The little weekly *Pennysaver*, however, was the only paper that would have complete details of the suit when it arrived in subscribers' mailboxes the next day.

Chapter Twelve

Lucy wasn't aware of her big scoop on Thursday morning as she went out for a run, conscious that she'd been neglecting her training program and time was running out before the Turkey Trot. It was a misty November morning, and Libby's black coat was soon gray with dew drops as she ran along, just ahead of Lucy. Libby always had to be first, which Lucy had heard meant the Lab considered herself the leader of the pack. Lucy didn't agree. She preferred to think that Libby was clearing a path for *Lucy* and guarding *her*, the actual leader of this very small pack.

When she got home, Bill was standing at the sink, rinsing the egg off his breakfast dishes. "Good run?" he asked, opening the dishwasher and loading the dishes inside.

"Great," said Lucy, panting and gently shoving him aside so she could fill Libby's bowl with fresh water. That chore completed she returned to the sink to get a drink for herself.

Bill closed the dishwasher door and wrapped his arms around her, nuzzling the back of her neck, tickling her with his beard. She enjoyed the familiar embrace and leaned back against him while she drained the glass of water. Once refreshed, she turned around for a proper kiss.

"Napoleon famously wrote to Josephine, telling her not to bathe before he returned from war as he enjoyed her natural scent," he said, stepping back, "but I gotta say a shower might not be a bad idea."

Lucy pouted. "You're not usually quite so fastidious and it seems to me that I put up with quite a bit of man sweat from time to time."

"Well, that's different. That's a sign that I've been working hard to bring home the bacon for you and the kids."

"Men are so weird. You just love all your various parts and bodily fluids. Must be the testosterone."

"Right," said Bill with a nod and a satisfied smile. "When you got it, flaunt it."

"Well, are you going to be flaunting it at the Cali Kitchen?" inquired Lucy, glancing at the antique Regulator clock that held pride of place on the wall between the windows. "It's getting late, isn't it?"

"That job's on hold," said Bill with a grimace. "The millwork truck was egged the other day when they were delivering windows and the tires on the electrician's van were slashed while he was working inside."

"Any idea who's doing this?"

"Probably some of those demonstrators. They're

not holding protests anymore. They've turned to vandalism instead. I don't know where it's going to end."

"I'm surprised that Rey is giving up," said Lucy. "He seemed so determined to move forward on the restaurant."

"He's not giving up, at least that's what he told me," said Bill, sitting down at the round golden oak table and grabbing the sports section. "He's just waiting for things to settle down a bit. He and Matt are taking a little vacation. They're going back to the West Coast for Thanksgiving with their family."

"I thought he was suspect number one for Ed Franklin's murder."

Bill shrugged. "He hasn't been charged."

"Interesting," said Lucy, heading up the back stairway to the upstairs bathroom for a shower. Pausing at the bottom stair she turned, struck with a thought. "You know, since you'll be at loose ends for a bit, you could paint the family room. And there's that closet door in Sara's room that's off kilter, and—"

"Enough, enough," he said, holding up a hand in protest. "I'll check in with some of the guys, see if they need an extra hand."

"Yeah, you wouldn't want all that testosterone to go to waste," said Lucy before making a quick escape up the stairs.

Freshly showered and blown dry, Lucy dressed for the day, keeping in mind that she would be meeting her friends for breakfast. Sue usually had something critical to say about her appearance so she took a bit of extra care, applying lipstick and mascara and choosing her best jeans and a new sweater she'd bought on sale.

She felt quite pleased with herself as she started the car and headed into town. Her route took her past O'Brien's Turkey Farm and she planned to make a quick stop there to pick up a turkey for the food pantry. She wasn't going to be cooking a big dinner for the family this year, so she wanted to give the turkey she didn't need to a family that wouldn't otherwise have one.

She passed the farm every day on her way to work and had seen the little turkey chicks grow into big, table-ready birds. *Table-ready* was just about the nicest thing you could say about the beasts, she thought, remembering that even as chicks they hadn't been cute. There was something prehistoric about turkeys, with their naked necks and long scaly legs, and she was only too happy to see that the pens that once held the birds were empty and the barnyard was quiet. O'Brien's turkeys had gobbled their last gobbles and were sitting in the refrigerator case, plucked and trussed and ready for roasting.

The farm store was quiet with only a few early-morning customers. Lucy wasn't in a hurry so she browsed, checking out the various turkey-related items the store offered. There were oversized turkey platters, basters, roasting pans, and packs of the O'Brien's own brining mix. There were also the usual T-shirts picturing a handsome Tom turkey in full display as well as aprons, dish towels, and pot holders. There were little onesies for babies, proclaiming BABY'S FIRST THANKSGIVING in big orange letters, with either a cartoon version of a tom or a hen with chicks. There were even turkey suits for pet dogs.

Lucy couldn't resist taking a closer look at the onesies, wondering if Toby and Molly might be planning to have a second child now that Patrick was getting older and they were more financially secure. She was admiring the little piece of clothing and dreaming of having a little grandbaby girl when a woman's voice broke into her reverie.

"Those are so adorable!" shrieked the woman in a voice that was much too loud.

Lucy turned to acknowledge her and recognized Eudora Clare, smartly dressed in a short fur jacket and carrying a huge Louis Vuitton bag that contained a tiny Yorkshire terrier. All that was visible of the dog was a little face with bright eyes, and a plastic pumpkin barrette attached between its ears.

"They certainly are," said Lucy. "I only wish I had a little grandbaby so I could buy one."

"Don't you know anyone who's expecting?" asked Eudora, examining one of the little garments with an expensively gloved hand. "I do." She laid the onesie over one arm and stroked it as if it was a pet cat, "but I don't know if she's expecting a hen or a tom."

"In that case, I'd go with the hen and chicks. They're cuter," said Lucy, who had noticed that while Eudora's face was smooth as a baby's bottom, evidence of a face lift, her wrinkled neck boasted wattles that a turkey would be proud of.

"I really shouldn't get her anything," said Eudora, stroking the onesie so hard that Lucy feared she would rub the design right off. "The mother, I mean. Face it, these presents are really for the mother and this one is nothing but a husband-stealing slut."

Lucy realized Eudora must be talking about Mireille, and was surprised she'd consider buying a gift for the woman she believed had broken up her marriage. Some of the allegations from the lawsuit ran through Lucy's mind and she couldn't believe Eudora was ready to forgive and forget.

"Of course," continued Eudora, spitting out the words, "it's not the baby's fault that her mother is a conniving little gold digger, and now that Ed and Allie are gone, the baby will be my only link to Ed." She turned and stared at Lucy with tear-filled eyes. "Isn't that right?"

Lucy felt uncomfortable being put on the spot and wondered if Eudora was somewhat unstable, perhaps even on some sort of medication. "I suppose you have photos and videos and memories . . ."

"It's not the same as a living person," said Eudora, dabbing at her eyes with a tissue in such a way that she wouldn't smear her heavy eye makeup. "That baby will have Ed's DNA. It might even be a boy and look like him."

"You have a son," said Lucy.

"Oh, Tag's not Ed's," Eudora said, crumpling the tissue in her hand. "I had him with my first husband. Ed adopted him, but he's nothing like my Ed."

"It's hard to let go of the past," said Lucy, "but you have to think of the family you do have, your son and husband."

"But don't you think I have a responsibility to this little mite? It's quite likely that a slut like you-know-who will be an unfit mother. What would happen then? Imagine, my Ed's child in foster care, abused and neglected." Eudora pressed her botoxed, glossy orange lips together. "It would be up to me. I would have to adopt the child. I would name him after Ed . . . Edward, Junior . . . or Edwina, if it's a girl."

"I think you're getting ahead of yourself," said Lucy, eager to get away from Eudora but somewhat concerned about her welfare. She was no psychologist, but this seemed extremely abnormal.

Fortunately, just as Lucy was looking around, hoping Eudora'd been accompanied by her husband or son, Jon Clare appeared, carrying a bulging shopping bag with the O'Brien's Turkey Farm logo.

"You mustn't chew this poor woman's ear off," he said, attempting to take Eudora's hand. "I've got the turkey—it's a beauty—and we can go home now."

"I'm not a child," hissed Eudora, yanking her hand away and stuffing the onesie into the Louis Vuitton bag, causing the dog to yip in protest. "Don't treat me like a child."

"Have a nice day," said Lucy, seizing the opportunity to make her escape. She crossed the store to the counter and placed her order, then watched as the squabbling couple made their way out of the store to a large Cadillac Escalade. As she watched Jon holding the bag with the shoplifted onesie while Eudora settled herself in the car, Lucy wondered if she should report the theft.

"This is a nice twenty-two pounder," said Carolyn O'Brien, grunting as she hoisted the heavy bird onto the counter and slid it into a reusable cloth shopping bag. "That'll be thirty-nine thirty-eight. The bag's complimentary."

Lucy couldn't believe that was right; she was used to buying Thanksgiving turkeys at the IGA for fifty-nine cents a pound. But when she checked the sign behind the counter, she saw that O'Brien's hormone-free, free-range turkeys were a dollar seventy-nine a pound. "Do you take checks?" she asked, deciding that O'Brien's Turkey Farm could certainly absorb the loss of the onesie.

Lucy was late for breakfast with the girls, having detoured to drop off the turkey at the food pantry. They were already seated at their usual table in Jake's when she arrived. Norine, the waitress, came and filled the mug that was waiting at Lucy's place while she seated herself and shrugged out of her jacket.

"Interesting choice of color, Lucy," said Sue, studying her new sweater. "I know orange was very big last year, but I think it's a tricky color for most people, and if you're going to go with orange I wouldn't combine it with blue. Brown or beige, maybe, even a creamy white, and, sweetheart, while I certainly appreciate the fact that you're wearing lipstick, nude would have been much better than that oh-so-sweet pink."

"It's my favorite lipstick and it's the only one I wear," said Lucy, who was used to Sue's critical comments and wasn't bothered in the least. Sue, she noticed, was immaculately turned out in a nubby white sweater and white wool slacks. "It's called Gentlemen Prefer Pink . . . and I got the sweater on sale."

"Cute name," said Rachel. "I think orange and pink together is very Lilly Pulitzer."

"That's what I thought," said Lucy, who didn't have a clue what or who Lilly Pulitzer was and wouldn't have recognized the company's colorful resort-wear designs.

"That sweater's the perfect color for this time of year," said Pam. "It's really more of a rust than orange, and they've done research that indicates warm colors like reds and oranges actually make you feel warmer and happier and thus more open to positive interactions with others."

"I had a very interesting interaction this morning," said Lucy, pausing to let Norine take their orders.

"Usual all round?" she asked, pen poised over her pad. Receiving nods she ambled off toward the kitchen, writing as she went.

"Who did you interact with in an interesting way?" asked Sue, who was running a perfectly manicured finger around the rim of her coffee mug.

"Eudora Clare," said Lucy, lifting her mug for that delicious first sip of coffee.

"Ed Franklin's first wife?" asked Rachel with a puzzled expression.

"The very same," said Lucy, setting her cup down. "It was at the turkey farm. She was acting kind of weird, talking about buying a Baby's First Thanksgiving onesie for Mireille's baby."

"Those onesies are really tacky," said Sue.

"I think they're cute," said Pam.

"In what way was she acting weird?" asked Rachel.

"She seemed kind of out of control, barely holding it together," said Lucy. "Her husband intervened and dragged her out of the store. She ended up shoplifting the onesie, but I don't think she meant to. She was pretty upset."

"Well, that's understandable. She must be grieving for her daughter and her ex-husband. I know they were divorced, but it's still traumatic when someone close to you is murdered," said Pam.

"Pam's right," said Rachel as Norine arrived with their breakfast orders. "She could be suffering from post-traumatic stress."

Norine plunked down a bowl of yogurt with granola for Pam, a sunshine muffin for Rachel, and hash and eggs for Lucy, then glared at Sue. "Anything I can get you?" she asked in a challenging tone.

"Just top off my coffee, thanks," said Sue, who, as far as anyone knew, existed on a diet of black coffee and white wine.

Norine went off to fetch the coffee pot, tut-tutting and shaking her head in disapproval.

"Just think about it," said Rachel. "Her husband left her for a younger woman then he divorced her, which research shows is every bit as stressful as a death. Then her daughter dies—that's a second stressor—her ex-husband is murdered, and to top it all off, the new, young wife is very visibly pregnant. That's a lot for anyone to deal with."

"I can't work up too much sympathy," said Sue, giving Norine a big thank-you smile as she added more coffee to her mug. "She's remarried, after all, and her son and the new husband seem very devoted to her, plus she's got plenty of dough. That's one thing she doesn't have to worry about."

"I guess she is worried, though," said Lucy, piercing the yolk of her sunny-side up egg with her fork. "She's contesting Ed's will, which leaves everything to the new baby."

"Going to court. That's another stressor," said Rachel, peeling the paper off her muffin.

"Well, I'll say this," said Lucy. "After seeing how she acted in the turkey store, I can understand why Alison went to live with her father and Mireille."

"That would be hard for a mother to take," said Pam. "It would be a real slap in the face."

"No rush. Any time you're ready," said Norine, tucking the bill between the salt and pepper shakers.

Sue picked it up and her eyebrows rose. "Talk about a slap in the face. Jake's raised the price of a cup of coffee."

Chapter Thirteen

When Lucy stopped by at the office to pick up her check, Ted was doing a little jig.

"What's gotten into him?" she asked Phyllis, who was resplendent in a sweatshirt featuring a bejeweled Tom turkey in full display, his chest and neck covered with sequins and his tail dotted with faux diamonds, emeralds, and rubies.

"It's your story about the lawsuit," she said, peering over the granny glasses perched on her nose. "He says AP and Gateway are picking it up and paying for the privilege."

"That's right, Lucy," he said, giving her a huge smile. "You got us a gen-you-wine scoop!"

"How about a little bonus for me?" she suggested, giving him a sideways look as she opened the envelope that was lying on her desk and noticed the usual paltry sum.

"How about I pay the heat bill?" he replied. "I suppose you'd rather work in a warm office—"

"Actually, it's not all that warm," said Phyllis, interrupting and rubbing her upper arms. "Barely above freezing."

"Well, with adequate heat and electric lights and computers and all—" said Ted.

"Point taken," admitted Lucy, slipping into her chair and powering up her computer. While she waited she noticed the light on her phone indicating she had a voice mail and dialed the code. Much to her surprise, Mireille Franklin had called and left a message, requesting an interview. Lucy immediately returned the call and was invited to "come right over."

"Why do I feel like I slipped into an alternate universe?" she asked after telling Ted and Phyllis about the invitation.

"Well, it isn't often that Ted is actually in a good mood," said Phyllis. "That alone is rather disconcerting."

"It's her sweatshirt that's disconcerting," said Ted, chuckling at his little joke. "You need sunglasses to look at it."

"I got it at the Harvest Festival. It's handcrafted," said Phyllis, smoothing the sequins. "I think what's disconcerting Lucy is the fact that somebody actually called requesting an interview. I don't think that's ever happened before."

"Well, that guy who puts on magic shows in the summer always calls," said Lucy.

"The Amazing Mr. Magic," said Phyllis with a disapproving snort. "He just wants free publicity."

"Not quite in the same league as Mireille Franklin," said Ted

"I bet she wants the same thing," said Lucy, "only in her case it's called *positive spin.*"

Whatever her motive, Mireille greeted Lucy at the door to the mansion, brushing aside the burly fellow dressed all in black—black shirt, black tie, black suit and shoes—who had opened the door. He had a rather obvious lump under his jacket that Lucy supposed was made by a gun.

"It's okay, Jack. I'm expecting company," said Mireille, grabbing Lucy by the arm and pulling her inside.

Jack looked Lucy up and down, frisking her visually, then asked for her bag so he could also check it. Finding no threat there, either, he handed it back to her. He turned to Mireille and said in a very serious tone, "I'll be right here in the hallway if you need me."

"Good to know," replied Mireille, who pressed one hand on her lower back and with a bit of a waddle, led the way to a small library at the rear of the house. The shelves were largely empty, apart from a handful of best-selling thrillers and business books, but there was a huge, wall-mounted TV above the gas fireplace. A comfortable sofa and arm chairs that swiveled were arranged around a large coffee table covered with a messy pile of magazines and newspapers. Both the gas fireplace and TV were on.

Mireille had been watching an old black and white Cary Grant movie, which she quickly turned off.

"It's pure escapism. I watch these old romantic movies. I love *Bringing Up Baby, The Philadelphia Story,* stuff like that."

"Me, too," said Lucy, who was waiting for an invitation to sit down. She thought Mireille was one of those women who couldn't help looking beautiful, even if her eyes were rather red and swollen, evidence she'd been crying a lot.

She was small-boned and had a touching air of fragility despite being nine months pregnant. Her tummy was a huge beach ball covered by a tight, stretchy turquoise top, which Lucy knew was the current fashion. Her hair was long and wavy, and the blond color seemed to be natural, though Lucy wouldn't have bet money on it. She knew from Sue, who was always urging her to "do something" with her fading hair, that hair color products had come a long way in recent years.

Mireille was wearing black leggings and her feet, only slightly swollen, were tucked into black ballet flats.

"Oh, please sit down," she said, flopping onto the couch and putting her feet up. "Would you like something to drink? Coffee? Tea? Herb tea? Kefir? I drink a lot of that."

"No thanks. I'm fine," said Lucy, choosing one of the swivel chairs and noticing that Mireille was nervously twisting her fingers.

"It's no trouble. I can just ring and someone will bring it," said Mireille, sounding as if this was a phenomenon she had not yet grown accustomed to.

"If you want something, go ahead," said Lucy. "I'm training for the Turkey Trot—"

She stopped suddenly, embarrassed. She should

never have mentioned the Turkey Trot, which Alison had also been training for.

"It's okay," said Mireille in a voice that was almost a whisper. "I know Alison was looking forward to running in the Turkey Trot. It was one of the positives in her life." She paused. "I'd run, too, if it wasn't for this," she said, patting her tummy.

"When are you due?" asked Lucy, pulling her notebook out of her bag. Spying her cell phone, and not wanting any interruptions during the interview, she turned it off.

"Any day," replied Mireille with a sigh.

"Well, thanks for the interview. I know our readers will be interested in what you have to say, and how you're coping with everything."

"Not very well, and that's the truth. The worst part is waking up and realizing this isn't a bad dream. It's my life." She snatched up a tabloid from the top of the pile and waved it around. "Anybody reading this rag would think I'm a coldhearted gold digger."

"Are you?" asked Lucy, taking advantage of the opening. She much preferred interviewing the defensive, angry Mireille than the weepy, grieving one.

"No! I don't care about money or houses or cars. I really don't. And I didn't break up Ed's marriage, either. He'd been wanting a divorce for a long time before we met and he pursued me, not the other way around. All that stuff that Eudora is alleging is absolutely false."

"How did you meet?" asked Lucy, jotting everything down in her notebook.

"I was working for a caterer, just to pay the bills.

I was taking drama classes and going to auditions. I was making progress, starting to get callbacks. He was very persistent. At first I turned him down, but he was hard to resist. He kept calling and sending flowers and he really won me over. After our first date I knew. I knew that even though he was old enough to be my father, he was the man for me. I know he had a reputation for being brash and hard-nosed in business, and some of his ideas weren't exactly PC, but with me he was nothing but kind and considerate and loving. He never raised his voice to me . . . or to Alison, for that matter. He said he liked having a peaceful, pleasant atmosphere at home."

"What about Alison?" asked Lucy. "What was it like when she came to live with you?"

"It was great," said Mireille, looking Lucy right in the eye. "I know what people think, that she must have hated me and the baby, but it wasn't that way at all. We got on great together. We were like sisters. She was so much fun and so excited about having a baby in the house." Mireille paused and plucked a tissue from the box on the coffee table, blew her nose, and dabbed at her eyes. "I really miss her and I hate the way she died in that cold, icy water.

"You know what she loved more than anything? Sitting by that fireplace," Mireille said, pointing at the flickering flames. "I think of her every time I turn it on. She loved to curl up by a nice cozy fire, reading or watching movies with me."

"It's a bit unusual, isn't it, that she moved in with you and her father? Wouldn't she naturally want to be with her mother?"

"I guess not. She moved in with us right after the wedding. That was about a year ago. She was just out of rehab."

"What about that?" asked Lucy, recalling the accusation that Mireille had gotten Alison back on drugs. "There are rumors that she was back on drugs and died of an overdose."

"No way!" exclaimed Mireille. "She got hooked after an accident . . . when she broke her ankle and they gave her painkillers. She hated drugs and was determined to stay off them. She was happy. She had friends and was doing well at college."

Lucy looked around at the comfortable, cozy room and thought of the huge, empty house beyond the closed door. It struck her that Mireille had carved out a little space for herself, almost as if she was holed up in a bunker with a guard at the door. "What about you? Are you going to stay on in Tinker's Cove?"

"I don't think so," she replied, stroking her tummy. "I'm just waiting for the baby and then I'll decide what to do. I'm not really a small town girl. I grew up in New York and I really miss it. It wasn't so bad here when Ed and Allie were, well—" She stopped and grabbed another tissue, quickly wiping her eyes. "I really miss them. I'm still in shock. I don't understand why anybody would want to kill Ed. I mean, I know he made enemies. He was so outspoken, but he didn't deserve to get shot like that." She chewed her lip. "And I don't like living like this, with bodyguards and all. It's scary and not just for me. I have to think about the baby."

"What about the guards? Do you think whoever killed Ed might try to kill you, too?"

"I don't know what to think, but it's a definite possibility. At least that's what they tell me. And they haven't ruled out murder in Alison's death, either."

"Who's they?" asked Lucy.

"Ed's people," Mireille said with a shrug. "You know, people who worked for him, like Howard Munn. And my mom. She's with me here. She says I can't be too careful."

"Will you be at the funeral?" asked Lucy.

"I really can't think about that now," Mireille answered, looking down at her tummy and giving it a pat. "I think a memorial service would be best after the baby's arrived and everyone's emotions have kind of settled down."

"Haven't you heard?" Lucy was so surprised that the words just tumbled out.

"What do you mean?"

"Howard Munn told me the funeral is this Saturday, eleven o'clock at Trinity Church."

"Which is Trinity?" asked Mireille. "The one with the big white steeple?"

"It's in Boston, at Copley Square," explained Lucy. "And there's a reception afterwards at the Copley Plaza Hotel."

"He must have called," Mireille said quickly, attempting a cover-up. "I haven't been checking my messages."

Lucy had a sudden realization Mireille was completely extraneous to the ongoing business empire that was Ed Franklin Enterprises, a situation that would certainly change once her infant child became the sole owner.

"I'm sorry," said Mireille, rising awkwardly from

the sofa by pushing against the padded armrest. "I hope you don't mind, but I really need to rest now."

"Of course," said Lucy, jumping up and spilling the contents of her bag onto the floor. Embarrassed, she fell clumsily to her knees and started stuffing everything back inside, including her notebook. Struggling to her feet, she apologized. "Sorry about that . . ."

"No problem," said Mireille. Sunshine was streaming through the window, backlighting her fair hair and making her look angelic.

"And thank you for your time," said Lucy.

"Thank you," said Mireille, suddenly dropping back down on the couch. "If you don't mind, I'm a bit . . . can you let yourself out?"

"Are you all right?" asked Lucy. "Can I get someone?"

"I'm ringing now," Mireille said, picking up a gadget like a TV remote.

A moment later, the door opened and a woman in nurse's scrubs hurried in and rushed to Mireille's side. Lucy was somewhat relieved to know she was leaving Mireille in good hands and stepped out into the hallway where she encountered a middle-aged woman also hurrying toward the library.

Seeing Lucy, the woman quickly changed direction, veering toward the front door where the bodyguard was slouched on a chair.

"What do you think you're here for?" she demanded, confronting him. "How did this woman get in? Why aren't you doing your job?"

The bodyguard jumped to his feet and his right

hand slipped beneath his jacket. "Mrs. Franklin told me to let her in. She said it was okay." His eyes were on Lucy, watching every move.

"It's true," said Lucy, making sure not to make any sudden movements and keeping her hands clearly in view. "I'm Lucy Stone from the *Pennysaver* and Mireille asked me to come and interview her."

"Oh, sorry, Lucy. I spoke to you on the phone. I'm Mimsy, Mireille's mom," said the woman, who Lucy realized was an older version of Mireille. She was heavier, and her frizzy hair was obviously colored, but beneath her carefully moisturized wrinkles, she had the same enviable cheekbones and little pointed chin. Like her daughter, she was casually dressed in yoga pants and ballet flats, though she had topped her T-shirt with a matching hoodie.

"I'm sorry about this," she added, giving the bodyguard an apologetic smile. "I'm a bit paranoid these days and I can't wait to get out of here. Believe me, if Mireille wasn't due any minute and hadn't made arrangements to have the baby here, we'd be long gone."

"I think you might want to check on her. She just rang for the nurse," said Lucy.

"Thanks," said Mimsy, hurrying across the hall to the library.

The bodyguard was standing by the front door, which he opened for Lucy.

"Take good care of them," she said, catching his eye.

"I certainly will," he replied with a serious nod.

Pausing for a moment on the front porch to take in the million-dollar view of the bay dotted with pine-covered islets, she felt a sharp stab of envy. Imagine being able to live among all this beauty, she thought, in a big, beautiful house with plenty of helpers just waiting to satisfy every whim. She grabbed the handrail and descended the stone steps carefully, comparing them to the scuffed wooden steps that led to her back porch.

And then she remembered that her husband was healthy and alive and so were her children, and even though she lived in a modestly-sized home, she didn't need a bodyguard. Ed Franklin's wealth hadn't protected him or his daughter from sudden death.

When she returned to the office, Ted was eager to hear all about the interview. "What's she like? What did she say?" he asked, looking up from his desk.

"I think she just wants everyone to know she's not a gold digger, she truly loved Ed, and she has nothing to do with his business affairs."

"If you believe that, I've got a bridge I'd like to sell you," said Phyllis.

"I do believe her," said Lucy, who was hanging up her jacket. "In fact, she didn't even know about the funeral Saturday. It came as quite a shock when I told her."

"That's weird," said Phyllis. "Planning a funeral without consulting the wife."

"That's what I think," said Lucy. "It's like Munn doesn't take her seriously, like she's kind of temporary."

"Well, she is very pregnant. Maybe he thought it would be too much for her," said Ted.

"I wonder whose side he's on," said Lucy, seating herself at her desk. "If the will stands, Mireille's baby will be the sole owner of Ed Franklin Enterprises. As the baby's guardian, she'll be running the show."

"I bet she's really a crafty little wench, out to make everybody think she's a little angel, while she makes off with the loot," said Phyllis.

"She's got the looks for the part," said Lucy, remembering how she'd been struck by Mireille's beauty. She went straight to her e-mails, catching up with the messages she'd missed while she was out. She couldn't miss the one from Zoe, which had arrived just minutes before, with the subject line in capitals: MATT ARRESTED.

Quickly opening the file, she found no details. There was only a terse message, also in caps. MOM, CALL ME.

Chapter Fourteen

Lucy immediately reached for the phone on her desk and called Zoe's cell phone, which Zoe must have been holding in her hand because she answered immediately.

"Why don't you answer your phone?" she demanded. "I called and called, but all I got was voice mail."

"I turned it off. I had an important interview and didn't want to be interrupted," said Lucy, fumbling in her bag for the forgotten phone and switching it back on. "But I got your e-mail. Is this true?"

"Yeah. Mom, he called me from California. He said he got a call from the DA that he was being charged with Ed Franklin's murder and there was a warrant for his arrest. The DA said he should turn himself in, otherwise the California cops would arrest him and Maine would start extradition proceedings."

"Well, it was nice of Aucoin to give him that option," said Lucy, thinking of the police shootings that were getting so much attention these days. By turning himself in, Matt would avoid being seized on the street in some sort of risky armed confrontation.

"Are you crazy?" demanded Zoe. "Being charged with murder isn't nice . . . especially if you didn't happen to do it."

"Did he say why they think he did it?" asked Lucy.

"He says it's because he used to date Alison."

"What did you say?" demanded Lucy, who couldn't believe what she was hearing.

"Matt used to date Alison. I thought you knew."

"I didn't know, but it explains a lot," said Lucy, thinking of the antagonism she'd witnessed between Matt and Ed Franklin.

"He said it's that thing about husbands and boyfriends being automatic suspects. You know how her father gave him a lot of grief. Franklin kept saying how Matt was a Mexican, and wouldn't let him come to the house or anything. I guess they think there was some sort of confrontation and he got real mad and killed him."

"I think there must be more to it than that," said Lucy, suspecting that Matt hadn't given Zoe the whole story. "They wouldn't charge him without evidence."

"You know, Mom, you're every bit as bigoted as Ed Franklin! People of color, people with Hispanic names, they get arrested all the time for crimes they didn't commit."

"That may be true but I don't think that's the case here—" Lucy broke off in midsentence, aware that Ted was frantically waving his arms like a demented sailor signaling by semaphore to get her attention.

"He's the darkest person in Tinker's Cove, Mom. Face it!"

"Right. Look, I'll get right on it," said Lucy, "I gotta go."

"Let me know what you find out, okay?" Zoe's voice had changed; she sounded like the little girl who used to beg Lucy not to go to work and leave her home in the care of her older brother and sisters.

Ted was waving his hand in a circle, signaling to Lucy to wrap it up, and she glared back at him in response, holding her free hand up in a "hold-on-a-sec" signal. She couldn't leave Zoe out on a limb. "I will, sweetie. I'll call as soon as I find out anything. Hang in there. Try not to worry."

"Are you kidding?" Angry Zoe was back. "Innocent people get convicted all the time. Our so-called justice system's rigged—"

"Maybe it is sometimes and some places," said Lucy, "but our *system* is made up of people, people like Phil Aucoin and Lt. Horowitz and Barney and all those Kirwan kids. They'll do what's right."

"I suppose," said Zoe, sounding chagrined. "I guess I forgot."

Reassured that Zoe had calmed down, Lucy ended the call. As soon as she said good-bye, Ted was on her.

"Pam wants you to call her—" he began, only to be interrupted by Lucy.

"Hold on a sec. My daughter got a call from Matt Rodriguez in California. He says Aucoin is charging him with Ed Franklin's murder and he's supposed to turn himself in and await extradition."

Ted looked puzzled. "Matt Rodriguez? Really?"

"The good-looking Mexican kid with the Corvette?" asked Phyllis, equally puzzled.

"Yeah," said Lucy, who was also struggling to reconcile the young man she knew with this disturbing new information. "Apparently he dated Alison, which means he was personally involved with Ed Franklin. It wasn't just the business about the restaurant." As she spoke, it occurred to her that Mireille hadn't shared this bit of information with her, and began to wonder if Mireille had really been as open and forthright as she'd thought. What else was she hiding?

"Thwarted love," mused Phyllis. "That's a strong motive."

"Well, I think they need more than a motive," said Ted. "There are plenty of people in this town with a motive to kill Ed Franklin."

"Like pretty much anyone who had to deal with the board of health," said Lucy.

Ted was already on the phone, calling the DA's office. "Hey, Phil," he began, in a friendly tone that implied they were old buddies. "What's this I hear about Matt Rodriguez being charged with Ed Franklin's murder?"

Lucy and Phyllis were all ears, but all they got

was a series of "I sees" and "Oh, reallys" and finally a "Thanks for your time."

Ted replaced the receiver thoughtfully and swiveled around in his desk chair, facing his two employees. Moving slowly and deliberately, he placed one hand on each thigh and pressed his lips together.

"So what did he say?" demanded Phyllis.

"What have they got on him?" asked Lucy.

"The murder weapon," said Ted, sounding surprised. "It was hidden inside the restaurant, dropped between two studs behind new Sheetrock."

"How'd they find it," wondered Phyllis.

"She's right," said Lucy. "Unless they used a metal detector. And what were they doing searching the restaurant, anyway?"

"Aucoin said they got a tip and were legally obligated to get a warrant and follow up."

"This is fishy," said Lucy, beginning to wonder if Zoe might be on to something. "It sounds to me like somebody planted the gun to set him up."

"Like who?" asked Ted.

"Well, there's the anti-immigrant, anti-Mexican bunch."

"I don't think they're smart enough to think up something like this," said Phyllis.

"It doesn't take a lot of smarts to hide a gun, especially if you used it to kill somebody," said Lucy.

"I don't see those guys as killers," protested Ted.

"Well, there's Ed Franklin Enterprises," Lucy pointed out. "That's a major operation that we don't know much about."

"Right," said Ted, looking as if a lightbulb had

turned on in the vacant space over his head. "We've got to find out who they are and what they do."

The phone rang and Phyllis answered, promptly transferring the call to Lucy. "It's your wife, Ted, and she wants to talk to Lucy."

Lucy picked up her extension and heard Pam's somewhat breathless voice. "Finally!" she exclaimed. "Didn't my husband tell you to call me?"

"He did," admitted Lucy, "but we're kind of caught up in a breaking story—"

"Well, this is breaking news, too. And good news, for a change. I want to get it in the paper. I'm here with the members of the Harvest Festival planning committee . . ."

Lucy could just picture the scene at Pam's kitchen table, where a group of earnest church ladies were listening as she made this big announcement.

"And we've just done the accounting and it turns out this year's festival was a record breaker, clearing just under ten thousand dollars!"

"That's terrific," said Lucy, eager to get back to the big story about Matt Rodriguez's arrest.

"It gets better," said Pam. "As you know, we usually distribute the money from the festival to local charities, but this year we decided to do something different."

Lucy had a somewhat disturbing thought, picturing the church ladies taking part in one of Pam's early-morning yoga classes on a Caribbean beach.

"We were discussing various options and one of our members mentioned that her nephew had become addicted to opioids and couldn't afford rehab

and, well, everyone seemed to know someone affected by this opioid crisis and we came up with
the idea of helping people who want to go to
rehab."

"That's a great idea," said Lucy, "but ten thousand dollars will send only one person to rehab.
Not that there's anything wrong with that. It
means saving a life."

"Believe me, Lucy, between the five of us we
knew quite a bit about addiction and rehab and
that's something we discussed. It was Michelle,
who is a social worker, who pointed out that simply
giving an addict a free ride to rehab would be
counterproductive. Addicts need to be account-
able, she said, so we've come up with the idea of an
interest-free loan program. Anyone who accepts
the money will have to pay it back so we can help
fund rehab for others. And we're not going to pay
the whole cost, either. Some medical insurance
plans provide partial coverage for rehab, and family members can usually help, too. And there are
charitable groups like the fraternal organizations
and the police and fire unions that would probably want to help."

Lucy had to admit the church ladies had come
up with a workable plan. "I think you're really on
to something."

"Well, we do, too, and we want to let everybody
know all about it and get the ball rolling."

"How soon will this money be available?" asked
Lucy, thinking of Hank.

"At the moment, it's just sitting in a bank account," said Pam. "But that doesn't mean we're going to write a check to someone for ten thousand

dollars. Every applicant will have to put together a financial package and formally request the amount they need and agree to pay it back on a regular payment schedule."

Lucy could just see those church ladies nodding along. "I see," she said, convinced that this was a rare opportunity for Hank, if she could convince him to take advantage of it.

"So you'll write the story?" asked Pam.

"Of course," said Lucy, struck by the absurdity of the question. "You're the boss's wife."

"Great. We'll write up an official press release and e-mail it to you today."

The wheels were already turning in Lucy's head, and she was convinced that simply writing up the details of the festival committee's plan was not enough. For the story to have a real impact it would have to show how the plan made a difference in someone's life, someone like Hank. But how was she going to pull something like this together?

First she'd have to convince him to agree to go to rehab, which he had said he wanted to do, but she wasn't entirely convinced he really meant it. And then he'd have to start putting a financial plan together, which seemed like a daunting challenge for someone struggling with drug dependency. He would definitely need help for that part, probably more help than she was in a position to provide. And finally, she realized, as her heart dropped with a thump, she didn't even know how to contact him. She knew he was no longer enrolled at the college, which meant he didn't have a dorm room of his own but most likely couch-surfed among his friends or even slept in his truck. She knew he still had his pickup because she'd seen him in it at Blueberry Pond . . .

"What does my wife want you to do?" asked Ted, crashing into her runaway train of thought.

"Hot lead. See you later," said Lucy, picking up her bag and grabbing her jacket as she hurried out the door.

Ted and Phyllis shared a puzzled glance.

"I thought I knew my wife," he said, shaking his head, "but now it seems she's brushing me off and giving news tips to Lucy."

Phyllis just shrugged and went back to editing the classified ads while Ted reached for his phone to call home.

Lucy knew it was a long shot, but it was the only shot she had. The drive home to the house took fifteen minutes or so, changing into her running clothes took another five, and then she was back on the trail to Blueberry Pond. Libby was thrilled at this unexpected treat and ran ahead with her tail held high, tongue and ears flapping.

Lucy suspected she was being ridiculous as she ran along the familiar path. There was only the slimmest chance that she would catch Hank buying drugs at the pond, and an even slimmer chance that she could get him to agree to go to rehab, much less figure out a plan to submit to the church ladies. What will be, will be, she told herself, repeating it like a mantra as her feet hit the path in an even pace. What will be, will be . . .

With a series of sharp barks, Libby announced their arrival in the Blueberry Pond parking lot and Lucy miraculously spotted Hank's parked pickup truck. She was panting as she approached the driver's side window where she could see Hank's head leaning against the glass. For a second she had a flashback to Ed Franklin's murder.

Then Hank moved his head and he saw her and the dog. "Hey," he said, rolling down the window

"Hey," said Lucy, eyeing him skeptically. He was unshaven and seemed lethargic, and he looked as if he could use a shower and clean clothes. "Are you high?"

He considered his state carefully. "Coming down, I'd say."

"You're good for a talk?" asked Lucy, chest heaving from exertion and also a certain amount of anxiety. She'd never done anything like this before.

"Sure. But I don't want a sermon."

"Funny you should say that," she began, launching into an outline of the church ladies' plan.

When she'd finished, Hank shook his head. "It's a great idea, but I wouldn't know how to begin."

"Your folks have got money," said Lucy.

"I'd have to tell them that I've been using," said Hank. "They don't even know I dropped out of college."

"Well, telling them would be an important step toward recovery. Believe me, I'm a mom and I'd rather know the truth about my kids. And besides, I think you're kidding yourself if you think they don't know. They certainly suspect something bad is going on with you."

He sat for a while and Lucy wondered if he was drifting off into a drug-induced haze. Then, all of a sudden, he shook his head and spoke. "And all that red tape with health insurance and finding a rehab place that'll take me . . ."

"I know a couple people who are brilliant at that stuff," said Lucy, suddenly inspired. "I'll bet they'll help you."

Again there was a long pause as Hank mulled things over. Lucy was feeling the chill and Libby had collapsed at her feet, resting her head on her paws. She was about to give up and head home when Hank made his decision.

"I'll do it," he said. "So who are these brilliant people who'll help me?"

Lucy was jogging in place. "Never mind that," she said, worried that the answer would cause him to immediately reject the idea, "just call this number."

"Hold on," he said, producing a cell phone. "Give it to me again," he requested, and Lucy obliged, with lots of stops and starts, until he got the right digits.

Back on the trail, she knew she'd done all she could and now it was up to Hank. She wondered if he would actually commit to getting clean or whether he would continue to use and simply slip away like so many others.

When she approached the house, she spotted Zoe's ancient little Civic in the driveway Her daughter met her at the door, ignoring the dog's enthusiastic tail-wagging greeting and demanding any news of Matt.

Lucy got herself a drink of water and filled Libby's bowl with clean water before sitting down at the golden oak table. She patted the chair Zoe usually used and waited for her to sit down, too, before breaking the news. "It's not good, I'm afraid," she said, somewhat out of breath. "The cops believe they found the gun that killed Ed Franklin. It was hidden in the restaurant."

As Lucy expected, Zoe promptly exploded, delivering an angry tirade. "That's absolutely unbelievable! It's so obvious that somebody set him up! How dumb are they? It's a construction site, right? Anybody could have gotten in and hidden the gun. Were there fingerprints? How do they know it was Matt's? That's crazy! It's . . . it's . . . it sucks," she finally said, running out of steam.

"It does," agreed Lucy, "but we don't know everything that the police know."

"Well, I know that Matt would never do something like that," said Zoe.

Lucy smiled. "Well, then, he's got nothing to worry about, right?"

"Oh, Mom," groaned Zoe, rolling her eyes. "You're so naïve."

Lucy stood up and rinsed out her water glass, then set it on the dish drainer. Zoe had remained at the table and was tapping away on her smartphone, which reminded Lucy that she needed to give Miss Tilley and Rachel a heads-up about Hank on the slim chance that he might follow up and call them for help.

Lucy knew that Miss Tilley had a way of getting her way and Hank wouldn't have a hope of evading rehab if he took that first step and called her. Rachel, who was Miss Tilley's companion and home aide, was a whiz with red tape and bureaucracy, and had the advantage of being able to get free legal advice from her lawyer husband, Bob.

"Ah, Lucy, I haven't seen much of you lately? Have you been avoiding me?" asked Miss Tilley when Lucy called.

"Not at all," said Lucy. "You're one of my favorite people."

"Well, I'd never know it, since you never visit," continued Miss Tilley.

"I know. It's been too long," said Lucy. "And now I'm going to ask a big favor of you and Rachel." She outlined the program the Harvest Festival planners had come up with and told Miss Tilley about Hank. "So I gave him your number, hoping you and Rachel could help him put together an application."

"That was rather presumptuous of you," said Miss Tilley, causing Lucy's hopes to wither.

"I know. I do hope you won't let that stand in the way . . ." she began, by means of apologizing.

"But of course we'll do it," said Miss Tilley. "Rachel has been so difficult lately, I've been at my wit's end trying to think of ways to keep her entertained."

"Right," said Lucy, suspecting that her old friend wasn't joking at all, but was quite serious.

She could only imagine how Rachel, who devoted herself to Miss Tilley's well-being, was reacting. Though, truth be told, she refused to let Miss Tilley's little jabs bother her, aware that the old woman's wit was her sole remaining defense against the inexorable deterioration of old age.

"I can't thank you enough for taking this on," said Lucy.

"We may not be taking on anything unless he calls," said Miss Tilley.

"I hope he does," said Lucy.

"So do I," replied her old friend. "So do I."

That task completed, Lucy glanced at the clock on the kitchen wall and realized it was time to think about starting supper. She opened the fridge and discovered it was quite empty; a look in the freezer revealed a whole chicken and nothing much else. She took out the chicken, which was frozen hard as a rock, and decided there was no way she could get it thawed and cooked before midnight. Nothing for it but to call for pizza.

Chapter Fifteen

Lucy couldn't believe it when Rachel called on Friday evening, looking for a way to get Hank to New Beginnings rehab in Portsmouth, New Hampshire. "They say it's not a good idea for him to drive himself," she explained, "as he might get cold feet and decide not to come. I'd do it, but I've got a rehearsal tomorrow."

Rachel was a gifted amateur actress, who often starred in the town's Little Theater productions. This year she was playing Scrooge's housekeeper in the group's annual production of Dickens' *A Christmas Carol*.

"You've done all this in one day?" asked Lucy, incredulous. "Put together the application, raised the money, got Hank to commit . . ."

"Well, yeah," said Rachel as if it hadn't been much of an achievement. "He called shortly after you did and came over that evening and I have to say he was very sweet and grateful for our help. He called his father and got a thousand from him. It turns out he has a trust fund from his mother's family and Miss Tilley got her to release some funds from that. He's on his parents' health plan so they're covering fifty percent, so he only needed a couple thousand from Pam's fund—"

"You did all this in one day? Including finding a spot in a rehab place?"

"That was the toughest part," said Rachel. "We got a list off the Internet and started calling and there were no openings, including this New Beginnings outfit you mentioned, but then they called back later and said they could take him. I think somebody may have decided not to go at the last minute, which is why—"

"I can do it, but we'll have to leave early. I'm driving to Boston tomorrow for Ed Franklin's funeral."

"Well, that's great, Lucy. Hank's sleeping here at Miss Tilley's tonight. We'll have him up and packed bright and early."

When Lucy arrived at Miss Tilley's little Cape-style house on Saturday morning, Hank was waiting by the door, every bit as nervous as a kindergartener on the first day of school. Rachel gave him a big hug,

Miss Tilley took his strong young hand in her age-spotted and blue-veined arthritic claw and gave it a pat. "You'll do fine, young man, and don't forget to write."

Hank was puzzled. "Write? You mean like Twitter?"

"I mean letters. You take a pen and paper and write down everything that's happening. I'll be looking forward to hearing from you."

Hank was thinking hard. "Wouldn't I need stamps for that?"

"E-mail will be fine," said Rachel, giving him a pat on the back and a little shove toward the door.

"That Miss Tilley's a funny old bird, isn't she?" he asked as he walked down the brick path with Lucy, dragging a wheeled duffel behind him.

"A word of advice," said Lucy, opening the rear hatch on her SUV. "Don't underestimate her and don't disappoint her, or you'll be sorry."

Hank loaded the bag inside, then turned to her. "You've done so much for me. Not just you, but Miss Tilley and Rachel and my folks and the Harvest Festival ladies. I really don't want to let anybody down."

"Well, don't," said Lucy, yanking the driver's side door open and climbing inside. She waited until he was seated beside her with his seatbelt fastened, then started the car and began the three hour drive to Portsmouth.

Hank was very quiet and when Lucy glanced at him she noticed his eyes were closed as if he had dozed off. Just as well, she thought, relieved that she didn't have to keep up a conversation.

It wasn't until they were going over the Piscataqua Bridge linking Maine with New Hampshire that he woke up, yawning and rubbing his eyes. "We must be almost there."

"Pretty close, according to the GPS. Did you have a nice rest?"

"Sorry about that. I haven't been sleeping much lately."

Lucy remembered how her son, Toby, when he was Hank's age, used to sleep for twelve hours at a stretch. She and her friends used to be amazed at the amount of sleep their teenage boys needed, and how difficult it was to get them up in the morning in time for the seven o'clock school bus. "How come?" she asked, wondering if insomnia was a side effect of addiction.

"I keep thinking about Alison," he said. "I keep seeing her dead, you know, drowned and all wet and ghoulish."

"I saw her body," said Lucy. "She looked just like herself. Not ghoulish."

He was silent, looking out the window as they drove down a main avenue dotted with stores and houses. Some of the buildings looked ancient, perhaps dating from the eighteenth century. "She wasn't on drugs. They say she was, but I know for sure that she wasn't. I tried to get her to use with me, but she wouldn't. She used to get mad at me, tell me to get clean or get lost."

"Was she dating anyone?" asked Lucy, thinking of Matt Rodriguez.

"Maybe. I don't know," he answered. "We were good friends for a while. We both have kind of messed up families, but we kind of drifted apart when I stopped going to classes."

"Do you know why she didn't want to live with her mother?" asked Lucy. "It seems kind of odd that she chose to live with her father and his new, young wife."

"She hated her mom, and she really hated her stepdad. She called him a weasel. She didn't always agree with her dad, she told me, but at least he was honest, even if all he really cared about was having a lot of money."

"You have reached your destination," the GPS informed her in a crisp British accent.

Lucy spotted a small, discreet sign announcing NEW BEGINNINGS on a patch of grass in front of a large Federal-style brick building. "We're here," she said, noticing that Hank seemed to have lost all the color in his face. "Are you okay?"

"I will be," he said, opening the door and climbing out.

Lucy popped the rear hatch and he pulled out his duffel, then he came around the car to her door. She hit the power button and lowered the window, expecting him to say good-bye.

But there was something else on Hank's mind. "Alison was really excited about having a little half sister or brother. She loved kids." He swallowed hard. "It's too bad she never got to have any of her own."

Lucy reached out the window and squeezed his shoulder. "This is about you," she told him. "Time for you to concentrate on getting well."

He nodded, looking very serious. Then he walked around the car and started up the brick path, dragging the duffel behind him. As Lucy watched him mount the stairs, she saw someone opening the door for him, greeting him with a welcoming smile.

She remained parked for a few minutes, entering her next destination—Boston's Trinity Church—into her GPS, and then shifted into DRIVE. As she pulled out into the street, she left with mixed emotions. On one hand, she felt satisfied she'd done all she could for him. On the other, she hoped and prayed that Hank would do the work he needed to do.

Lucy was familiar enough with Boston to know that she wouldn't be able to pull up next to Trinity Church and park the car, so she was on the lookout for a parking garage when the GPS told her she was approaching her destination. She pulled into the first garage she saw and, after getting over the shock of the price listed on a sign by the entrance, took the ticket and began a long descent into the bowels of Boston. Finally finding a vacant spot, she parked, took the elevator to the surface, and began the short walk to Copley Square.

Her mother used to scoff that Boston was a "small town" compared to New York, but Lucy found Boston pretty exciting after living so long in Tinker's Cove. The streets were lined with tall buildings and the sidewalks were filled with people of all ages and ethnicities, all intent on going somewhere. The shop windows were filled with interesting, and no doubt expensive, temptations.

Arriving at Copley Square where a steel drum band was playing beneath the bare trees, she paused to take in the scene. The square itself was filled with people, some listening to the music, others feeding pigeons or simply taking a rest on one of the benches. The Boston Public Library faced the square on one side, the stately Fairmont Copley Plaza Hotel stood on another, and Trinity Church itself stood beneath the gleaming mirrored walls of the sleek Hancock Tower, which was designed to reflect an image of the church.

A steady stream of people were pouring into the church and Lucy joined them, making sure to have her ID and press pass ready for presentation. As she shuffled along in the line, she recognized some well-known people—the governor of Massachusetts, the mayor of Boston, the senior senator from Massachusetts, Bob Kraft who owned the Patriots football team, and a couple newscasters she'd seen on TV. The line moved right along as people were identified and escorted to pews in the Romanesque church, but when Lucy handed over her credentials to the gatekeepers she was directed to a small doorway. There she encountered a steep staircase that led to the choir loft, which offered a terrific view of the church below, but was too small for the large number of media people assigned to cover the funeral.

She was fortunate enough to squeeze herself into a spot in the front row, where she stood in a corner and prayed that whoever designed the 150-year old church had thought to make sure the choir loft was strong enough to hold a large crowd. She wasn't the only one who had that thought.

The cameraman from Channel 5 was clearly uncomfortable. "I covered a balcony collapse—a triple-decker—last week," he told her. "Bunch of college kids. Two were killed."

"That's terrible," said Lucy. "I hope that doesn't happen to us."

"What are the chances?" he asked. "An old building, constructed before today's building codes . . ."

"Back when people weighed less," added newscaster Monique Washington, who was a beautiful, large black woman.

"We don't get no respect," said a young guy sporting a fashionable day-old beard whose lanyard identified him as working for the *Boston Globe*. "They want good press, but they don't want to provide decent accommodations for us. They just crowd us in behind fences like we're a bunch of cows or stick us up in the attic. Jeez, it's hot up here."

"You said it," agreed Monique, fanning herself with the order of service she'd picked up off a chair. "So do you think we'll have any drama? The wives encounter each other and start ripping off black veils?"

"That'd be something," said the guy from the Globe in a hopeful tone.

"Well, here comes the current wife, the show girl," said the cameraman, swinging his camera to focus on Mireille.

She was walking slowly down the aisle, leaning slightly backwards and holding onto her mother's arm. From her vantage point, Lucy could only see her back. Mireille was dressed in low heels and a simple black cloth coat that provided a dark contrast to her flowing blond hair. Mimsy was also dressed simply in a navy pantsuit. A navy and white checked beret was on her head. They were following an usher, who led them to the first pew on the left-hand side of the church.

"Very understated, very tasteful," admitted Monique with a raised eyebrow. "I'm kinda surprised. I thought she'd be brassier somehow."

Lucy wanted to defend Mireille but bit her tongue, unwilling to share her privileged one-on-one interview with the entire press corps.

"You gotta wonder with a young wife like that, if she's kinda glad the old boy is gone or whether she'll really miss him," said the cameraman.

"She won't have to go on Match.com, that's for sure, not with a billion or two in the bank," said the guy from the Globe.

"And she's got the looks, or will have, once she has the baby," said the cameraman. He was swinging the camera once again, this time picking up the arrival of Ed Franklin's divorced wife, Eudora. "Here comes the hag," he announced.

"Oh my gosh. She's gone over the top," said Monique, rolling her eyes.

Peering down, Lucy had to agree. Eudora had swathed herself in layers and layers of black gauze, which gave the impression that she was a Muslim woman required to cover every inch of herself with a suffocating chador. Apparently unable to support her grieving self, or perhaps unable to see through the dense layers of fabric, she was supported by her son Tag on one side and her husband Jon on the other. The trio were led by an usher and followed by an entourage that included two beady-eyed security agents and a couple assistants carrying briefcases and black leather portfolios.

Lucy would have loved to hear what her companions thought of Eudora and company, but anything they might have said was drowned out by the organ music, which began with a thunderous chord that practically blew the crowd of media representatives right off the balcony. The pipes of the church's organ were located behind the choir loft, giving the media the full benefit of that magnificent instrument's awesome power.

The service was long. Many famous people eulogized Ed Franklin. A famous opera singer sang his favorite song ("I Did It My Way"), and the congregation stumbled through a number of unfamiliar hymns, which didn't matter because the organ drowned everyone out. Lucy was feeling quite dizzy and nauseous when the casket containing Ed Franklin's remains was finally lifted off its support and carried down the aisle on the shoulders of six strong men. There was an anxious moment when Eudora and Mireille faced off on opposite sides of the aisle, but Mireille graciously yielded to Eudora, who was determined to be seen as the principal mourner.

"First wives go first," said Monique with a smirk.

Lucy regretted taking that prime spot in the front row of the choir loft as it meant she was one of the last to leave. She seemed to be having some sort of low blood sugar problem. Or maybe it was the noise of the organ or the heat in the church, or the fact she hadn't had anything to eat since breakfast. She was feeling quite unsteady when she finally reached the stairs and began descending.

She held on to the railing for dear life and concentrated on getting through the crowd to the door, hoping that all she needed was some fresh air. At the bottom of the staircase she encountered Eudora's assistants, who were distributing packets of press releases. She grabbed the thick folder and slipped through the crowd to the porch, where she grabbed a handy pillar for support and breathed deep breaths.

She spotted a CVS store across the square and made a somewhat unsteady beeline to its candy counter, where she bought herself a lifesaving Snickers bar and a bag of peanut M&Ms. She ate them all while standing outside the store, watching the great and good—the celebrities and the politicians—stream from the church and make their way to the Copley Plaza. All except for Mireille and her mother, who Lucy saw leaving by a side door and getting into a waiting black town car unnoticed by the chattering crowd.

She felt much better after her chocolate and sugar binge and was sorely tempted to cruise down Boylston and back up Newbury for a bit of window-shopping . . . or maybe even some actual shopping if she found something irresistible that wasn't too expensive. Then she remembered the price of the parking garage where the meter was running and decided she'd better head back to Tinker's Cove. She had a long drive ahead of her, after all, and a long list of weekend chores that weren't going to do themselves. There were no little fairies (or even family members) who shopped for groceries like she did, taking advantage of coupons and sales, nor any who remembered to pick up the dry cleaning or knew which brand of dog food to buy.

She was somewhat nervous about the traffic in Boston, which was known for its notoriously bad drivers, but she made it to the expressway in one piece, and then joined the bumper-to-bumper traffic crawling through the Big Dig tunnels to the dramatic Zakim Bridge. Things gradually improved as she headed north and traffic steadily thinned out. She was approaching the Hampton tolls, where her EZPass allowed her to fly through the formerly clogged toll booths, when her cell phone rang.

She picked it up, she saw Zoe's picture, and quickly answered. "What's up?"

"It's Dad, Mom. He's in the hospital."

Lucy felt as though she'd been hit with a sledge hammer. What could it be? A heart attack? An accident? "What happened?"

"I'm not sure. I'm on my way there now. Barney called. He said the restaurant was firebombed."

Lucy had lots of questions, but the only thing that mattered was getting back to Tinker's Cove and Bill as fast as possible. That was all she thought about as she pushed her car beyond the speed limit, rushing to her husband's side.

Chapter Sixteen

The drive from New Hampshire had never seemed so long to Lucy, even though she was risking getting a speeding ticket. She kept trying to call Zoe or Bill or even the Tinker's Cove police department on her cell phone, desperate to learn what had happened and, more important, Bill's condition. She struggled to divide her attention between the phone and the road, unwilling to lose time by pulling over into a rest area. Her fingers kept fumbling and she couldn't get a signal and when she nearly ran off the road, she gave up.

She ran out of freeway in Brunswick when she had to exit onto Route 1 and that was when the state trooper appeared in her rearview mirror, blue lights flashing, and she had to pull over.

"I know I was going too fast," she told the trooper, "but my husband's been injured. It was an explosion, and I'm desperate to get to the hospital in Tinker's Cove."

"License and registration," said the trooper, unmoved by her plea. "Turn off your engine."

She obeyed, turning the ignition key and producing the documents, and watched in her side mirror as he took them back to his cruiser, where she knew he'd run them on his computer. Minutes ticked by slowly and it seemed like hours before he returned and handed them back to her.

"It seems you're known to the department," he said, still expressionless. "I'm supposed to escort you to the hospital. Follow me."

"Great," said Lucy, amazed at this surprising turn of events.

Moments later he passed her, blue lights flashing, and she followed as he sped along the local road clearing the way. Traffic was fairly heavy this time of day when people were heading home for supper, but vehicles scattered before him as drivers pulled over to the side. When an inattentive motorist failed to spot the cruiser and forced him to slow he hit the siren, producing a couple short barks, and the driver quickly moved out of the way.

Lucy found she had to pay close attention in order to keep up as they whizzed along the narrow two-lane road, sometimes pulling into the oncoming lane, and she had to put her worries about Bill out of her mind. She'd never driven like this, weaving through traffic at speeds approaching eighty miles per hour, and she found it terrifying. It was a huge relief when they finally made the turn onto Main Street in Tinker's Cove and she spotted the illuminated emergency room sign at the cottage hospital. The trooper turned off his flashing lights and drove off, giving her a cursory wave as she pulled into an empty parking space.

Getting out of the car, she was assailed by fear, dreading what she might find. What if Bill hadn't survived the blast? What would she do then? She couldn't imagine living a single day without her husband. It would be like losing part of herself. Or what if he was gravely injured and required constant care? How was her life going to change? Was he suffering?

It was that last thought that propelled her forward, toward the plate glass doors that opened automatically at her approach. She went straight to the reception desk where she was surprised to see Babs Culpepper, her friend Barney's sister.

"Lucy, you're here," she said in a bright voice. "Bill's in that first exam room. Go right on in."

"How is he?" Lucy asked.

"I'm not supposed to say," replied Babs. "But he's in pretty good shape, considering."

Lucy wasn't sure how to take that. "Pretty good shape, considering" could cover a lot of territory. But when she opened the door, she saw Bill was sitting up on the gurney, with his arm in a sling. Zoe was there, sitting on a chair, and State Police Lieutenant Horowitz was standing beside him, dressed as always in a gray suit. Lucy and Horowitz had a long history, and while they often conflicted, they shared a mutual respect for each other. She was rather dismayed to notice his hair was also entirely gray, and his pale blue eyes made him look more tired than ever.

"Did you enjoy the escort?" he asked, stepping aside so Lucy could reach her husband.

"Was that you?" she asked, occupied in studying Bill's condition and deciding if she could hug him.

His face and head were scraped and bruised, as was the hand that emerged from the black sling. He held out his other hand and she grabbed it with both hands.

"What's the damage?" she asked.

"Broken arm, a few bumps and bruises," he answered with a smile. "I was darned lucky. I was standing by the door, which happened to be open, and I was blown outside by the force of the explosion. I guess I must have instinctively used my arm to try and break my fall, which is why it's broken."

"You should see the place, Mom," said Zoe. "The entire front wall is gone and there was a lot of damage from the fire. It looks like a bomb hit it."

"That's what we're trying to determine," said Horowitz, looking very serious. "The fire marshal is investigating whether the explosion was caused by a device or a gas leak. I was just asking your husband if he smelled gas beforehand."

Lucy couldn't take her eyes off Bill. She was studying every scab and bruise, and kept hanging onto his hand as if afraid he'd disappear if she let go.

"I don't remember much," said Bill, mumbling a bit.

"Does it hurt to talk?" she asked, and he gave her a nod.

"Can you question him another time?" asked Lucy, turning to Horowitz. "He's clearly in pain."

"I really don't know what happened," said Bill, speaking slowly with effort. "I opened the door and pow! Next thing I knew I was flat on my back in the parking lot and the pub was in flames." He sighed. "I wish I could tell you more. I really do."

"Okay," said Horowitz with a decisive nod. "I'll be in touch." He turned to go.

"Thanks for the police escort," said Lucy, walking the few steps to the door with him. "It was quite an experience."

"Glad to be of service," he said, opening the door. "Besides, from what I heard, you were a menace out there on the road."

"Well, thanks again," said Lucy as he stepped into the hallway.

Once she was sure he was gone, and the door closed, Lucy had a million questions for Bill and Zoe. She had to wait to ask them, however, as a nurse popped in with a clipboard full of papers for him to sign.

"Once we finish this business you can go," she announced, flipping the pages and pointing where to sign.

"Good thing it was my left arm," he said, scrawling his signature where she'd indicated. "I'm right-handed."

"I've got a prescription for painkillers for you," she said, handing him a blue square of paper. "Don't try to be a hero. They're not addictive and you'll be a lot more comfortable if you take them."

"Will do," said Bill. "I'm no hero."

"I can pick up the prescription on my way home," offered Zoe.

"That would be great," said Lucy, giving her the blue slip. "That way we won't have to stop and can go straight home with your dad."

The nurse gave him a hand and helped him off the gurney, and then they all walked through the ER and out through the waiting room to the door.

"Safe home," said Babs, and Lucy gave her a big smile and a little wave before stepping outside.

"Do you want to wait here and I'll bring the car over?" asked Lucy, but Bill shook his head and headed straight for her SUV, albeit walking rather more slowly than usual.

Zoe headed in the opposite direction, toward her little Civic.

Watching her go, Lucy had a sudden inspiration and called after her, "Zoe! Pick up a pizza for dinner!"

"Again?" asked Bill with a groan.

Zoe turned back and gave her a nod. "Will do!"

Bill grunted a bit as he settled himself in the passenger seat, and he winced as Lucy helped him with his seat belt, arranging it so it didn't press against his broken arm. Then she started the car and they were on the way home.

"So what really happened?" she asked, braking at the exit.

"It's like I told the lieutenant," said Bill. "I opened the door and the place blew up."

"Do you think it was a gas leak?" she asked, making the turn onto Main Street. "Or did somebody set a bomb, like maybe one or more of those anti-immigration demonstrators?"

"Could be either of those," said Bill. "Or it could have been Rey."

Lucy couldn't believe what he was saying. "Rey?"

"Yeah. Why not? He's running into a lot of problems here. His son is facing criminal charges, he's got to pay a lot of money for a lawyer to defend the kid, and he's already soaked a lot of money into a project that he probably figures is never going to be profitable. "

"You think he did it himself for the insurance money?"

"Wouldn't be the first time somebody tried that," said Bill, leaning back and closing his eyes. "Or the last."

When they got home Lucy helped him into the house and got him settled on the sectional in the family room where he could rest and watch the evening news on TV while she threw together a salad. When the segment about the explosion came on, he called her and she hurried to watch.

Looking at the images of the damage, which was extensive, she thought it was a miracle that Bill had survived. As Zoe had told her, the entire front of the pub was gone, and the inside was a charred mess. Tables and chairs had been tossed this way and that, the remaining walls were streaked with soot, and the swinging door that led to the kitchen was hanging askew. A lace curtain that remained where a window had once been blew in the breeze.

"What happened here?" a reporter asked fire chief Buzz Bresnahan. "Was it arson?"

"We don't know yet. The fire marshal will conduct a complete investigation. I'm just glad it wasn't worse. One man was injured, but there were no fatalities."

Overcome by the thought of what might have been, Lucy plunked herself down on the coffee table and took Bill's good hand. When she started to talk he shushed her.

"All's well that ends well," he said with a wry grin. "And I think Zoe's here with the pizza—and the pills."

Lucy met Zoe in the kitchen and they put together trays so they all could eat in the family room. Lucy read the instructions on the bottle of painkillers and counted out two tablets, which she placed in a custard cup on Bill's tray. He swallowed them immediately when she gave him his dinner tray, washing them down with a big swallow of cola. He had switched off the news and found a college football game, and the roar of the huge crowd, punctuated by blasts from the college band, provided a welcome distraction as they ate their pizza and salad.

When there was a break in the action and the chains were brought out to determine if Iowa had made a first down, Zoe spoke up. "I don't think I should go to Montreal," she said, referring to her planned departure after class on the coming Tuesday, two days before Thanksgiving. "Dad's gonna need help while Mom's at work and I'm sure Renee will understand."

"But you've been looking forward to seeing Renée," said Lucy, referring to their young neighbor from the housing development on nearby Priscilla Path who was attending Concordia University.

"And I'll be fine," said Bill, who had polished off his first piece of pizza and was well into his second.

"I'm really nervous about leaving and I know I'd be terrible company. I'd just be worried about Dad and Matt and, well, it's just a lot coming on top of Alison's death."

"I think you should go, the sooner the better, for your own safety," said Lucy. "I've got a bad feeling that Tinker's Cove isn't safe right now."

Bill was about to take a bite of pizza but, hearing this, set it back down on his plate.

"Don't be silly, Lucy. That explosion was probably due to a loose gas connection, something like that."

"I don't think so, Bill. I think it was purposely set off by somebody, some evil person who didn't care if someone got hurt. Maybe it was for insurance, maybe it was to send a message. I don't know. But I do know that the whole town feels different. It's like people are afraid to meet each other's eyes. Admit it. You've felt it, too. There are people who don't like the fact that you've been working for Rey Rodriguez."

"Some idiot did throw some rotten garbage into my truck," he said with a shrug.

"When was this?" demanded Lucy. "Why didn't you tell me?"

"A couple days ago. I didn't think it was a big deal," he replied.

"It is a big deal!" exclaimed Lucy. "It's escalating and I'm afraid it's only going to get worse."

"Mom, you're being paranoid," said Zoe.

"Well, maybe so, but better safe than sorry. I think you should give Renee a call and say you can come earlier than you planned, okay?"

Zoe didn't answer but looked at her father, waiting for his thoughts.

"I'm not sure your Mom is right, but I do think

you could use a change of scene," said Bill. "It would be good for you to spend some time with Renée . . . and you can brush up on your French."

"I think you should give Renée a call. See if you can go tomorrow," suggested Lucy.

"But what about Matt? I want to support him . . ."

"I'm pretty sure he'll be relieved to know you're safe," said Lucy. "And he sure won't want you visiting him in jail."

"If he's got any decency at all," added Bill, who was never a fan of his daughter's boyfriends.

"Okay," agreed Zoe, deciding further resistance was futile and turning her attention to her salad she speared a chunk of lettuce. "Will you keep me posted?"

"Absolutely," promised Lucy, taking a bite of pizza. She was chewing when a Notre Dame player made a ninety-yard run for a touchdown. Realizing Bill was strangely quiet, she turned to look at him and saw that he'd drifted off, still holding the tray with his half-eaten pizza in his lap. She gently removed it and covered him with an afghan, giving him a little kiss on his forehead as she tucked it around him.

Sunday morning was busy. Bill needed help getting showered and dressed, and took out his frustration with the situation on Lucy. She'd made him a big breakfast of ham and eggs, thinking it would please him, but he snapped at her when he couldn't manage to cut the ham by himself and had to ask for help. Zoe couldn't decide what clothes she needed to pack for Montreal and kept appearing in the kitchen, holding up various garments and asking her mother's opinion. Lucy was at her wit's end by the time Bill retreated to the family room, where he promptly fell asleep on the sectional sofa.

When the phone rang, she was surprised to hear Rey's voice.

"How is Bill?" he asked, concern in his voice.

"He's doing okay," said Lucy, taking the phone into the kitchen so she wouldn't disturb Bill. "He's in some pain, I think, but he doesn't want to admit it."

"What a terrible thing. I feel responsible. Let me know if there's anything I can do."

Lucy was tempted to say that he'd done enough, thank you, and to please leave them alone, but then she remembered that his son was facing murder charges, which was much more serious than a broken arm and a few bruises. "What's going on with Matt?"

"I believe they're transferring him today, bringing him back to Maine for arraignment on Monday. The lawyer says there's little chance he'll get bail, but we're going to try."

"I'm very sorry," said Lucy.

"I guess it was inevitable, given the situation, that they would try to pin Franklin's murder on him. He's innocent, of course, and I believe the truth will come out in the end."

"I certainly hope so," said Lucy.

"The reason I called is I'm coming to Maine for the arraignment, and to see Matt, and I'd like to meet with Bill about the restaurant project."

"I don't suppose you want to continue—" began Lucy.

"On the contrary," he said, interrupting her. "I'm determined to go ahead, I'm meeting with the insurance adjuster tomorrow and I'd like Bill to be there, if he's able."

"I'm not sure," said Lucy when Bill appeared in the doorway.

"Who's that?" he asked.

When she said it was Rey he took the phone himself and, before she could object, had agreed to meet him at the burned-out pub first thing in the morning.

Lucy was furious. "You're always telling me to mind my own business and to stay out of trouble," she reminded him, "and here you're walking right into a hornet's nest. Maybe you should take your own advice."

"I'm not committing myself to anything. I'm just going to a meeting," he said, turning his back on her and shuffling back to the family room.

A series of thumps emanating from the back staircase preceded Zoe, who appeared with her enormous duffel bag, ready to leave for Montreal. "You're sure you don't need me here, Mom?" she asked, setting the suitcase on the floor.

"No, we'll be fine. Give your dad a kiss."

Zoe disappeared into the family room, only to emerge a moment later. "He's gone back to sleep. You'll have to say good-bye for me."

"Okay," said Lucy, her voice thickening. "Drive carefully and be, well, you know, it's a big city. Take care of yourself."

"I will," said Zoe, laughing, as she put on her coat. "I won't go wandering off with any strangers, not even if they're incredibly cute and have charming French accents."

"If only I could believe that," said Lucy, tying a long scarf around her daughter's neck and giving her a big hug.

She stood at the kitchen window, watching as Zoe dragged the heavy bag down the path and loaded it into her car. She paused before getting in the car and gave her mother a wave, then she was gone.

Lucy was headed down to the cellar with a load of laundry when her cell rang and she saw the caller was Zoe. "What's up? Did you forget something?" she asked, resting the laundry basket on her hip.

"No, Mom, I didn't forget anything. It's this billboard. I thought you'd want to know about it. It must have just gone up, right out here on Route 1. It's a big blown-up version of the newspaper photo of those three drug dealers that got arrested a few weeks ago, with those police ID placards that have their names on them, all Latino of course, and then in big red-white-and blue letters it says AMERICA FOR AMERICANS!"

Chapter Seventeen

Bill might have been able to drive one-handed, but the fact that he was also taking pain meds meant that Lucy had to chauffeur him to the early Monday morning meeting with Rey. His truck was damaged in the blast and was in the body shop, so they went in her SUV. The sun was just rising when they arrived at the harbor and shafts of morning light filled with dancing bits of dust streamed through the burned outer wall of the restaurant. The place reeked of smoke, charred wood, and melted plastic. Lucy and Bill stood outside the cordon of yellow tape and studied the scene, amazed that Bill survived the blast that created so much damage.

"I was sure lucky," he said, taking Lucy's hand.

"I can't think about what might have been," she said, turning away. Looking across the mostly empty parking lot dotted with a few pickup trucks and boats shrouded in white plastic, she spotted a white sedan coming down the hill. "I bet that's Rey."

Moments later the sedan slid into the parking spot next to Lucy's SUV and Rey got out, giving them a wave. The passenger side door opened and a young woman stepped out and came around the car to join him.

"This is my daughter Luisa," said Rey, introducing her.

She was a petite version of her brother, with the addition of a gorgeous mane of black, wavy hair. She smiled, revealing dazzling white teeth and two dimples, one in each cheek.

"It's lovely to meet you," said Lucy. "We're both very sorry about Matt. Have you seen him?"

"Not yet," said Rey. "I imagine we'll be able to have a minute or two with him after the arraignment."

"He's very strong," said Luisa, sounding as if she was trying to reassure herself. "He'll be all right."

"I'm sure he will," said Bill. He indicated the burned out pub with a wave of his hand. "So what do you think?"

Rey stepped up to the yellow tape and walked along it, studying the damage and shaking his head. Bill, Lucy, and Luisa stood together, silently watching him.

"I'm interested to hear what the adjuster has to say," he said, joining them. "I think that may be him."

The *him* turned out to be a *her* dressed in mannish Carhart overalls, sturdy work boots, and a hard hat. "I'm Donna Dewicki from National Assurance," she said, sticking out her hand.

"Rey Rodriguez." He shook hands with her and introduced the others.

"I've got permission from the fire department to take a look inside," she said, pulling a flashlight out of her pocket. "I'll be back in a jif."

The four stood together, watching as Donna stepped inside the burned shell of the pub and following the progress of her dancing flashlight.

After a few minutes she returned. "This is a total loss. It doesn't look to me like anything can be salvaged."

"So that means the company will pay the entire amount of the policy?" asked Luisa.

"That depends on the results of the fire marshal's investigation," said Donna, giving Rey a once-over. "If the explosion was caused by a gas leak or an electrical fault, then the company will pay, but if it's arson, there will need to be a further investigation."

"Are you implying I might have done this myself?" asked Rey.

"I'm not saying that. I'm saying that it's been done before and the company will want to be certain that it's not the case. We have a responsibility to our shareholders."

"I'd like to point out that I was in California when this happened," said Rey.

"Point taken," said Donna. "But there are people who would do the job for a price, and there are plenty of people who think a couple thousand dollars is a small price to pay for a million dollar pay-out."

"I can't believe this," fumed Rey, who was building up a head of steam.

Luisa rested a cautionary hand on his arm.

"It's okay, Papa. They have to investigate all the possibilities, but we know that we had nothing to do with this."

"I hope that's the case," said Donna, thrusting a clipboard in front of Rey. "Sign here, please. It's just an acknowledgement that I was here and examined the premises."

Rey scrawled an oversized signature on the small line marked with an X and handed the clipboard back with a little shove.

Donna responded with a raised eyebrow, but didn't say anything and quickly turned and strode across the parking lot to her van. No doubt she had learned through the years to avoid confrontations with policyholders. Lucy herself had been furious with her own insurance agent when he informed her that, even though their auto policy would cover some of the cost of repairs to the truck, they would have to pay a hefty deductible.

"Come on, Papa," said Luisa. "Let's look at the view before we leave."

Rey shook his head. "I want to talk to Bill. I want to know what he thinks."

"I'll walk with you," offered Lucy. "You can see Quissett Point from here."

"Okay," agreed Luisa with a smile.

The two women strolled to the end of the pier, watching in silence as a little red boat headed past the lighthouse, rounded the point, and went out to sea.

"It must be awfully cold out there," said Luisa with a little shiver.

"You bet." Lucy wondered if Luisa knew about the developing relationship between Matt and Zoe, but wasn't sure how to ask. After they stood in silence a few moments, gazing at the gleaming surface of the water and the little pine covered islands and the boats bobbing on their moorings, she decided to just go for it. "You know, Matt seemed to be taking an interest in my daughter, Zoe."

"He told me. He said she was the first girl since Alison that he really liked."

"Zoe's in Montreal, visiting a girlfriend there," said Lucy.

"Probably a smart move, considering all this," said Luisa with a nod in the direction of the burned-out pub.

Lucy was quick to add, "But she's very worried about Matt. She made me promise to keep her posted on developments."

"I'll let him know," said Luisa with a little smile.

"Thanks," said Lucy. "Was he very serious about Alison?"

"I think so. He dated her for quite a while. She was practically part of our family. They met in LA. She was a student at UCLA and he was working as a sous chef at the Four Seasons. I think they met when they were both running. You know, they had the same routine and saw each other every morning and finally started saying hi, that sort of thing. But then she had that accident and got into drugs and they broke up."

"Wow, it really is a small world. Girl from Maine meets boy in California."

"You know those Venn diagrams, those circles that overlap?" asked Luisa. "I'm into math and that's how I think about things. We all travel in circles, you know family groups, interest groups, economic groups, age groups, and when people share a certain number of factors it's pretty likely that their circles will overlap and they'll meet."

"So Matt and Alison shared a number of factors?" asked Lucy.

"Yeah. They were both young, they were both runners, they were in the same city, and they shared the same fantasy. She saw herself as a damsel in distress and he saw himself as a knight in shining armor."

"So what was Alison's dragon?" asked Lucy. "Drugs?

"No. It was her family. She didn't get along with them at all. I used to think that it wasn't so much Matt who she liked as our whole extended family. You know, the parties and dinners with all the uncles and cousins and aunts."

"Well, Ed Franklin wasn't the easiest guy to get along with . . ." began Lucy.

"Oh, no, it wasn't her father. It was her monster mom and her slimy stepfather. Her words, not mine. And she hated the half brother, Trot or Trig. I forget his name. She said he was awful."

"In what way?" asked Lucy, fascinated.

"I'm not sure, exactly," admitted Luisa, "but Matt told me that she had him install a deadbolt on her bedroom door so she could lock herself in at night."

"Oh," said Lucy as they turned to walk back. She knew from her work as a reporter that sexual abuse in families was not uncommon and often had tragic consequences. "Do you think that she might have killed herself?"

"No. She would never have committed suicide," said Luisa, certainty in her voice. "I'm sure of that. And she didn't use drugs, either. She got addicted to pain killers after an accident, but she went to rehab and after that, she wouldn't even take an aspirin."

Bill and Rey were shaking hands and saying good-bye when the women returned and joined them.

Lucy also took Rey's hand and said, "I hope everything goes well at the arraignment. Be sure to give Matt our best wishes."

"I most certainly will," said Rey, taking Luisa's arm and walking with her to the rental car.

Lucy and Bill were quiet as they walked to the SUV, but as soon as they were inside Lucy asked if Rey had come to a decision about the future of the pub.

"He wants to go ahead," said Bill. "He says it's a blessing in disguise and he's hiring an architect to design his dream restaurant and he wants me to build it."

"I guess that depends on the insurance company."

"I guess it does."

Lucy took a detour on the way home, driving out to Route 1 to see the AMERICA FOR AMERICANS billboard. It was exactly as Zoe had described it, and it dominated the view. You couldn't avoid seeing it even if you wanted to. Lucy suspected a good number of people probably agreed with the anti-immigration sentiment.

"I wonder if Rey and Luisa saw it," said Bill as Lucy drove on past.

"I think they must have. Of course, they would have thought it utterly ridiculous since their family was here long before the American Revolution."

"But it's not really about immigration, is it? We're all descended from immigrants after all. It's about race and ethnicity. You know how they say a picture is worth a thousand words? Well there are only three words on the sign, but the picture of those mug shots of the three accused drug dealers says that Mexicans are criminals."

"I wonder who's behind it," said Lucy, switching into investigative reporter mode. "Those billboards are expensive."

"I have a feeling you're going to find out," said Bill as she turned off Route 1 onto Shore Road, heading back to Tinker's Cove and home.

Lucy was running late when she was finally able to leave for work, and she knew that Monday morning was always busy. There were usually new developments over the weekend, and a lot of people seemed to have nothing better to do on Sunday afternoon than to write e-mails to the local paper, which had to be answered.

Phyllis greeted her with a smile, and asked how Bill was doing. "Everybody's talking about that explosion," she said, peering over the zebra-striped cheaters perched on her nose. They matched her sweater and also her fingernails.

"Bill's got a broken arm," said Lucy, studying Phyllis's manicure. "How do you get stripes like that on your nails?"

"They're stickers. I heard the explosion, you know, and the sirens. It was scary. I thought the whole town was going to blow up."

"It was a heck of a blast," said Ted, turning away from his computer screen. "He was lucky he wasn't blown to bits."

"That's what he tells me," said Lucy, attempting a joke while hanging up her coat. She didn't like to think about the explosion and what might have been. Now she was realizing, for the first time, that the blast hadn't affected only her family and the Rodriguez family, but had literally sent tremors through the entire town.

"I'd like to interview Bill, if he's up to it," said Ted. "That blast is a big story and I'd love to get a first-person account."

Lucy plunked herself down at her desk, feeling overwhelmed. It was one thing to cover the news, quite another to *be* the news. "I was on my way home from Ed Franklin's funeral when Zoe called. I was only thinking of Bill. I wasn't thinking like a reporter."

"That's perfectly understandable," said Ted. "But it's the biggest thing that's happened in Tinker's Cove since the big ropewalk fire. I'm running it on page one."

"They had mutual aid," said Phyllis, referring to

the system by which the local fire departments helped each other. "Trucks came from Gilead, Elna, and Dundee."

Lucy found herself growing misty, thinking of all those people who came to help Bill and put out the fire. "He says he doesn't remember much, but I'm sure he'd like to tell you as much as he can."

"Great," Ted said. "I'll give him a call and set a time. I want to interview him face-to-face. You're writing up the Franklin funeral. There's the selectmen's meeting and I think the finance committee is meeting—"

"What about the billboard? I want to do a piece on that, find out who's behind it," said Lucy.

"What billboard?" asked Ted.

"The one out on Route 1 that says *America for Americans*, with bigger than life mug shots of those three drug dealers that got arrested."

"I hate those things. They spoil the view," said Phyllis. "I was so happy when they finally took down that one of the governor."

"I'll swing out that way and take a look on my way to the interview," said Ted, reaching for his jacket. "Meanwhile you've got plenty to do, Lucy."

Lucy had finished up her story about the Franklin funeral and was trying to think of a way to write an interesting story about the selectmen's debate as to whether or not the town had an adequate supply of road salt for the coming winter when Ted called.

"I saw the sign and it's too big to ignore," he said. "Go ahead and find out who's behind it."

"Great," she said, only too happy to switch gears. She immediately called the owner of the sign, Maine Message, and spoke to a sales rep who was enthusiastic about the benefits of roadside advertisements.

"We have hundreds of billboards throughout the state. Surveys show that billboards are one of the most effective forms of advertising."

"I'm not interested in renting a billboard," said Lucy, explaining that she was a reporter with the *Pennysaver* newspaper. "I'm working on a story about a billboard that just went up on Route 1 and I need to know who is responsible for it. It's got an anti-immigrant message, America for Americans."

"I know the one. I sold that," said the rep. "We're not responsible for the message, you know. We just provide the space. We've had people propose marriage on our billboards. One guy rented one to announce the birth of his grandson. We do have limits. No profanity, no libel or slander, that sort of thing. If you want to call your neighbor a thief or a liar, you have to paint that on a piece of plywood yourself and nail it up on a tree on your own property."

"Good to know," said Lucy. "Can you tell me who put up the *America for Americans* sign?"

"Sure. I'm just checking my files . . . Ah, here it is. It's actually a group called America for Americans, and the contact person is Zeke Bumpus."

"Thanks," said Lucy, abruptly ending the call. She didn't need any further information. She knew exactly who Zeke Bumpus was and where to reach him.

He lived on Bumpus Road where his family had lived for hundreds of years without doing much to improve the place. The family home was a compound of ramshackle buildings surrounded by an assortment of things that might come in handy someday—things like busted washing machines, old cars propped on cinder blocks, and various pieces of rusting machinery. Family members supported themselves by occasionally working on lobster boats or helping local building contractors, but generally avoided full-time jobs.

Zeke operated a firewood business, and Lucy found him in a patch of woods next to the family compound, running logs through a splitting machine. The machine was noisy and she caught his attention by waving her arms.

He reluctantly silenced the machine. "Whaddya want?" he asked, scowling. Zeke was only in his mid-twenties, but looked older due to his thinning hair and growing waistline. He was dressed for work in a faded plaid flannel shirt, filthy jeans, and a pair of unlaced work boots.

"Hi, Zeke. It's a nice day for outdoor work, right?"

He scowled at her. "I'd rather be hunting, but I gotta do this. We got a big order from the Queen Vic."

"Yeah, they advertise fireplaces in every room." Lucy was familiar with the town's upscale B&B.

Zeke cocked his head and looked at her with a puzzled expression. "Are you here for wood? I can give you a half-cord."

"No, I'm all set with firewood," she replied. "I'm actually here to ask about that billboard, the one that says *America for Americans*. How'd that come about?"

"Is this for the newspaper?" he asked, narrowing his pale blue eyes suspiciously.

"Of course. People are wondering who's behind the sign. It's causing quite a stir."

"Great. That's what we want. We want folks to realize that these immigrants, these Muslims and Mexicans and Somalis, are taking our country away from us. It's white people like you and me that built this country and now folks like us can't get jobs. All the jobs have gone overseas to places like Bangladesh and China. Do you know our country owes millions and billions of dollars to the Chinese? What's gonna happen if they decide it's time to pay up, huh? It's crazy the way we're letting these Mexicans flood the country with drugs, and they're sending us their criminals, too. Rapists and murderers, attacking white women and leaving them with little brown anchor babies."

"I'm sure a lot of folks agree with you," said Lucy when Zeke had run out of steam. She didn't want to risk angering him further, so she ventured cautiously into the territory she wanted to explore. "Do you have some sort of organization people can join?"

"Sure, America for Americans. We've got a website and everything."

"Those are expensive, aren't they? And that billboard must have cost a pretty penny, right?"

"Money's no problem. That's for sure."

"Really? How come?" Lucy seriously doubted Zeke's little firewood business earned the kind of money needed to rent a billboard.

"'Cause a rich donor gave us a big, fat check."

"Who was this donor?" asked Lucy, who had a good idea.

"Ed Franklin himself, before he died. I'm president, you see, but the sign was his idea. He worked out the design and the details. It came out real good."

"His death must be a huge loss to the organization," said Lucy.

"Yeah," agreed Zeke, nodding. "But we're going to have a big rally in his memory . . . on Thanksgiving Day, our national holiday."

Lucy couldn't resist. She had to say it. "But you know, Thanksgiving was started by the Pilgrims, who were actually immigrants."

"They were American immigrants," said Zeke, pointing a finger at her. "Remember that. American immigrants. America for Americans."

"It's been great talking to you, Zeke," she said, managing a halfhearted smile. It really wasn't worth pointing out that the Pilgrims arrived in 1620, a hundred and fifty-six years before the colonists rebelled against English rule. "Thanks.'

"Anytime, Lucy," he said, picking up a log and starting up the log splitter. It roared into life and even though his lips were moving she couldn't hear what he was saying.

She gave him a wave and headed for her car, feeling somehow soiled by his hateful, ignorant words. If only you could wash off intolerance and prejudice like you rinse off salt after a swim in the sea. But all too often, it seemed, these ideas stuck and wormed their way into people's minds, where they grew like cancer.

Ed Franklin was dead, she thought, but he had left behind a hateful legacy that would live on, poisoning minds and quite possibly ripping the Tinker's Cove community apart.

Chapter Eighteen

Lucy glanced at the dashboard clock when she started the car and was startled to realize it was almost noon. She wasn't far from home, so she decided to stop by to see how Bill was doing and have lunch with him before heading back to the office.

Reaching Red Top Road, which was usually deserted this time of day, she was surprised to see a number of cars coming the opposite way. The drivers usually stuck an arm out the window and gave her a wave or a friendly toot on the horn. When she got to the house perched on the top of hill, she saw an extra car in the driveway. Franny Small was bent over taking something out of her little Chevy, and when she stood up, Lucy saw she was holding a foil-covered dish.

"Hi, Lucy," she said, waiting while Lucy got of her SUV. "I hope Bill likes American chop suey. I made some for him. I thought he might like a hot lunch."

"Thanks, Franny. It's one of his favorite meals." Lucy neglected to mention that she hadn't made it for him in years, considering all that macaroni and ground beef much too fattening. "Why don't you come in and have lunch with us."

"Okay," said Franny, who was a single lady, now retired from a successful business career. "That would be nice. I do get a little tired of eating alone."

Once inside the kitchen, Lucy saw the golden oak table was full with a number of covered dishes. "What's all this?" she asked when Bill popped out of the family room.

"People have been stopping all morning, bringing food," he said. "There's cookies and banana bread and mac and cheese and I don't know what all."

"I guess I've brought coals to Newcastle," said Franny.

"Never you mind. I'm going to clear this away and we'll have your American chop suey," began Lucy, transferring a couple pies to the counter.

"American chop suey!" exclaimed Bill. "That's my favorite, and Lucy never makes it anymore."

Franny blushed, setting the foil-covered dish on the table. "I know it's the sort of hearty dish most men enjoy eating."

Lucy took Franny's coat and hung it up with her own, then quickly set the table with placemats, dishes, and silverware. She put the kettle on for tea and they all sat down to eat. Bill's broken arm hadn't spoiled his appetite, and he pleased Franny no end by eating seconds and thirds. When the kettle whistle sounded, Lucy made a pot of tea that they had along with Lydia Volpe's pizzelle cookies for dessert.

When they were finished eating, Franny insisted on helping Lucy with the dishes. Bill went off to the family room, rubbing his tummy and yawning as he went. The phone rang a couple times, but each time, he picked up the extension in the family room before Lucy could dry her hands to answer. When the dishes were done, Franny and Lucy exchanged thanks and good-byes—Franny thanked Lucy for inviting her to lunch and Lucy thanked Franny for bringing lunch and they both did this several times before Franny finally left. Lucy went into the family room expecting to find Bill sound asleep, but he was still talking on the phone.

"Waller's Garage has offered to cover the deductible when they fix the truck," he said when the call ended. "No charge."

"That's great," said Lucy, who had been fretting about that hefty deductible ever since her conversation with their insurance agent. She'd made the decision to raise the deductible some years ago in an effort to reduce the cost of their car insurance, which had increased sharply when the kids began driving.

"And the kids in the church youth group want to come and rake leaves for us."

"My goodness," said Lucy, feeling rather overwhelmed.

"Miss Tilley is going to bring me some books," he

said, "and Hattie Gordon from the garden club is
bringing a harvest-themed wreath, whatever that is."

Lucy was going to tell him, but the phone was already ringing again. She left him to answer it and
headed back to work, taking along one of the four
loaves of cranberry bread they had received. It
would be good for an afternoon coffee break.

As she drove, she thought about all the good
and kind people in Tinker's Cove who were always
quick to reach out and help their neighbors in
times of trouble, and she thought of Zeke Bumpus
and the America for Americans faction. She wondered if the groups overlapped, like the circles in
Luisa Rodriguez's Venn diagrams, or if they were
clearly distinct circles. Reaching town and making
the familiar turn onto Main Street, she concluded
that they probably did. People weren't necessarily
consistent and the woman who baked cranberry
bread for her ailing neighbor might also fear that
an influx of immigrants would change the character of her town.

Lucy was passing the town common when she
noticed that the chamber of commerce's huge cornucopia had been erected in the bandstand and
decided to snap a photo for the *Pennysaver*. Volunteers had built the horn of plenty, which was constructed of painted canvas stretched over a wood
frame, and the chamber set it up every year to collect the canned foods that were the entry fee for
the Turkey Trot race. A photo of the empty cornucopia would remind everyone to bring donations,
whether or not they were competing in the 5K.

She parked alongside the green where the grass

was now brown and grabbed her camera, noticing that the cornucopia had already drawn a couple passersby. Drawing closer, she recognized the two women who were studying the display as Mireille Franklin and her mother, Mimsy.

"Do you mind if I take a photo of you two admiring the cornucopia?" Lucy asked, raising her camera.

"Maybe not," said Mimsy, grabbing her daughter's hand in a protective gesture. "Mireille needs to keep a low profile."

"Don't be silly, Mom," said Mireille. "A couple figures will make the photo more interesting."

"I can take you from behind and I wouldn't have to identify you," offered Lucy.

"Okay," agreed Mimsy somewhat reluctantly.

"I was going to suggest that, in any case," said Mireille. "I'd rather not be photographed with this huge belly."

"I thought you'd be a mom by now," said Lucy, smiling.

"Me, too," said Mireille, stroking her baby bump. "This little one is in no hurry to come into the world, and I can't say I blame him."

"Or her," added Mimsy, holding up her hand with two fingers crossed.

"Are you still planning to leave Tinker's Cove after the baby's born?" asked Lucy.

Mimsy answered, her assertive tone leaving no doubt about the matter. "Absolutely. Mireille needs to get away. The sooner she gets that house on the market, the better."

"You haven't done that yet?" asked Lucy.

"I know I should," said Mireille with a sigh, "but

I'm not ready to leave Ed and Alison. I know it's weird, but I like visiting their graves . . ."

"It's morbid. That's what it is," snapped Mimsy. "And you shouldn't go alone to that cemetery."

"No, it's not morbid. I like being with them, just me and them, remembering them as they were when they were alive." Mireille paused, smiling. "Sometimes when I go there I think I hear them talking to me. They don't seem sad. Ed's mad that he isn't around to manage everything. He's not convinced that I can get along without him. Alison is more at peace. She says she's watching over me and the baby."

Mimsy didn't like hearing this one bit. "Come on, Mireille. You must be tired. You need to go home and get some rest."

"I'm fine, Mom," said Mireille, protesting.

"That's what you think, but it's not true," countered Mimsy. "You're not yourself and you're not behaving sensibly." She took her daughter by the arm, then turned to face Lucy. "Do you know what she did? She fired the bodyguards. All of them. Says she doesn't need them. Now does that sound like a sensible thing to do?"

Put on the spot, Lucy didn't know how to respond. "I really don't know."

"I didn't like having strangers in the house," said Mireille with a wan smile.

"Well, they were there to protect you and your baby," said Mimsy. "And if you end up dead like Ed and Alison, I'm not going to be visiting your grave so you can just hold your peace. Don't try talking to me, because I won't be there to listen!"

"Point taken, Mom," replied Mireille, allowing

Mimsy to lead her away across the dead brown lawn to their car.

Lucy decided to jog the short distance to the *Pennysaver* office, chiding herself for not taking her Turkey Trot training regimen more seriously. She had lots of excuses, she told herself, but she definitely needed to make her morning runs a priority. Time was running out with only a few days until the race.

When she got to the office, Phyllis was bursting with news. "Lucy!" she exclaimed, "You'll never guess what's happened."

"Martians landed?"

"No! Jason Sprinkle and Link Peterson have been arrested for torching the pub."

"That was quick," she said, glancing at Ted.

"Those two are not the brightest bulbs in the pack," he said. "At first they claimed they were out of town, but the cops have witnesses who saw them at the harbor just before the explosion. There's even video from the harbormaster's shed of them leaving the parking lot moments before the explosion. The chief told me they're saying they didn't notice the blaze, and that's why they didn't call for help. Little bastards insist it was Hank DeVries who did it."

"There's no way he could've done it. I took him to rehab in New Hampshire on Saturday," said Lucy.

"Next thing they'll be saying Santa Claus did it," said Phyllis.

When Lucy called Bill to give him the news, he wasn't convinced that Link and Jason were the arsonists. "They're not bad kids. I can't believe they did it. They knew I was in the building. I spoke to them in the parking lot. They asked me what I was doing working for those Mexicans and I told them I'd probably be needing help and asked if they'd be interested in some work. I figured even they could do demo."

"Looks like they did it for free," said Lucy.

Bill chuckled. "I don't think so. They seemed pretty interested in the fifteen dollars an hour I offered to pay them."

"Who else was down there?" asked Lucy. "Did you see anyone?"

"Yeah. Lots of people. It was Saturday afternoon and there was lots of activity. Even some tourists."

She heard the doorbell ring and Bill ended the call, saying someone was at the door and so far they had received six loaves of banana bread, but only one with chocolate chips, which he was eating.

"I should take out an ad," she told Ted and Phyllis. "No more banana bread, please!"

When she fired up her computer, she wondered if Link and Jason had actually seen the arsonist, but mistook him for someone else. When you thought about it, you realized there were a number of fair, tall young men in town.

That impression was confirmed that evening when she was driving home from work. Lucy was approaching the stop sign at the intersection of Main and Summer streets when a speeding car shot right through, causing her to brake abruptly. She was thinking it was a good thing she hadn't been going too fast, and strained to see who was the reckless driver. At first she thought it was

Hank, then remembered he was supposed to be in rehab in New Hampshire and also that he certainly wouldn't be driving a shiny new Audi. It was probably Tag Franklin, she decided, wondering if he could possibly be the arsonist who firebombed the pub. He seemed a more likely suspect than Link and Jason, if he subscribed to his adoptive father's anti-immigrant views. But it was also a terribly dangerous thing to do, and why would he risk blowing himself up, or getting caught and going to jail? All indications were that he had a cushy lifestyle as the pampered offspring of wealthy parents.

When she reached home she saw a MINI Cooper parked in the driveway and figured that Bill had yet another visitor. Poor guy, he certainly wasn't getting much rest, she thought, opening the back door and finding Rev. Marge standing in the kitchen.

"I was just leaving," she told Lucy. "But Bill and I worked it out that the youth group will come on Friday afternoon to clean up your yard."

"Great," said Lucy. "We really appreciate the help." Her eyes were traveling over the kitchen table and counters, which were loaded with every imaginable form of baked good.

As Bill had told her, there were indeed six loaves of banana bread, as well as three loaves of cranberry bread, numerous Bundt cakes, plastic containers of cookies, even a few pies. The freezer, too, was loaded to bursting with homemade soups and casseroles.

"I don't know what to do with all this," she said. "Can you use some for coffee hour at the church?"

"Coffee hour is all set," said Rev. Marge. "Why don't you take it to the jail?"

"The jail? Will they take donations of food?"

"Sure," said Rev. Marge. "As long as there's no saws or chisels inside."

"Not that I know of," said Lucy, chuckling.

"I visit there every week as part of my ministry and I often take day-old baked goods from the IGA. Joe Marzetti donates them and I drop them off around back at the kitchen. The gals really love the sweets, especially anything chocolate, but the men like them, too. They get good food, but it's very plain, institutional cooking. They appreciate the sweets. I think it's also the fact that somebody is thinking of them and believes they deserve a treat."

"I'll do it," said Lucy. "There's somebody there I ought to visit, anyway."

"Bless you," said Rev. Marge by way of farewell.

Next morning, Lucy ran in the woods despite a chilly drizzle. When she got home she asked Bill to pick a few baked goods to keep while she showered, then she loaded the rest into the SUV and drove off to Gilead and the county complex. She had never gone around back at the county jail as Rev. Marge had suggested, but found there was no problem at all gaining admission to the delivery entrance. A guard was stationed at the gate in the fence, which was topped with razor wire, but when she explained her mission and showed him the baked goods he opened the electronic gate and waved her in.

She pressed the buzzer at the door marked for deliveries and it was promptly opened by another guard, who summoned several prisoners assigned to work in the kitchen and supervised as they unloaded the goodies. Lucy had visited the prison many times before, but only to visit individual prisoners involved in stories she was covering who were awaiting trial; she had never had much contact with actual convicts. She knew that the prisoners in the county jail were usually serving sentences for lesser offenses, those convicted of serious felonies were sent to the state penitentiary. At first, she was somewhat wary of the men, but gradually realized that these criminals were folks just like the people on the outside, except for the fact that they had made a mistake that got them into trouble. The guys joked as they carried in the foil-wrapped desserts, and made a point of politely thanking her for the donation.

As she drove around to the front of the jail, she felt the happy glow of knowing that she'd done her good deed for the day. She parked in the visitors' lot and made her way to the forbidding entrance. There she presented identification and allowed the guard to search her bag, then walked through a metal detector before she was buzzed through a second door that led to the visitor's room. That area was busy on weekends as family members usually visited then, but on this weekday morning the large room was empty. She seated herself at one of the cafeteria-style tables and waited for Matt.

When he appeared and saw her she noticed that his face fell in disappointment, and she suspected he had expected to see Zoe, not her mother. He quickly recovered, however, and greeted her with a big smile as he seated himself opposite her on the round stool attached to the table.

"Thanks for coming," he said. "How's Zoe?"

"She's fine. She's in Montreal, visiting a friend."

"Just as well, considering everything that's happening. I heard about the pub. How is your husband?"

After telling him that Bill was recovering from his injuries, Lucy asked if he had any ideas as to who might have torched the pub.

"I heard they arrested two guys, but I haven't seen them. They've been keeping me kind of separate from the others. I think it's because I'm charged with such a serious crime."

"How are they treating you?" asked Lucy.

"I don't have any complaints. The guards seem pretty decent. Of course, I haven't been convicted. I'm still legally innocent. I've got a good lawyer and I'm hoping to get out on bail, though I know it's a long shot."

"You seem to be taking all this remarkably well," said Lucy, struck by his attitude.

"Well, I know I'm innocent. I didn't kill Ed Franklin, and I've got faith in the justice system. Plus, I've got a lot of advantages most people accused of crimes don't have. I've got money and can afford a good lawyer, I've got family and friends who support me and believe in my innocence, and I've got connections to influential people." He gave her an apologetic shrug. "The system might be rigged, but it's kind of rigged in my favor."

Lucy couldn't help smiling. "That's one way of looking at it."

"I'm a glass-half-full sorta guy. I doubt I'll be

brought to trial. Dad's got a private investigator who is working with the lawyer, and I'm sure they'll turn up something. And Dad's already working on winning over public opinion. He's planning a big Thanksgiving dinner for the entire town."

"That's a really good idea," said Lucy. "But how's he going to pull it off?"

"Not problem. Trust me. If he says he's going to do something, he'll do it." Matt paused. "I only hope I get out of here, so I can go." He licked his lips. "I don't want to miss my dad's turkey tacos."

Chapter Nineteen

Lucy had no sooner walked through the door at the *Pennysaver* before Ted sent her right back out on assignment. "Pam tells me the ladies at the Community Church have volunteered to help Rey with this Mexican Thanksgiving Feast and she wants me to run a story. Can you go over there and see what's cooking?"

Phyllis, dressed from head to toe in a blaze of autumnal orange, rolled her eyes and groaned at the pun. "I sense a headline: A Recipe for Reconciliation? Cooking Up Cooperation? Stirring Up a Better World?"

"Those are a good start," said Ted in all seriousness, "but they need work."

"I was joking," protested Phyllis, again rolling her eyes. "You know"—she turned to Lucy—"he has absolutely no sense of humor."

"Oh, I do, believe me," said Ted. "How else do you think I manage to put up with you two?"

"Well, I'm outta here," said Lucy. "I'll leave you guys to your verbal sparring." She was at the door when the perfect headline came to her. "How about A Feast for the Season?"

When she reached the church, she was encouraged to see the parking lot was almost full, and when she stepped inside the kitchen, she was met with a wave of delicious odors and a cheerful bustling atmosphere. Rey was clearly in charge, passing out recipe cards and answering questions from cooks who were unfamiliar with the ingredients and techniques. Luisa was there, too, giving a hand.

"You're sure this sausage goes in the pumpkin soup?" asked Toni Williams, sounding very doubtful. "It's very spicy."

"That's chorizo. It's delicious," replied Rey.

"And how exactly do I cut this thing up?" asked Betsy Coolidge, holding up a mango as if it was a hand grenade about to go off.

"I'll show you," said Luisa, grabbing a paring knife. "It's going to make the most delicious mango salsa."

Lucy snapped a few photos of the volunteers, then approached Rey for a brief interview. "What's on the menu?"

"Oh, my goodness, everything but the kitchen sink," he said. "We'll start with chorizo pumpkin soup, move on to turkey tacos and enchiladas, roast stuffed pork, a variety of salsas, and for dessert, we'll have flan, bread pudding, and traditional pies like pumpkin and apple. How does that sound?"

"It sounds delicious," said Lucy. "Am I invited?"

"Everybody's invited," said Rey with a big smile. "It struck me, when I realized Matt wouldn't be able to come home for our family feast, that there are a lot of people who are in similar situations— people who've lost loved ones, people who are separated from their families by long distances, old folks who've outlived their friends. I thought it would be nice to do something for them, give them an opportunity to enjoy a delicious meal along with good fellowship. We'll even have some music and dancing afterwards so people can burn off some calories."

"That sounds great," said Lucy, who recognized herself in Rey's description. "You can count on me and Bill. The kids are all away this year and it's just the two of us."

"Great. I'll see you on Thanksgiving," Rey said, turning his attention to Angie DiBello who had a couple prickly pear paddles in her hands and a puzzled expression on her face.

Lucy didn't want to leave without saying hi to Pam, and spotted her and Rachel in a far corner of the large hall. The two were unpacking groceries from a number of cardboard boxes and arranging them on a long table where the cooks could find them.

"Thanks for coming, Lucy," said Pam, as Lucy approached them. "Time is short, Thanksgiving is fast approaching, and we need to get the word out so people will come."

"Look at all this food," said Rachel, setting two huge cloth bags of corn meal on the table. "Rey must have spent a fortune on this stuff."

"Where did it all come from?" asked Lucy, who knew that Marzetti's IGA did not carry prickly pears, Mexican chocolate, and chorizo, or many of the other items she saw on the table.

"He had it trucked in from some ethnic grocery in Portland," said Pam, who was looking worried. "I'm just afraid this is all going for naught. Who wants to eat roast pork on Thanksgiving? Or turkey tacos?"

"I do," said Lucy. "I'm pretty excited about trying some new foods."

"I suspect you might be alone in that," said Pam. "It's not Thanksgiving without turkey and stuffing and cranberry sauce."

"There's going to be cranberry salsa," said Rachel.

"Not the same thing at all," said Pam, checking the recipe card. "It's got hot peppers!"

"I'd like to come, but I'm not sure Bob and I will be welcome," said Rachel. "Bob's defending Link and Jason, you know."

"I didn't know," said Lucy, "but I'm sure you'll be welcome. Rey will understand. He knows how the system works. Everybody's entitled to legal representation whether they're innocent or guilty."

"That's the thing," said Rachel, lowering her voice to a whisper. "Link and Jason still insist they're innocent, that if it couldn't have been Hank DeVries, it's someone who looks a lot like him, but Bob's not buying it. He thinks they probably did it, but they didn't act alone. He suspects they were egged on by someone else to firebomb the pub, but they won't say who."

"That's not like Link," said Lucy, thinking that he and Jason may have grown up but were still behaving like naughty children, relying on the bully's tried and true tactic of blaming others for their own misdeeds.

"A lot of people are saying it was Rey himself," said Pam.

"No way," said Lucy. "I know for a fact that Rey wants to rebuild. He's hired an architect and he wants Bill to be the contractor. And look at this dinner. He wouldn't be doing all this if he wasn't sticking around. He wants to be part of the community."

"Bob thinks Zeke Bumpus was involved," said Rachel.

"There's a big difference between talking hate speech and committing hate crimes," said Pam.

"I heard someone say that it's not so much what people say as what people hear," said Lucy. "Maybe Jason and Link misconstrued something Zeke said."

"I don't think that gets him off the hook," said Rachel. "He still bears some responsibility."

"I wonder what Zeke's got to say about that," mused Lucy, planning to give him a call. But first she had to make her escape from the kitchen where her friends seemed to expect her to put down her notebook and camera and pick up a knife and a cutting board. "I wish I could stay and help"—she gave an apologetic shrug—"but I've got to take Bill to see the bone doctor today."

She made the call to Zeke while driving back home to pick up Bill.

As she expected, he vehemently denied any involvement in the firebombing.

"America for Americans is strictly nonviolent. We're sort of a National Association for the Advancement of White People, and we follow Dr. King's strategy of passive resistance."

Lucy found this claim hard to swallow. "But some of the statements you've made do seem to encourage violence. It seems pretty suspicious that the pub was firebombed after your anti-immigrant demonstration."

"America for Americans held a demonstration and put up a billboard, all activities that are protected by the Constitution. We didn't have anything to do with the explosion at the pub—no how, no way."

"But some folks might have taken your anti-immigrant rhetoric a step too far," said Lucy.

"Well, that's their problem, not mine. And what about folks like you, in the media?" he continued, challenging her. "Time after time I've seen my words twisted just so you guys can sell more newspapers."

Lucy knew this was an argument she couldn't win. Just as patriotism was said to be the last resort of scoundrels, blaming the media seemed to be their first, knee-jerk reaction. "So, for the record"— she spoke slowly and carefully—"you insist that America for Americans had nothing whatever to do with firebombing the old pub?"

"Absolutely not," said Zeke, "but I'll be amazed if you print that."

"Prepare to be amazed," said Lucy, ending the call as she reached the top of Red Top Road and turned into her driveway.

Bill was ready to go, waiting for her at the kitchen table where he'd been doing the word jumble in the morning paper. "Any idea what *c-l-e-t-t-e-u* could be?" he asked as he got to his feet.

"Lettuce," said Lucy, not missing a beat. "How's the arm?"

"Fine, thanks to the Vicodin, once it's in the sling, and I don't move it or bump it," said Bill.

Lucy knew he was putting on a brave front. She'd seen how badly bruised his arm and shoulder were, and how painful it was for him to get dressed and undressed. He couldn't wear anything that involved raising his arm, like a pull-on T-shirt or sweater, and instead chose shirts that buttoned. Even so, he couldn't shove his broken arm into a sleeve but had to carefully slide it on, inch by painful inch. Getting dressed was no longer a quick matter of automatically throwing on a few garments but was a slow process that left him white-faced and exhausted. He couldn't even tie his shoes and, too proud to ask for help, had switched to a pair of casual suede slip-ons.

"Well, we'll see what the doctor has to say," she said while he settled himself in the passenger seat and struggled to fasten the seatbelt with his good arm.

Coastal Orthopedics and Sports Medicine was housed in a modern office building that had only recently been built on the outskirts of town near the Winchester College campus. It took about fifteen minutes to drive there, and there was plenty of parking in the adjoining lot.

As she walked into the waiting room with Bill, Lucy was reminded of the many times she'd brought the kids to see Doc Ryder. The old family doctor was now retired, and Bill was her husband, not her child, but there was still a bit of that déjà vu feeling. She was on her way to the receptionist's desk to announce their arrival when Bill caught her by the wrist, signaling that he was fully capable of managing that business by himself. She took a seat, and he joined her in a few minutes, settling down on the next chair and watching CNN on the wall-mounted TV. When his name was called they both got up, but he gave her a little head shake, indicating that he would see the doctor by himself.

She waited for what seemed a very long time, flipping through tattered issues of *Real Simple,* and growing increasingly discouraged about the chaotic condition of her home, her finances, her health, and her wardrobe. After learning of the various options for simplifying her life by repackaging her liquid dish detergent in a variety of attractive containers she decided to abandon the quest for lifestyle improvement and looked up, glancing through the glass doors of the waiting room to the outer lobby. There, much to her surprise, she saw Jon and Eudora, along with Tag, coming through the outer doors. Curious as to what brought them to the professional building, she decided to head for the ladies room which was conveniently located in the lobby.

The three were standing together, waiting for

the elevator, and didn't notice her walking behind them and down the hall toward the ladies room. The elevator arrived and they stepped in, so Lucy quickly ducked into the nearby staircase. Reaching the landing to the next floor she peeked through the small window in the fire door and spotted the group walking down the hallway. She waited a few seconds, then stepped out and followed them, careful to remain some distance behind.

Unlike the first floor where the orthopedics practice took up the entire floor, the second floor was occupied by a number of smaller offices arranged on a long hallway. Placards on the doors identified a CPA, a lawyer, a dentist, and other professionals, none of whom seemed to be terribly busy this morning. The hallway was empty apart from Eudora and the two men with her; they had stopped in front of an office and Eudora was shaking her head, refusing to step through the door. Wishing to advance closer, Lucy pulled the notepaper on which she'd jotted down the time and place for Bill's appointment and studied it as if looking for the correct office. As she proceeded down the hallway, she made a show of checking the names on the doors against the paper in her hand. Approaching the trio, she heard Jon and Tag arguing, but when she passed them they lowered their voices and she couldn't catch the words.

She reached the end of the hallway where she turned and planned, if they noticed her, to say she must be on the wrong floor. That proved to be unnecessary, however, as Eudora suddenly exclaimed, "I'm not going in there!" and marched

off down the hall toward the elevator, arm in arm
with her son, Tag. Her husband Jon, looking quite
defeated, trailed behind them.

Lucy followed and saw them enter the elevator
together just as she reached the office that Eudora
had so vehemently refused to enter. She wasn't really surprised to see it was occupied by a psychiatrist.

Interesting, thought Lucy, hurrying down the
stairs in hopes of returning to the waiting room
before Bill's appointment was over. She was back
in her seat, watching CNN announce that the president had officially pardoned a turkey, sparing it
from certain death as the main course for someone's Thanksgiving dinner, when Bill appeared.

"How'd it go?" she asked.

"I got a prescription for more painkillers and an
appointment to come back in four weeks."

"No surgery? Not even a cast?" she asked.

"Nope. They took X-rays and the break is too
close to my shoulder for a cast. I'm supposed to
stick with the sling and start physical therapy in a
couple weeks." He paused. "The good news is that
my shoulder's not dislocated."

"What about all that bruising?" asked Lucy as
they left the waiting room and walked outside and
across the parking lot.

"Normal."

"And how long before you can go back to work?"
she asked.

"Six, maybe eight weeks."

"That's after Christmas." Dismayed, she opened
the car door for him. "How are we going to manage?"

"We'll manage somehow," he said, climbing into the passenger seat. "We always do. I can probably pick up some work at the hardware store. They'll need extra help with Christmas coming and I don't need two hands to help people find Christmas lights and coffeemakers."

Lucy did some calculations involving the checking account, the savings account, and their usual monthly expenses while she walked around the car and got in the driver's seat. It wasn't an encouraging exercise, but they weren't in any immediate danger of bankruptcy or foreclosure so she shoved her concerns to the back of her mind and started the car. "You'll never believe who I saw while you were with the doctor."

"Who? Santa Claus?"

"No. Eudora Clare, Ed Franklin's ex-wife, along with her son and present husband. It looked to me like they were taking her to see a psychiatrist, but she balked at the door and wouldn't go in."

"She does seem to have a screw loose," said Bill as they turned out of the parking area and onto the road.

"What's really interesting is that it was Jon, the husband, who was pushing her to see the psychiatrist, but it seemed like Tag, the son, seemed to side with her against Jon," said Lucy, thinking aloud as she drove. "A witness identified Hank as the arsonist, but when you think about it, Hank and Tag look a lot alike. It might have been Tag who blew up the pub. Maybe Ed planned the whole thing before he was killed and Tag followed through as a sort of final tribute to him. Or maybe he had some sort of cockeyed idea that Mireille was on the same page with Ed about Mexicans and blowing up the restaurant would please her and she'd share her child's inheritance with him."

They were passing a little inlet where a couple handsome old houses sat on the shoreline over-looking a million-dollar view of rocky seacoast when Bill challenged her.

"Where exactly did you see this little drama? The sports med is the only office on the first floor."

Lucy knew she'd said too much. "Uh, well, I saw them come in and, um, followed them upstairs."

"Are you crazy? You can't follow people around. What if they saw you?"

"I was going to pretend I was looking for an office and was on the wrong floor."

"And you think that would convince them? You suspect this guy is an arsonist, someone who's willing to hurt and possibly kill other people, and you think it's smart to follow him around?"

They'd passed the inlet and were passing stands of leafless trees and fields of drooping cornstalks.

"It wasn't like I was creeping around in the dark or something. I was in a professional building in broad daylight, well actually under bright fluorescent lights. There were no windows up there. It was a brightly lit hallway and I had every right to be there."

"Yeah, well, I had every right to go about my business in the pub and look at what happened to me," declared Bill.

"So you do think it might have been Tag?" asked Lucy, making the turn onto School Street.

"I don't know and I don't care," said Bill. "And I

want you to promise to stop this crazy nonsense and mind your own business. You should hear yourself. You sound as crazy as this Eudora woman."

"Well, this is my business," argued Lucy, braking for the stop sign at the bottom of Red Top Road. "When you got blown up it became my business."

"Stop. Stop the car," ordered Bill.

"Why? Do you think you can drive one-armed?"

"I'm not driving, I'm getting out. I'll walk from here."

"That's crazy," said Lucy, beginning the climb up the hill.

"I mean it. Stop the car."

"Okay, okay," she grumbled, pulling off to the side of the road.

She turned, giving him a questioning look, but he didn't notice.

He had already shoved the door open and was getting out. Then he shut the door hard without looking at her and marched off, striding up the hill without a backwards glance.

If only *Real Simple* had had an article advising how to have a productive argument with your husband, she thought, watching as he strode along, clearly driven by anger.

She made a three-point turn and headed for the office, aware that it wasn't only his arm that was injured in the blast, but also his pride. She knew she'd handled things badly. He'd given her clear signals that he didn't want to be mothered or babied, and that he would take responsibility for his injuries and for the family's welfare, too. By the time she reached the office she'd resolved to be more tactful in the future . . . and to keep her investigative reporting activities to herself until it was time to break the story in the *Pennysaver*.

When she got to the office, Phyllis greeted her with a stack of press releases to be entered in the listings, and Ted informed her that he'd sent her story about the selectmen's meeting back to her for a rewrite, so she knew she'd be working late. That was actually fine with her since she was in no hurry to go home and face Mister High and Mighty Grumpy Pants. If he was so darn independent, he could zap a frozen mini-pizza for himself. She was pretty sure he wouldn't need two arms for that little chore.

When she sat down at her desk she found a press release from the DA announcing that the state crime lab had found no trace of any opiates in Alison Franklin's body and therefore her death from drowning was considered accidental and the case was officially closed. There was also a voice mail from Mimsy, asking Lucy to give her a call as soon as possible, as it was a bit of an emergency. Lucy's curiosity was piqued, wondering if the call was a reaction to the news about Alison, and she returned the call immediately. The phone rang numerous times before it was answered.

"Sorry, I was stuck in a closet," said Mimsy, sounding rather breathless. "Mireille got a bee in her bonnet about getting the house ready for the Realtor and she's had me clearing out all sorts of junk."

"Maybe it's that nesting thing," said Lucy. "I bet she'll go into labor any minute."

"I can only hope," said Mimsy with a sigh. "She's

working me ragged, and she's got me worried, too. You know she fired the bodyguards and I'm terrified for her safety, especially since I found"—she paused and dropped her voice to a whisper—"I found committal papers that Jon sent to Ed. He wanted to have Eudora committed and wanted information from Ed about their marriage. He specifically wanted to know about any incidents of violent behavior." Again she paused. "What if she goes after Mireille?"

"What do you mean? Do you really think Eudora is prone to violence?"

"It's not what *I* think. It's what her husband thinks. And Eudora's made it very clear that she hates Mireille."

Lucy thought about this and had to admit Mimsy had a point if Eudora truly was an unhinged psychopath. Lucy wasn't convinced that was the case. True, she'd witnessed Eudora refusing to see a psychiatrist, but that didn't mean she was a danger to herself or others. As her friend Rachel often said, mental health was a continuum, and people moved through various periods of stability and instability throughout their lives, but that didn't mean they were crazy. Eudora had clearly been through a lot, and she might very well be close to a breakdown, but her husband seemed to be dealing with the situation. He was clearly in contact with a psychiatrist and even if Eudora wasn't ready to cooperate was probably getting sound professional advice.

"I don't think you have anything to worry about," said Lucy, recalling her encounter with Eudora at the turkey farm. Then she'd seemed on the verge of hysteria, understandably shaken by the dual loss of her ex-husband and daughter. "Eudora is a small, slight middle-aged woman. If anything, she seems to be struggling with her emotions. Grief takes people differently. It's terrible to lose loved ones, even if you're estranged. Sometimes that makes it worse."

"I don't buy that," said Mimsy. "Eudora might look fragile, but she's been absolutely horrible to Mireille. She blames her for losing Ed. And remember, it doesn't take a lot of muscle to pull a trigger." Mimsy sighed. "I thought you'd be able to help me. That's why I called. I don't really know anybody but you in this stinky little town and I thought maybe you could talk some sense into Mireille."

Lucy sensed Ted looming over her and when she looked up, he handed her a freshly issued brochure from the state outlining new hunting regulations. A yellow sticky note had been attached to the front cover, on which the words *summarize this* were written in his neat block print.

"I've really got to get back to work," said Lucy, "and I don't see how I can help you. Mireille's all grown up. She seems quite capable of taking care of herself and her baby. If you're really worried about Eudora, I think you should share this information with the police."

"From what I've seen so far, they're a pretty useless bunch," said Mimsy.

Ted hadn't budged. He was still standing behind her chair.

"Well, that's all I can suggest," said Lucy. "Thanks for calling. I'll keep this information in mind." She hung up and turned to face him. "So what do you want now?" she demanded.

"I just wanted to tell you that Rey Rodriguez

dropped off some apple cider and donuts. The cider's in the fridge and the donuts are by the coffee pot."

"Oh," said Lucy, somewhat deflated. "Thanks. I could use a donut."

Her emotions were in turmoil as she ate three donuts in quick succession and gulped down at least a pint of apple cider. She didn't really taste any of it as she tried to rationalize the way she brushed off poor Mimsy. She felt horribly guilty, but told herself that Mimsy and Mireille's problems weren't her problems. She had plenty of her own, the most pressing of which was the pile of work that was sitting on her desk. That wasn't all, however. Bill was languishing at home, not only coping with considerable pain but also depression about his inability to work. It didn't help matters that they'd parted the way they did, with him stomping off in an angry huff.

It was bad enough that she was swamped at work, but knowing that Bill was mad at her made her feel completely overwhelmed. She didn't have time for self-pity, she told herself. All she could spare was a nod and a prayer. The nod was an acknowledgement of the whole messy situation—the deaths, the grieving families, the accusations against Matt Rodriguez, the simmering intolerance that had suddenly flared up in the little town, and Bill's injuries. The prayer was for help and guidance in seeing her own way through, for justice to be done, and for everyone involved to find peace and healing.

Even so, she couldn't forget the terrible morning when she'd discovered Alison's body and the whole mess began. No matter how hard she tried, she couldn't seem to erase the image of the lovely girl's drowned body and the streaming hair that floated around her bluish face in the freezing water. That popped into her mind with disturbing frequency. If only she could remember some clue, some bit of information she missed, that would shed light on Alison's death.

What could possibly have prompted Alison to venture out on thin ice? She wasn't a child. She was an intelligent young adult familiar with seasonal changes and she certainly would have known the danger. There must have been some reason, some very strong reason that caused her to disregard her own safety and go out onto the thin ice.

She wondered if Alison might have spotted a dog that was in trouble, or even a wild animal like a deer. It was heartrending to witness an animal struggling for survival and Lucy knew from her own experience that it was almost impossible to resist the impulse to help, even when you knew it could be life threatening. She had once seen a mother doe and her fawn stranded on a chunk of floating ice in the pond and had felt terrible about leaving them to their fate, even though she knew there was nothing she could do that wouldn't endanger her and possibly leave her own family motherless.

On impulse she hurried back to her desk and put in a call to her friend, Barney Culpepper, who had been one of the first police officers to respond to her call that awful morning.

"Barney, I was just wondering. Did you see anything the morning that Alison Franklin drowned that might explain why she went out on the ice? We just got a press release from the DA that says they didn't find any trace of drugs."

"Sorry, Lucy," he replied in a mournful tone. "I keep worrying about that myself. I can't seem to put that pretty young thing's face out of my mind."

"I think maybe she saw a dog or a deer that got in trouble."

"Could be, Lucy. It seems something like that happens every year. Some do-gooder tries to help and falls through. And half the time, the animal manages to save itself and is just fine. The stupid dog gets itself back on shore, gives a good shake, and wants to go home for a good meal."

"But did you see any sign of anything like that?"

"Nope. But that doesn't mean it didn't happen that way," said Barney. "That's most likely what happened. It's the only thing that makes any sense to me."

"Me, too," said Lucy, reaching for the booklet of revised hunting regulations. Flipping it open to the first page, she saw a bold red headline advising hunters to hunt safely. First on the list of dangers to watch for was thin ice.

Chapter Twenty

Thanksgiving Day dawned bright and clear, but with a cool breeze that made it perfect weather for running. Bill's temper had eventually cooled, helped by a Skype session with his grandson Patrick in Alaska and his favorite supper of meatloaf and mashed potatoes.

Both he and Lucy were in high spirits as they parked the car alongside the town common and joined the crowd of people gathered around the registration table for the 5K race. Everyone was talking about the cornucopia on the bandstand, which was already full to overflowing with donated food for the Food Pantry. Bill had volunteered to help collect the canned goods that were the entry fee for the race, along with a nominal $10 fee, but since he had to work with only one hand he was assigned instead to distributing the highly coveted Turkey Trot T-shirts. Many of the competitors were wearing shirts from previous years. Each featured the cartoon running turkey and the year in big, bold numbers. The older the shirt, the greater the prestige.

After signing in and receiving her T-shirt, Lucy pulled it on over her running togs and got busy stretching out her muscles. She didn't have any real hope of winning the race, especially since her training had been so spotty, but as she checked out the other runners who were also busy warming up, she realized that there were very few in her age category. Most women her age, she figured, were much too busy this morning getting their turkeys stuffed and in the oven to even think of running in the race. Maybe, she thought as her competitive spirit rose, she might actually have a chance of placing and getting a medal. It was certainly worth a try. Vowing to give the race every bit of energy she could, she joined the other runners assembling behind the starting line. She noticed lots of familiar faces, including Phyllis's husband Wilf, several of Dot Kirwan's kids, and even Roger Wilcox, chairman of the board of selectmen.

Rev. Marge offered a short prayer and announced that this years' donations for the Food Pantry had topped all previous records. Then she raised the starting gun, said the traditional "Ready, Set," and pulled the trigger.

They were off. Runners who had placed in previous years' races got the best positions just behind the starting line, and they led the pack. Others, like Lucy, had to wait a bit before they even reached the starting line. As she shuffled along, Lucy pictured the route in her mind, picturing the race

course. The route was clearly signed and led from
the town common along Parallel Street with its antique sea captain's homes, then gradually climbed
up to Shore Road. There the route passed roomy
shingle-style summer cottages and newer McMan-
sions and offered beautiful views of the bay dotted
with rocky, pine-covered islands and bound by
Quissett Point in the distance. The course then
turned at the gate to Pine Point, the Van Vorst estate, and continued along a pine needle strewn path
through the woodsy Audubon sanctuary, emerging onto Church Street by the old cemetery and
continuing down Main Street to Sea Street, where
the runners descended to reach the finish line in
the harbor.

Lucy was trapped in a crowd of runners when
she reached the starting line where she gave a
wave to the cheering crowd of onlookers and
jogged along with the group. The pack of runners
began to thin out as they proceeded alongside the
town common and Lucy could finally begin running. The race attracted runners and walkers of
various levels of fitness. Some were keen competitors who raced regularly, while others were simply
out for a pleasant bit of exercise that also happened to benefit a good cause. That meant that
the pack stretched out for some distance along the
course, with the dedicated competitors far out in
front of the rest, followed by slower runners and finally, the walkers bringing up the rear.

Reaching Parallel Street, Lucy found her rhythm
and began passing the slower walkers and joggers.
The running became automatic. The steady *thump-
thump* of her running shoes hitting the asphalt be-

came a kind of background music, and her mind began to wander as she left Parallel Street and began the climb up Shore Road.

There, the air seemed to thin and a brisk ocean breeze refreshed and cooled her heated body. The sky and ocean were deep blue, a few oak trees still held on to rattling russet leaves, and dark green pointed firs stood sentinel on the rocky coast. The handsome homes that lined the road, most only occupied during the summer, had interesting architectural features that captured her imagination. Here a spacious porch where the railing was dotted with drying beach towels all summer long, there a tall tower where a telescope could be seen in the window, pointing out to the sea below.

Approaching the Franklin mansion, Lucy was struck once again by its enormous size. It almost seemed terribly foolish, perhaps even tempting fate, to build such a grand house. A house was meant to shelter its inhabitants, and this house had clearly failed. Ed was dead, so was his daughter Alison, and now his pregnant wife couldn't wait to leave.

A water station had been set up in the mansion's driveway and Lucy grabbed a paper cup, slowing slightly to swig a few gulps before discarding the cup in one of the barrels set out for the purpose. Something about the house caught her fancy. She thought the large, hulking edifice looked a bit like Ed Franklin himself. There was something unsettling about it, just as there had been about the man. Something a bit off-kilter or out of proportion. Something not right. And then she saw a young woman with long blond hair stepping out of the house and she stopped in her tracks, certain it was Alison.

It wasn't, of course. She realized immediately it was one of the volunteers bringing a fresh pack of paper cups out to the water station. Lucy shook her head, trying to clear her mind as she resumed running, but she couldn't get that easy rhythm back. Once again, the image she couldn't seem to shake, the vision that kept reappearing—Alison's white face and long, swirling hair just beneath the surface of the water—came back to haunt her. What on earth possessed the girl to go out on that ice?

That was the question that bedeviled Lucy. It was such a foolish, dangerous thing to do. Why did Alison do it?

Lucy was running more steadily as she approached the gates at Pine Point. The *thump-thump* had become a *why-why, why-why*. And suddenly, clear as day, she remembered doing something remarkably similar. Something so foolish and risky, she could hardly believe she'd done it.

"My bag! I dropped my bag!"

Lucy heard the panic in the voice, and she quickly stooped down and grabbed the bag off the tracks moments before the train came thundering into the station.

She could still hear the frantic urgency, and the memory of that close call was so strong that it took her breath away and squeezed her heart, stopping it for a moment. The pain was excruciating, piercing, and then it began to ease.

She was running. She was running again and she was certain she knew who had sent Alison onto the ice.

But what about Ed Franklin? Did the same person kill Ed? It was possible, she thought, even likely. As Mimsy had pointed out, it didn't take a lot to pull a trigger, especially if you were gripped by a powerful emotion. Cops who feared for their lives shot unarmed people. It seemed to happen all the time. Gang members who'd been dissed took their revenge on city streets, often missing their intended targets and killing innocent bystanders. Lost souls were recruited by terrorist organizations and turned into lethal killers, and mentally unstable people heard voices that urged them to kill. Even love could sour and turn to murderous hate, as children rose up and killed parents or spouses took advantage of intimacy to pull a gun from beneath the pillow.

By the time she reached Church Street and the turn back toward town, Lucy found herself practically alone. She could see the backs of the elite runners ahead of her, but they were some distance away, and she knew that most of the others were behind her. She decided to try to catch up to the leading group of runners as she approached the ancient cemetery where former citizens of Tinker's Cove were presumably resting in peace beneath lichen-covered tombstones that leaned this way and that.

She turned to catch a glimpse of a favorite grave marker, a Victorian angel that bowed sadly over little Rose Williams, barely three years old when she died in 1854, but couldn't make it out as a flash of bright sunlight momentarily blinded her. Curious, she slowed. As her vision cleared and the angel came into view, she realized to her horror that the blinding flash had not come from the sun but came instead from a huge carving knife. That knife was held in Eudora Clare's hand and she was brandishing it wildly over Mireille's prone and struggling body.

Momentarily at a loss, Lucy didn't know what to do. She was alone, she was tired and out of breath, and she didn't have a weapon of any sort. She did hear the runners approaching from behind, however, and thinking quickly, grabbed one of the signs marking the course and turned it so it pointed to the road leading into the cemetery. Then she raced to intervene, praying that the other runners would be deceived and follow her into the grave-yard.

As she drew closer to the statue of the hovering angel, she realized that Mireille had been trussed up with duct tape and was lying on her back on a raised stone grave, twisting from side to side in a tremendous effort to avoid Eudora's knife thrusts. Lucy could hear Eudora's voice cooing like a de-mented mourning dove, admonishing Mireille to lie still.

"It won't hurt a bit and will be over in a minute." Eudora aimed the knife for Mireille's dome of baby belly. "Won't hurt a bit. Not a bit," she crooned over and over as she brandished the knife. "You took them all, my Ed and my little Alison, and now you have to give me your baby." The knife con-nected with Mireille's breast, slitting her shirt. "It's not your baby." Eudora shook her head sadly and thrust the knife yet again, slashing Mireille's upper arm which began to bleed. "It's my baby. My baby."

Lucy realized with horror that the unbelievable

was actually happening. Eudora was attempting to cut Mireille's baby from her body.

"You can't do that! Stop! Stop!" Lucy yelled, leaping over gravestones and throwing herself at Eudora, attempting to knock the knife from her hand.

Eudora wouldn't let go, even though Lucy had grabbed her arm with both hands, desperately trying to pry the knife from her grip. She was surprisingly strong, and Lucy found she had a tiger by the tail. She had to hang on for dear life. She couldn't use her hand to punch or strike the crazed woman for fear Eudora would slash or stab her. She tried to use her feet, kicking at Eudora's shins in an attempt to knock the woman down, but Eudora was able to dodge her running shoes.

Lucy found herself weakening, tired from the race and the struggle. Her hands were slipping and she knew it was now or never. She had to gain control of Eudora. She took a deep breath and using both hands, forced Eudora's arm upward, then threw herself at the woman, knocking her down on the ground. Lucy was in an awkward position, and although she had pinned Eudora beneath her, she was stuck on top of the struggling woman. She was beginning to doubt she could continue to restrain her when the first of the pack of runners arrived, feet pounding, and yelling.

Eudora quickly dropped the knife and began screaming, claiming Lucy was trying to kill her.

"What's going on here?" inquired Roger Wilcox, giving Lucy a hand and helping her to her feet.

Wilf Lundgren did the same for Eudora, careful to place his substantial bulk between the two combatants.

"She attacked me," claimed Eudora, pointing at Lucy. "She tried to kill me with that knife!"

Her claim was quickly rebutted as Lily Kirwan, who was studying to be an EMT, pulled the duct tape off Mireille's mouth.

"Don't believe her!" Mireille cried. "Lucy saved me! Eudora was trying to take my baby!"

Hearing this there was a general gasp of horror, which gave Eudora a chance to attempt to dart away. She was stopped by the quick action of Wilf, who grabbed her arm and held her tight.

"Nobody's going anywhere till this is sorted out," he said as a siren was heard in the distance.

Lucy wanted to go to Mireille, but felt that since she'd been accused, she had to wait for the police. She had to be content to let Lily and a few of the runners attend to Mireille, comforting her, stripping off the duct tape, and bandaging her bleeding arm in fourteen-year-old Finn Thaw's T-shirt, which he had pulled off. Lucy was also concerned about keeping an eye on the knife, which was still lying on the ground, and keeping a wary eye on Eudora, who had given up struggling and stood silently in place with a sulky expression on her face.

The wailing siren grew closer, bringing Barney Culpepper to the scene in a squad car. He surveyed the scene, taking it all in. He saw Mireille sitting on the grave, accompanied by a handful of caregivers, her arm wrapped in a blood-stained cotton T-shirt with a pile of duct tape neatly arranged beside her. He saw the knife on the ground and collected it as evidence. He examined Eudora, noting the spatters of blood on her hands.

Finally, he turned to Lucy. "What's going on here? Some of the runners reported a scuffle at the cemetery."

"I was running in the race and I saw Eudora in the cemetery, flashing a knife. She had tied up Mireille and was trying to cut the baby from her body. She kept saying 'It's my baby,' over and over. I tried to stop her. I tried to get the knife."

"That's right," said Roger. "When I arrived, Lucy had tackled Eudora and was struggling with her on the ground."

"Lucy saved my life," said Mireille.

Barney nodded and produced handcuffs, which set Eudora into a fit of hysterics.

"They're lying. They're all lying," she screamed, twisting free of Wilf's grip and starting to dart away, but running instead right into Finn Thaw's wiry young body. A member of the high school JV wrestling team, he wrapped his arms around her, pinning her arms to her sides and restraining her until Barney applied the handcuffs.

They were all watching him escort a protesting Eudora to the squad car, when Mireille suddenly moaned.

"I'm in labor," she said, panting and clutching her stomach. "I've got to get to the hospital!"

Nobody could talk about anything else at Rey's Mexican Thanksgiving Dinner, which had attracted a huge crowd that somehow managed to squeeze into the basement hall at the Community Church as evening fell.

"There's plenty of food, plenty of food for everyone," Rey said, busy ladling out bowls of spicy pumpkin soup and piling plates with turkey burritos, roast pork, and plenty of cranberry salsa.

Lucy had signed up to help serve at the dinner, but he had insisted that she should sit this one out, considering her heroic actions that morning. She and Bill were seated at one of the long tables, along with Miss Tilley, Rachel and Bob Goodman, and Miss Tilley's best friend, Rebecca Wardwell. Rebecca was almost as old as Miss Tilley, and was rumored to be a witch, but that was probably only because she kept a tiny owl as a pet.

"Well, as usual, Lucy, you seem to have been up to your shenanigans," said Miss Tilley, digging into her burrito with gusto.

"Honestly, I was just running when I saw Eudora raising that knife. If it hadn't been for the beam of sunlight that hit it, I never would have seen a thing."

"A higher force was at work," said Rebecca, taking a bite of a turkey taco.

"Talk about crazy," said Rachel, stirring her soup. "That woman was completely round the bend."

"What about your famous continuum?" asked Lucy. "You know, how our mental states fall along a continuum throughout our lives, sometimes more balanced and sometimes less."

"I can say with confidence that Eudora fell off the continuum," said Rachel with a nod. "Absolutely loony-tunes, completely crazy, psychopathic, out of her mind."

"Evil. She was possessed by the evil one," said Rebecca, sounding like someone who had first-hand knowledge of the demonic, and had the battle scars to prove it.

"Well, whatever you want to call it, we're all a lot better off now that she's in jail, along with her son."

"What I don't understand," said Miss Tilley, scooping up cranberry salsa, "is why her family didn't take care of her. At the very least, she should have been under the care of a psychiatrist, perhaps even confined."

"They tried," said Lucy. "Her husband tried to enlist Ed Franklin and Alison to commit her, but Eudora found out. That's what began her murder spree. First Alison, who she somehow managed to lure onto the ice—"

"Whoa there," said Bob. "Where'd you get that idea?"

"It came to me while I was running. I remembered how my mother had dropped her purse on a train track and I foolishly grabbed it for her just as the train arrived. I would never have done such a stupid thing except it was for my mother, and she was so upset about losing her bag." Lucy paused. "It's amazing, the things you'll do for your mother— especially if you feel guilty about something."

"Alison probably felt guilty about leaving her mother's house and moving in with Ed and Mireille," said Rachel.

"That is exactly why Eudora wanted to kill her," added Lucy. "If she couldn't have Alison, she certainly wasn't going to let Ed have her."

"But why wasn't killing Alison enough?" asked Bill.

"Mimsy said she found a letter from Jon to Ed asking him for help committing Eudora," said Lucy. "That's why Eudora killed Ed. She shot him while he was sitting in his car, supposedly waiting for Tag. Ironically, she used a gun which he had given her so she could protect herself. According to Barney, she confessed everything, even hiding the gun at the old pub to cast suspicion on Matt.. She was quite proud of herself.. And, believe it or not, she fingered her own son, Tag, for the fire-bombing. She said it was her idea . . . to divert attention from the murders of Alison and Ed."

"But what about Mireille? Did Eudora really think she could perform an al fresco caesarean?" asked Bill. "And how did she manage to truss up Mireille? She's a healthy young woman, even if she is pregnant."

"Eudora said she found Mireille sitting on that raised slab chatting with Ed's spirit, and she conked her on the head, then wrapped her up in duct tape."

"But what was Eudora thinking?" demanded Bob. "You can't carve a fetus out of a woman's body and expect it to live."

"It's hard to know what Eudora was thinking," said Lucy. "Maybe she did want the baby. Maybe she did believe that Mireille stole Alison and Ed from her, but there's also the fact that Ed's will left his entire estate to his children, which meant that Mireille's baby will get it all. Maybe Eudora wanted the baby in order to get the money or maybe she just wanted it out of the way."

"Quite extraordinary," said Miss Tilley, who had moved on to a large helping of refried beans.

"The one who puzzles me is Tag," said Bill.

"He's smart and good looking. He's well-educated and has great connections. Why did he risk it all by firebombing the restaurant?"

"An Oedipus complex?" suggested Rachel. "To please his mother?"

"Probably, plus he might well be a bigot like Ed," suggested Bob. "And it could be he wanted to gain some cred with the America for Americans crowd."

"Maybe he's every bit as crazy as his mother," suggested Lucy.

"The evil one at work, again," said Rebecca with a sigh.

"Well, all's well that ends well," said Bill. "Mireille's in good hands in the hospital—"

He was interrupted by Rey, who was tapping a glass tumbler with a spoon and beaming.

"I have good news to report: Mireille has given birth to a healthy little boy."

Both Miss Tilley's and Rebecca's faces fell at this news, and they shared a look.

"A girl would have been so much nicer," whispered Rebecca.

"I have it here, eight pounds, fourteen ounces, and twenty-one inches long."

This news was met with great applause and a few cheers.

"And his name is Lucas," Rey added.

"Lucas," repeated Bill. "I think he's named after you, Lucy."

Hearing this, Lucy blushed. "I'm sure she just liked the name," she said.

"Let's all raise a glass to Lucas," said Rey. "May he have a long and happy life."

"To Lucas," they all said, standing and clinking glasses.

"And also, I'm happy to announce that my son Matt will soon be joining me and managing our new restaurant, Cali Kitchen, which my friend Bill Stone is building. Construction will begin immediately and Cali Kitchen will be open in time for the summer season."

This news was greeted with wild applause and a few whistles.

When the crowd quieted down, Rey approached Lucy and Bill's table.

"How do you like the food?" he asked.

"Delicious," said Lucy.

"Really good," said Bob.

"Terrific," said Rachel.

"And what about you, Miss Tilley?" asked Rey.

"Well . . ." she began. "Personally I prefer roast turkey, stuffing, and giblet gravy . . . but I think I could manage a bit more of that spicy cranberry salsa. And, oh dear, don't tell me the burritos are all gone?"

"For you," said Rey as they all laughed, "I will make some more."

Lucy's energy began to flag when dessert was served, but she wasn't about to miss tasting the pumpkin flan that everyone was raving about. She was clearly exhausted, however, and Bob drove her and Bill home in Lucy's SUV, followed by Rachel in their Volvo. The familiar route took them past the town green where Zeke Bumpus and the America for Americans group were scheduled to hold their much-publicized demonstration demanding tougher immigration policies.

"Where's the demonstration?" asked Lucy as they passed the green where Zeke stood entirely alone, draped in an American flag and holding an AMERICA FOR AMERICANS placard.

"I think they're all over at the church, eating Rey's Mexican Thanksgiving Dinner," said Bob, and they all laughed.

Much has happened since Leslie Meier first intro-duced her beloved sleuth Lucy Stone with Mistletoe Murder. *Many holidays and bake sales have come and gone, Lucy's children have all grown up. But even after twenty-four books into the bestselling series, murder is never out of the picture . . .*

As Tinker's Cove, Maine, buzzes over a town-wide silver wedding anniversary bash, Lucy is reminded of her nuptials and ponders the where-abouts of Beth Gerard, her strong-willed maid of honor. Lucy never would have made it down the aisle without Beth's help, and although the two friends lost touch over the years, she decides to reach out. It only takes one phone call for Lucy to realize that a reunion will happen sooner than later—at Beth's funeral.

Beth, who was in the process of finalizing her fourth divorce, had a reputation for living on the edge—but no one can believe she would jump off a penthouse terrace in New York City. The more Lucy learns about Beth's former husbands, the more she suspects one of them committed murder.

Summoning her friend's impulsive spirit, Lucy vows to scour New York from the Bronx to the Brooklyn Bridge in search of the killer. With each ex dodgier than the last, it's not long before Lucy's investigation leads her to a desperate criminal who will do anything to get away—even if it means si-lencing another victim . . .

Please turn the page for an exciting sneak peek of Leslie Meier's SILVER ANNIVERSARY MURDER now on sale wherever print and e-books are sold!

Chapter One

"Honestly, I'm surprised he hasn't killed her," whispered Harry Nuttall, leaning over the deli counter at the IGA in Tinker's Cove, Maine. He was speaking to one of his regular customers, Lucy Stone, who was doing her weekly grocery shopping.

Lucy was a part-time reporter for the *Pennysaver*, the local weekly newspaper, and had developed the habit of shopping after the paper's Wednesday noon deadline, taking advantage of the free afternoon, which also happened to be a time when the usually crowded supermarket had few customers.

"So is it the usual?" Harry pulled on a fresh pair of plastic gloves. "A pound of ham, sliced thin, and a half of Swiss?"

"I guess I'll live dangerously," said Lucy, turning to watch Warren Bickford, Harry's potential murderer, presenting his wife and likely murder vic-

tim, Sylvia, with his wrapped cold cuts. Then remembering the task at hand, she turned back to
Harry. "Throw in a half pound of turkey breast,
too."

"Do you want it sliced like the ham?" asked Harry.
Lucy's attention had returned to the Bickfords;
Warren's deli purchase had clearly not satisfied
Sylvia. She glared at the label on the package
through heavily made-up eyes, ran her red-tipped
nails through her obviously bleached blond hair,
pointed at the label, then roughly thrust the
packet back to Warren. "Black Forest, Warren. I
told you Black Forest! Honestly, how many times
do I have to repeat myself?"

Warren bent his head and seemed to offer an
apology, then trotted obediently back to the deli
counter.

"Same thickness as the ham?" Harry asked
again, the grin on his face revealing his amusement at Lucy's fascination with the Bickfords.

Lucy considered asking him to slice the turkey a
bit thicker than the ham, but aware that Warren
was under the gun to deliver the correct order,
changed her mind. "Same," she said, turning to
give Warren a big, warm smile. It seemed the least
she could do for the poor, henpecked husband.
"Nice day," she said, referring to the lovely, mild,
May weather that was such a treat after the bitter
cold Maine winter, which this year had been followed by an especially blustery March and extremely muddy April.

"Sure is," replied Warren, unzipping his jacket.
Lucy guessed he was in his early fifties, and like
most middle-aged men in Tinker's Cove, he was

wearing khaki pants and a sports shirt topped with a light sweater. His thinning hair was combed in the standard left-parted barbershop cut and he was developing a bit of a paunch. That growing tummy was probably the result of an occupational hazard; as owner and operator of a limo service he spent a lot of time sitting behind the wheel. "Sorry to bother you, Harry, but I got the wrong ham. I should've asked for Black Forest. I hope it's no problem."

"No problem," said Harry, placing Lucy's three packages on the counter. "It's already wrapped. I'll save it for the next customer who wants Virginia ham."

Warren let out a relieved sigh. "Thanks, Harry." It seemed he was about to say something more, perhaps a reference to his wife, but thought better of it and bit his lip instead, rocking slightly from one sturdy Timberland shoe to the other while waiting for Harry to slice his Black Forest ham.

Lucy put her packages in her cart and pushed it along, heading for the meat counter, which ran along the back wall of the supermarket. She paused at an island displaying English muffins—buy one get two free, a deal that was hard to pass up—and witnessed Warren rejoining his wife and presenting the correct ham, rather like a little girl offering flowers to the queen.

"Warren, you always do this. You don't speak up and people take advantage of you. Just look—this ham is sliced much too thick. Not that I blame Harry. He isn't going to shove that slicer back and forth any more times than he has to, if people don't speak up and ask for thin slices."

Warren stood like a statue, letting his wife's crit-icisms rain down on him. "Do you want me to take it back, *dear*?" he asked, with the slightest note of sarcasm in his voice.

Sylvia expelled a large sigh. "No, Warren. We don't have time. We have a big order this week." She flourished her shopping list. "Do you think you could manage a simple task like getting the coffee while I look over the meat? Beef chuck is supposed to be on sale, but I'll be amazed if they have any left this late in the week. They probably sold it all on the weekend. Not that they'll get away with it, not with me. I'll insist on a rain check."

"You do that, dear," said Warren. "Quite right. Now, do you want decaf or regular, and what brand? Or should I go for price?"

"It never ceases to amaze me, Warren. How long have we been married? Twenty-five years next month, and you don't know what brand of coffee we drink?"

"Well, it's usually the one in the red package, but sometimes it seems to me we have the blue kind."

"*The red kind? The blue kind?* Honestly, Warren, you sound like a child." She rolled her eyes. "Get the Folgers, unless Maxwell House is on sale for half price. And don't fall for that foul French roast stuff. Can you do that for me?"

"Yes, dear." Warren trotted off in the direction of the coffee aisle, and Sylvia, as promised, attacked the meat counter. Lucy, hoping to avoid witnessing any more of Warren's humiliations, slipped off into the cereal aisle. Distracted by a special on canned soups on the end cap, where she was searching for chicken noodle but only finding minestrone and vegetarian vegetable, she wasn't quick enough to miss Warren's presentation of a green can of coffee.

"Green is decaf, Warren; everybody knows that," declared Sylvia, in a voice that could probably be heard on Metinnicut Island, ten miles across the bay.

"But it's Folgers, like you said." He attempted a weak defense. "They could have changed the package, you know."

"No, Warren, they haven't changed it." Sylvia paused to sniff a cello-wrapped piece of chuck, then replaced it. "Now, take this back and get the red Folgers. And do hurry. We've got a lot to do and I'm going to have the butcher cut me a fresh piece of chuck. The nose knows—you can't fool my nose. This meat has probably been sitting out here since Sunday."

"Right, dear," said Warren, obediently hurrying back to the coffee section to complete his assignment. Watching him go, Lucy thought Harry might have a point. Some day, maybe some day soon, Warren was bound to snap.

Diverting as that thought was, Lucy had a long shopping list that demanded great concentration as she frequently consulted the weekly ad for specials, checked prices, and thumbed through her coupon file. From time to time she heard Sylvia's strident voice berating Warren for something or other, but she didn't actually encounter the Bickfords again until she reached the checkout counter.

Warren was busy bagging their order when Dot Kirwan, the cashier, announced the amount due.

"A hundred and forty-seven dollars!" exclaimed Sylvia. "We don't want to buy the store, do we, Warren? We just want to eat for a week."

"Should we put this back, dear?" suggested Warren, who was holding a large bottle of expensive olive oil. "We could get a smaller one."

Sylvia shook her head. "The larger one is a better value, Warren. You ought to know that. It's cheaper per ounce. Now pay the bill and stop grumbling."

"Yes, dear," said Warren, pulling his wallet out of his back pocket and handing a credit card to Dot.

"Let me see that!" demanded Sylvia, snatching the card out of Dot's hand. "Just as I thought. It's the wrong card!"

Dot's eyes met Lucy's, and they both struggled to maintain neutral facial expressions while Warren fumbled with his wallet. The two women were of like minds and Lucy had great respect for Dot, who was the widowed matriarch of a large family. Most of her kids and grandkids worked for the town, filling positions in the fire and police departments, which made Dot a valuable source of inside knowledge for Lucy.

"Oh, give me that wallet!" demanded Sylvia, losing patience. He obliged and she flipped it open, pulling out a wad of plastic cards. "My word! What is all this? Exxon, Sears, Shell, Visa, Plenti . . . Ah, finally! This is the one that gives us rewards, Warren." She waved the colorful bit of plastic underneath his nose. "Only use this one, from now on, only this one. You don't need the rest. You might as well cut them up and throw them away."

"I'll do that, dear," said Warren, who had continued packing the groceries and was holding the disputed can of Folgers coffee.

"Just slide the card on the keypad," urged Dot, and Sylvia complied, signing with a flourish. Warren carefully placed a plastic bag containing their eggs on the child seat and pushed the cart toward the door, followed by Sylvia, who was checking the register tape as she walked.

"Thank you and have a nice day," said Dot. Unable to stifle her laughter any longer, she burst into a fit of giggles. "I call them the Bickersons," she whispered to Lucy, as the automatic door opened and the Bickfords exited the store.

Lucy felt a certain sympathy for Sylvia as Dot finished ringing up her order, which amounted to nearly two hundred dollars despite her coupon clipping. Sylvia was right about one thing, she decided, as she pushed her heavily loaded cart out to the parking lot, and that was the price of groceries. The sun this afternoon was very bright, and she paused in the shady overhang to put on her sunglasses only to find they were missing. They weren't in the usual pocket on the outside of her purse, and they weren't inside, along with her wallet, granola bar, numerous pens, phone, and reporter's notebook, either. Sighing, she gave the cart a shove and stepped into the sunlight, squinting. She'd almost finished loading everything into her trunk when it came to her: she'd pulled the sunglasses off when she got to work earlier that day and set them down on her desk. They were most likely still there, so she'd have to swing by the *Pennysaver* office to retrieve them.

Lucky for her, there was a vacant parking spot

right in front of the weekly newspaper's Main Street office and Lucy swooped right in, then dashed into the office, setting the little bell on the door to jangling. Somewhat to her surprise, she was greeted not only by the receptionist, Phyllis, but also by her editor, Ted, who didn't usually stick around the office after deadline. The two were standing at the reception counter, heads bent over a press release.

"What's up?" asked Lucy. "Breaking news?" Late breaking news was a problem for a weekly, which had to wait an entire week before printing stories that by then had become stale.

"Not hardly," said Ted, chuckling. He was not only the editor, but also the publisher and chief reporter for the paper, which he'd inherited from his grandfather. That celebrated New England journalist's rolltop desk still dominated the old-fashioned newsroom and was Ted's most prized possession.

"You've got to see it to believe it," said Phyllis, laughing so hard that her sizable bosom was jiggling as she handed the press release to Lucy. Phyllis was celebrating spring's late arrival by wearing a pink bouclé sweater that matched her pink reading glasses and her hair, also dyed pink.

Lucy quickly scanned the press release, which announced in bold capitals that Sylvia and Warren Bickford were soon to celebrate their twenty-fifth wedding anniversary in June by renewing their vows, that joyous ceremony to be followed by a reception to which the whole town would be invited. And that was not all, promised the press release, which went on to invite all the ladies of the town to participate in a fashion show of wedding gowns from the past by modeling their own dresses. All those interested should contact Sylvia at her shop, Orange Blossom Bridal.

"This is so funny," said Lucy, when she'd finished reading. "I just saw the Bickfords, who Dot Kirwan calls the Bickersons, at the IGA. She picked on him mercilessly; the poor guy couldn't do anything right. Harry, the deli guy, said he was surprised Warren hasn't murdered Sylvia. A divorce would be more appropriate than renewing their vows. The whole town is going to be laughing at them."

"It's pretty smart, if you ask me," said Ted. "It's great publicity for her bridal boutique, and also for his limo company."

"It could backfire," said Lucy. "Everybody knows it's an unhappy marriage. Nobody'd be surprised if Warren bailed out, or worse."

"Oh, I don't know," said Phyllis, in a thoughtful tone. She was a bit of a romantic, having found her great love, Wilf Lundgren, rather late in life. "There must be something that keeps them together, despite outward appearances. I think it's kind of sweet."

Lucy spotted her sunglasses, exactly where she had left them, and grabbed them, perching them on top of her head in Jackie Kennedy style. "Speaking of sweets, I gotta run before my ice cream melts—see ya tomorrow!"

Lucy thought about marriage as she drove the familiar route through town, down Main Street, and out to Route 1, then turning onto Red Top Road and up the hill to the handyman's special she and Bill had restored and in which they'd raised their four children. Sometimes the glue held, even for couples like the Bickersons, who didn't seem terribly happy, and sometimes that glue dried up and crumbled, like the stuff she'd spent hours scraping off the back of an antique picture frame she'd recently picked up at an estate sale. There had been rough spots in her marriage to Bill—she remembered fights but not exactly what caused them—but she'd never seriously considered divorce. Maybe, she admitted to herself, that was because she was far too practical to attempt to raise four children by herself, especially considering the mostly low-wage jobs available to women like her in coastal Maine. She didn't want to spend her summers juggling a couple of jobs, chambermaiding by day and waitressing by night as many local women did.

That wasn't quite fair to Bill, she thought with a smile, pulling into the driveway. She loved him. She'd been distant at first, when he began chatting her up in college, but through sheer persistence he'd gradually won her over. Now, after the house and the kids and grandson Patrick, he was so much a part of her that she couldn't imagine life without him.

Though, she admitted to herself as she began toting the heavy recyclable bags of groceries into the house, she could use a little help from him right now. What was it her mother used to say, when her father was nowhere to be found? Something about wishing she could put on her hat and walk out the door, though that didn't quite take into account the fact that Dad was just going to work. She knew that Bill, who was a restoration carpenter, was hard at work on a big project, transforming an old, abandoned church into a vacation home for a successful Portland restauranteur and his family.

Still, it was a big job, toting all the groceries that would feed herself and Bill, and their two daughters who hadn't yet flown the nest. The fact that Sara, now a graduate student at nearby Winchester College, was a vegetarian, and Zoe, an undergraduate at the same institution, was avoiding gluten, didn't make things any easier. Her grocery list was now filled with the special foods the girls demanded: quinoa, kale, organic yogurt, free-range eggs, hormone-free milk, on and on it went. She dropped two heavy bags on the kitchen table and went out for more, eventually making three trips to get everything inside. And then there was the unloading, the sorting and the storing.

When she'd finally folded the last bag and tucked it away with the others in her bag of bags, she sat down at the round, golden oak kitchen table and considered making herself a cup of tea. Entirely too much work, she decided, opting instead for a glass of water. She sipped it thoughtfully, thinking of Sylvia's challenge: could she possibly fit into her wedding dress? Setting down her glass, she decided she had to find out.

The dress, shrouded in a garment bag, hung in the back of her closet. She hadn't looked at it in years, had almost forgotten about it. Like most mothers, she had a vague hope that one of her daughters might wear it for her wedding, but so far that hadn't happened. Even Elizabeth, her oldest, who worked for the tony Cavendish Hotel chain and was currently living in Paris, hadn't shown any interest in marriage, much less in wearing her mother's dress. It probably wouldn't suit her, thought Lucy, climbing the steep, back stairway that led from the kitchen to the bedrooms on the second floor. She would surely want something more high fashion.

Entering the bedroom she shared with Bill, Lucy opened the bifold closet doors, which stuck a bit and which Bill kept meaning to fix. She slid the clothes along the rod until she came to the long garment bag, which she pulled out and laid on the bed, then unzipped it to reveal the white dress.

It was a simple design with short sleeves and a jewel neckline. The bodice was made of Alençon lace, ending in a slightly raised waist. The full skirt was heavy satin ending in the slightest suggestion of a train, and fastened with a wide ribbon sash at the waist. It was slightly crushed from hanging in the closet all these years, and the veiled headpiece, which she had tucked into the bottom of the garment bag, was flattened.

She took it out, reshaping it with her hands, and set it on her head, fluffing out the white tulle veil, and looked in the mirror. She was much older now, but if she brought the veil forward, over her face, she almost looked like the young woman in the wedding picture that stood on Bill's dresser. But not quite, she decided, snatching the coif off and tossing it on the bed.

Picking up the dress, she held it at arm's length and studied it. It was a pretty dress but nothing like the strapless sheaths the girls wore these days, and not like the heavily beaded and hugely skirted cream puffs that had been fashionable for a while. Turning to the full-length mirror on the back of the bedroom door, she held the gown against her body and sighed. It was obvious, without even trying it on, that she could never fit into it. She wasn't fat, not by a long shot, but she'd given birth to four children, and she'd breast-fed them all. Her body had changed and she was no longer the little slip of a thing who had worn that dress.

Standing there and studying her reflection, she thought it wasn't just her body that had changed; she had changed, too. She was much more confident these days and much more assertive than she had been as a young bride. She was more openminded, too, and less opinionated. Back then, she thought, she'd been a bit of a prig, convinced there was a right way to do things and a wrong way. Nowadays she was no longer convinced that food colorings were poison, that childbirth had to be natural, and all plastic should be banned.

She realized now that her strongly held beliefs had been a defense against an uncertain world. That had become obvious when she stepped inside the church vestibule on her wedding day and panicked, completely terrified to take that first step down the aisle to the altar where Bill was waiting for her.

"Ready, sweetie?" her father had asked, cocking his elbow and inviting her to take his arm.

Not at all, she'd realized, wanting only to turn tail and run right out the door. She would have fled, she remembered, except for the fact that everything was going black and she was about to faint. It was Beth Gerard, her best friend and maid of honor, who had produced from somewhere a brown paper lunch bag, which she gave to Lucy, instructing her to breathe into it.

Dad had held her up as Lucy breathed in and out, deep breaths, into the paper sack. "I thought this might happen," said Beth.

"I can't do this," said Lucy. "The wedding's off."

"It's rather late for that," said her father.

"Look, if it's no good, you can get a divorce, or an annulment. But today, you have to get married," said Beth.

"It's not Bill, it's me. I can't go down that aisle."

"Oh, yes you can," said Beth. "Just imagine they're all naked."

Standing there, in front of her mirror, Lucy smiled, just as she had on her wedding day when she followed Beth and the other bridesmaids down the aisle on her father's arm. Afterward, everybody said they'd never seen such a radiant, happy bride.

It was time, thought Lucy as she replaced the dress in the garment bag, to call Beth. She hadn't spoken with her in a long time, and she knew Beth would love hearing about the Bickersons and reminiscing about the wedding. No time like the present, decided Lucy, knowing that unless she made the call immediately the moment would pass and she would be distracted and forget. She perched on the side of her bed and picked up the phone from the bedside table, punching in the number she knew from memory.

The voice that answered wasn't Beth's; it was male.

"Is Beth there?" asked Lucy, puzzled.

"I'm afraid not. Who's calling?"

"I'm an old friend, Lucy Stone. Could you please tell her I called?"

"I'm afraid not, Lucy," said the voice, which was close to breaking. "This is Dante."

Lucy knew Dante was Beth's son, whom she remembered as a skinny, mischievous kid. Now, from his deep voice, it was clear he was all grown up. And it was also clear to her that something was wrong. "Is everything all right, Dante?"

"No. It's not. Oh, Lucy, everything's wrong." He gasped, letting out a sob. "My mother is dead."

Connect with Us

Visit us online at
KensingtonBooks.com
to read more from your favorite authors, see books
by series, view reading group guides, and more.

Join us on social media

for sneak peeks, chances to win books and prize packs,
and to share your thoughts with other readers.

facebook.com/kensingtonpublishing
twitter.com/kensingtonbooks

Tell us what you think!

To share your thoughts, submit a review,
or sign up for our eNewsletters, please visit:
KensingtonBooks.com/TellUs.